To Mark,

The Schoolgirl
and
The Seamstress

By
JD BADROCK

Thanks for your help
and support.
Junee X

?
Question Mark Press

First published in 2024 by Question Mark Press

1

Secondary School East London, England.
December 2015

Fourteen-year-old Mari Lone fidgeted on her chair. Her best friend Carly was off sick, and the previous week their history teacher had threatened them that there would be a project to work on.

'Get into pairs, please,' Mrs McCurdy commanded.

Mari had feared hearing those words; she had guessed she would be paired up with one of the nearby Muslim girls, and the teacher confirmed it. There were three of them in her class; normally they were allowed to work together but Carly's absence gave her teacher the perfect excuse to split them up. She sensed Mrs McCurdy's intention before she voiced it.

'Mari? You can work with Razia today.'

Mari turned to look at Razia Rahman, who smiled back at her, brushing her hand over her hijab as if to acknowledge Mari's discomfort. Both turned back to listen to their teacher outline their task for the day.

'This is going to be a project as part of the Mayor's History of East London initiative. What I want you to do is search an area of London. I'll give you a map, and I want you to find out about any famous people, places, events, or notable pieces of art, including sculptures, in that area. You have two weeks to do it and if your work is good enough, I'll submit it to the Mayor's Office in the new year.'

She paused to look around the class. 'Any questions?'

There were moans and groans and many exchanged glances among the pupils.

'Does that include boxers, Miss?' one lad ventured.

'Indeed it does,' came the reply, which surprised the recipients. Maybe this wasn't so bad, they thought collectively.

'Footballers?' A girl asked.

'Definitely.'

'Fast food places,' someone whispered. It was answered with an eye roll.

'Prisons?'

'Yes, even prisons. London has a very long and rich history, and all these things have added to it over time. Art galleries, museums, parks, graveyards. Almost every building has a story. It's up to you to look for it.'

She paused again. 'Any more questions? No? Then pull your desks together and I shall come round and talk to you all.'

Mari and Razia looked at each other but this time with a little more enthusiasm. 'Could be interesting,' Razia nodded.

'I suppose.'

Mari was less sure. She wasn't particularly sporty but did like looking at old houses and walking the old alleyways near her flat. She stood up and pushed her desk to meet Razia's. Razia smiled, and with a tacit agreement, the two girls waited quietly until it was their turn for the teacher to come and talk to them.

'Here you are.' Mrs McCurdy handed them each a piece of paper with a photocopy of a map on it. 'This is your area, marked with the red pen.'

Both girls studied the paper. Razia was the first to comment. 'Our mosque's in there. Can we do that?'

'Of course,' Mrs McCurdy nodded. 'Religious buildings always have interesting histories.' She looked at Mari, who was still studying the map. 'Mari?'

She looked up. 'Our church is there. So that counts too. I know it's very old.'

'Good. Find out what you can about both buildings. But don't forget to look around the area too. You may find something even more surprising.'

When the class finished, Mari and Razia chatted enthusiastically.

'Come over to ours tonight,' Razia suggested. 'I'll take you to our mosque, then maybe tomorrow you can take me to your church.' Mari bit her lip. 'We don't bite,' Razia smiled.

'It's not that, it's... Well, I don't go to church much, to be honest. But I'll talk to Mum.'

'Tonight then?' Razia pressed.

2

'If you like,' Mari replied, noting that Razia seemed to be much more energised than she had been previously.

'Good.' Razia replied, almost as if she had heard Mari's thoughts. 'I do enjoy these projects and my friends...' she nodded her head towards the two girls. 'They're too interested in Kim Kardashian.'

That made Mari smile. 'Shall we meet after school?'

'Definitely.'

When the school bell rang at the end of the day, Mari's enthusiasm waned when she saw Razia with her two friends. She began to have doubts, but Razia clearly had none. She beckoned Mari over. 'We're getting started on the project tonight,' she explained to them.

'I'll let Mum know,' Mari said, tapping into her phone.

When they arrived at Razia's house, Mari was a little envious. This was a proper house with a front garden, not at all like her tiny flat on the fourth floor. Razia opened the door and immediately pulled off her hijab, noting Mari's shocked face with a grin. 'Did you think I slept in it or something?'

'Well, I... ' Mari began, but before she could continue, she was saved by Razia's mother, who appeared in the hall.

'Hello, my dear. What is your name?'

'Mari. It's Irish.'

'What a coincidence. I am Maria. That's Arabic and Italian and all sorts. Welcome to you, Mari.'

Mari stepped inside and gazed around the colourful hall.

'Are you Irish like your name?' asked Maria. 'Sorry, I don't mean to be nosy but... '

Razia squirmed. She hadn't thought about Mari's complexion before. 'Mum...' she began, but Mari was not at all bothered.

'Mum's Irish. My father was Pakistani.'

'That explains your lovely colour. Oh...' Maria hesitated. 'I'm sorry. You said *was*.'

Mari, used to explaining, was untroubled by this. She trotted out her usual response. 'He was a soldier.' She suddenly realised that this time, it might provoke a different reaction. But she had no idea how to rephrase it to accommodate any sensitivities. 'He was killed in Iraq.'

3

'Oh, my poor dear. How terribly sad. You must be so proud of him.'

'I am. But I hardly remember him.'

'What was his name?' a curious Maria asked.

'They called him Wolf, but his real name was Mo. Mohammed Lone.'

Maria digested this before exclaiming. 'Lone wolf? Ah, I see.' She nodded her understanding.

Mari didn't react. She was being drawn further into the house, gazing at the richly coloured furnishings and family photos on the walls. 'This is lovely,' she said.

Maria opened the door to the kitchen and smelled the wondrous flavours of what she presumed to be their tea. 'That smells delicious,' she said.

'You must stay for tea,' Maria declared.

'Oh, but... ' Mari began.

'Call your mother. Ask her if it's all right.'

Mari nodded in reply.

'Come upstairs,' Razia held out her hand. 'Let me show you my room.'

Mari was a little disappointed. Razia's room looked every little bit like her own, except it was smaller, if that were possible. 'So you liked One Direction then?'

Razia blushed. 'Oh, I used to when I was younger. I should take that silly old poster down.'

'Don't worry; I liked them too,' Mari confided. She rang her mother to explain what was happening.

Razia looked at her watch. 'We should go now. It's a good time to see the imam; he can tell us about the mosque.'

'Am I OK like this?' Mari looked down at herself.

'Of course. You'll have to take your shoes off, that's all.'

4

2

Mari and Razia arrived outside the Mosque entrance to curious looks from the people emerging.

'In here,' Razia guided her in, pointing to the shoe rack where two pairs of shoes were already resting.

'Not very busy, is it?' Mari noted as she took off her shoes.

'It's not prayer time yet.'

Razia went inside, Mari following tentatively. She gazed up at the domed ceiling. 'It's all patterns!' she exclaimed. 'Why are there no pictures?'

The imam approached the girls with a welcoming smile. He had overheard Mari's comments.

'No. It is not explicitly forbidden in the Quran but many, the majority, believe it is not appropriate. There was a declaration a few hundred years ago so now there are never any images in mosques. And Allah is omnipresent, we do not need to see him, we feel him.' He turned to Razia. 'Hello, Razia, and who is this young lady?'

'This is my school friend, Mari. We are doing a school project about important places in this area so I brought her here.'

'Excellent. Would you like to know more about the history of the mosque?'

'Yes please!' the girls replied in unison.

'This is a very interesting mosque,' the imam began. 'All mosques are, of course, interesting, but this one has a particular place in London's history.'

Mari and Razia listened carefully to what he said. How they had raised the money to build it. How this building was built on the site of the first one. That Prince Charles had been to visit.

When the history lesson was over, Mari was enthusiastic and curious. 'What about religious beliefs?' she asked.

'That is a very large subject,' he replied. 'Do you have specific questions?'

'Yes. Do Muslims go to heaven?' she asked.

'I will give you a simple answer for now. For Muslims, our entire life is lived with the aim of getting into heaven, so yes,

Muslims – anyone – who believes in Allah can go to heaven. Does that help?'

'Oh. Yes, thank you. I've really enjoyed coming here. It's been so interesting.'

'Yes,' Razia added, sounding a little impatient. She turned to Mari. 'We should go now. Tea will be ready.'

The girls returned to the house to find Maria looking flustered. The dining room table was already laid with dishes of food in the middle of the table. 'Ah, at last, you two. Sit. It is ready.' She waved the girls in and directed Mari to sit down. 'Mari, will you have some chicken and rice?'

Mari looked around the table. There was an empty place set. Maria caught her eye and explained. 'That's for Razia's brother, Saeed. He'll be here soon. My husband will eat when he comes home from work. Chicken?' Maria reminded her.

'Yes please.'

'Are you used to eating curries?' Maria asked.

'When Mum can be bothered to make them. We usually just have something out of a jar.'

Maria said nothing and began to spoon the rice and then meat onto each plate. Mari watched as the other two paused before eating. She said grace in her head before taking a small mouthful.

'This is lovely.'

'Thank you, Mari. I am pleased you like it.'

The meal was eaten accompanied by talking and laughing. Maria was good company and the rapport between her and Razia made Mari a bit jealous.

Mari was beginning to wonder about the missing brother but just before they had finished eating, the door was flung open and Saeed entered. She was startled as he came in. He was very good-looking, about sixteen or seventeen she guessed. He gave her a strange look as he sat down. Mari smiled at him as he continued to stare at her. Maria served him a large portion of rice and chicken.

'You're late,' she scolded. 'Lucky for you it's still warm. Where have you been?'

'Who's that?' Saeed spoke just before shovelling a large spoonful of food into his mouth.

6

Maria tapped him on the back of his hand with her unused spoon and winked at Mari. 'I asked you a question first.'

'I have been helping that idiot Nadeem with his maths.' He looked at Razia for an answer.

'The imam's son? I'm impressed that you keep such good company,' Maria smiled. 'It's nice to know once in a while where you are.'

Saeed sighed. He looked from Mari to Razia.

'It's my friend Mari. And don't be so rude,' Razia retorted.

'As if you have any friends.' He gave her a sarcastic look and turned to Mari. 'Nice to meet you. I'm Saeed.'

Saeed's face broke into the loveliest smile Mari had ever seen. He had such kind and expressive eyes. She was dazzled but he carried on eating, unaware of his impact on her .

Razia, too had failed to notice; she looked at her brother who was hoovering up his meal. She saw that, like herself, Mari had finished her meal. 'Come on. Let's go up to my room and see what we've got for our project so far.'

Mari looked away before returning to glance at Saeed briefly. 'Nice to meet you too.' She turned to Razia. 'Yes, we must.'

***

Mari walked home fantasising about having a boyfriend. Maybe a boyfriend like Saeed. Maybe Saeed. She trudged up the concrete staircase and then walked along the passageway to her flat, taking out her key as she walked. The door opened straight into the living room and there she found her mother, Sinéad, sitting on the sofa in her dressing gown, wine glass in hand, watching TV.

'So you're back then?' She spoke without turning around.

'Yes.' Mari looked around her own home. It was shabby, almost bereft of colour with scant decoration. For the first time, she felt ashamed of her mother and thought how wonderful, colourful, and busy Razia's home had been by comparison.

'You're quiet. How was your tea?'

Mari walked over to the dining area and perched on a plain wooden chair. 'It was lovely.'

'Would you like to invite that girl back here?'

Mari shook her head before speaking. 'No,' she said.

Sinéad did not query it nor did she explain.

'Do I have any other family? I mean on Dad's side. You never talk about him.'

Mari could see her mother tense up but she didn't turn around.

'Not today, love. I'm watching this. We'll talk tomorrow. OK?'

'OK.'

Mari went into her bedroom and smiled at the poster of One Direction. Then she thought again of Saeed. Was she too young? Would her mother approve? It would be hypocritical if she did. She wondered again how old he was. She'd never seen him at school so he must be at college. *Did he think I was pretty?* Some boys had told her she was. He'd stared at her. Then he'd smiled...

Her phone pinged. It was a text from Carly. She grabbed her phone and looked at the message.

It's me.

How R U?

: (: (: (

When U back?

C U tomorrow.

OK XX

Mari remembered the project and went to talk to her mother.

'I said not now.'

'No, this is something else.'

'What?'

'Do you think it will be all right if I take Razia to church tomorrow?'

'Why ever would you want to do that?'

'It's for the project at school. We went to her mosque today.'

Sinéad hesitated. 'OK. I'll ring Father George. I'll text you if it's OK. You should bring her here, really, for tea. If you went there.'

'I'll ask her then. Night Mum.'

'Night, love. We will talk tomorrow. It's just that...'

'I know. Night.'

3

'You are such a stubborn woman!' Aram shouted through the half-open door of the little stone house. 'They will kill you. If they do not kill you they will steal your house. They will take all your money. You should leave with us while you still can.'

'I have work to do,' Maryam Rabka replied with quiet determination, not even lifting her head to acknowledge him.

'Stubborn *and* foolish.' Now she looked up and smiled at him, catching his eye. 'Where will your work be when everyone else has gone?'

'The Lord will provide.'

'And He will also be the death of you. Hide it away!' Aram pointed to the cross around her neck. 'That is a signpost to them.'

'Never,' she replied, her hand automatically clutching the precious pendant.

Aram turned away and made a spitting gesture as he went on his way, along the dusty tarmac road. No trees to shade the route here; the village houses merged into an abstract pattern of creams and sands, bright against the blue sky.

Maryam mused that there had been a time when the little street would be busy with people. Today, Aram cut a lonely figure. He had disappeared round a curve in the road when she gave her reply, her hand still clasping her precious cross. 'Bless you, Aram. God will provide. Whatever is His will, it will be done. I am not afraid.'

She shut the door and turned around, catching her reflection in the mirror. It was not there for vanity, at least not hers. It was there so that her customers could inspect their garments before settling up. But today she made use of it for herself and examined her simple white chatta blouse and mundu. She was tall for a woman and had to stoop a little to look properly at herself. Her topknot of long grey hair exaggerated her height. It was an old habit acquired from her meticulous approach to her work. No human hair should catch in the needle of the machine or the seams of her craft.

The garments were assessed with a critical and expert eye. 'The seams are straight and complete. There are no stray strands of cotton. The fit, is, of course, excellent. You'll pass for another year.' She smiled at herself, briefly savouring the smells of recently chopped garlic, olive oil and spices waiting for her in her little kitchen. They would soon be subsumed into her cooking pot along with some chicken. It would be a small but perfectly sufficient meal.

Maryam returned to her sewing room to finish her day's work which had been loudly interrupted by Aram's insistent knocking. But it had made her think, yet again, of what she should do for the best. She caressed her old but well-loved sewing machine. The source of not just her income, but also so many memories. Hardly a wedding, baptism or funeral had passed in the village without someone wearing something she had made on that very machine. Times were so very different now.

And where would she go, even if it was possible? Even if she wanted to? There was no family left to join. For sure, there would be friends happy to help. Nearly all of those living around her had already fled. They'd run to stay with other family members in safer parts of the country, or other countries.

Friends like Aram were precious in good times. He, or another, might well be happy for her to join them for a short while. But without income, how long would the friendship last?

'I will not be a burden,' she murmured. 'I have made my decision and nothing will make me leave. Far better to stay where I can do God's will.'

She surveyed the heaped garments which still demanded her attention. Even these made a smaller pile than in the weeks before. Nowadays it was mending. Nobody had the money for new clothes; it was all about making things last. But how many of her neighbours would last?

Maryam looked at the faded photograph on the top of her sewing cupboard. A young man's face looked out. He was smiling at her. 'You would understand, Bahir.'

She sighed as she remembered her young husband and murmured a small prayer to Jesus Christ to forgive her for the sin of wanting children. Bahir had lost his life many years before. A man of peace, he could not deny his service in the army, and there he was chosen. She accepted that this was the path God had chosen for her, and she had never met another man she could have married. Sewing, she decided, was her life. 'You always told me that God gives us talents which we must use as best we can. I am a good seamstress, and if that's what God wants of me, so it shall be.'

The outside light was fading and the electricity supply was unreliable. She had a kerosene heater but was running low on fuel. Pulling a shawl around her shoulders to ward off the cold a little longer, she lit a candle and sat at her sewing desk. She licked the end of the thread, fashioning it into a point with her fingers before bending down and peering at the needle, carefully guiding the end into the awaiting eye. As always she smiled as she succeeded and said out loud, 'Thank you, Lord.' Adding for the benefit of herself, 'No riches will ever prevent me from entering your kingdom.'

4

Hertfordshire, England.

Detective Sergeant Karen Thorpe sat at her desk, all her procrastination about to be ended. After Jim Westbury, the man who had murdered her mother, had finally been sentenced to life imprisonment, she'd had no more excuses and had taken and passed the legal exam, the next step on her career ladder to Inspector. She'd passed with a result of 84%, if not quite the highest in the country, probably the highest ever in Hertfordshire.

Her boss, DCI Winter had congratulated her at the time, but she'd always managed to avoid his efforts to talk to her about progression. 'I've got five years,' she retorted. He hadn't been impressed. She drummed her fingers on the desk while waiting for the door to his office to open. When it finally did, she jumped.

'Karen?' he yelled.

She stood up and looked around the room watching all the heads drop as her laser gaze surveyed them. *They all want to see the back of me*, she thought, not entirely unreasonably. She was not a popular figure in the office although she had developed a habit of confounding all her colleagues with her exceptional results in solving near impossible cases. Also, although it had absolutely nothing to do with her at all, the only other senior officer on DCI Winter's team, Detective Inspector Harris, had been absent from service due to continuing mobility problems after being run over by a criminal, who was now safely behind bars. But, to Karen's annoyance, he came in regularly to visit, always bringing cakes and smiling a great deal.

There had been a series of temporary replacements, and it seemed that all of them were much nicer than her. She also knew that Detective Constable Macy Dodds was snapping at her heels, already mugging up for her sergeants' exams next spring.

'Yes, Guv.' Karen sat in front of her boss.

They respected each other, that was true. They had even worked very closely together – and made a surprisingly good team. But career-wise, they were worlds apart. Karen knew that DCI Winter craved the relative peace and quiet of retirement. A career copper, he'd mainly kept his head down and progressed through the ranks happy at management responsibility, less so when he was out in the field. She knew he had a plan for his department and that it would go much more smoothly if she finally played ball and took a step up the ranking ladder. He'd told her that he admired her skills and dedication to police work, and that in time, if she behaved herself, she would become a real asset to the force. Especially at a high rank.

'You can't pussyfoot around any longer,' he announced. 'Besides, I've got a placement for you which will satisfy, and possibly extinguish, all your yearning for action.'

Karen sat up. 'An Inspector placement with lots of fieldwork?'

'Yes,' he nodded. 'I know how much you enjoyed your spell with the Met. Well now. How about an assignment in East London?'

Karen frowned. 'Isn't that all council estates, gang violence, and drugs, Guv?'

'No doubt those things will cross your path. But it's real life for millions of people, Karen. And it's hardly comparable to the pleasant leafy suburban sort of crime you've had to deal with before. Have you forgotten the knife attack in Leytonstone?'

'The terrorist attack.' Karen gulped. *Is he right? Have I had it soft all this time?* She wondered whether this could be the challenge she was looking for. Certainly, she had relished her time with the Met but had been pleased to get back to base. It had left her with some sad memories of a fellow cop. *But he was a DCI and he certainly saw lots of action...*

'Karen? Are you with me?'

Karen jumped out of her reverie. 'Sorry, Guv. What's the timescale?'

'New Year, Karen.

'And when do I have to decide?'

DCI Winter gave her a withering glance. 'Any time in the next five minutes will do.'

Karen gaped. 'What's the urgency?'

'The station is low on manpower and needs someone to parachute in as quickly as possible. And four weeks, less if you include Christmas, is a long time to get prepared.'

'But where will I live?' Karen asked.

'Are you serious?' DCI Winter rolled his eyes. 'You can commute. It's not the other side of the world.'

'Oh!' Karen banged her head with the side of her hand. 'I suppose I can.'

'Give me strength,' DCI Winter shook his head. 'Is that a *yes*?'

'Yes, Guv. I shall look forward to it. Just one thing.'

'Go on.'

'Will there be a place for me here when I pass my probation?'

'I thought you'd set your heart on the Met?'

'I just want to know where I stand.'

DCI Winter looked serious. 'Well, that depends,' he replied.

'But you're down a DI at the moment!' Karen said.

'Not for long. DI Harris is returning to duties on the seventh of January.'

'What?' Karen gaped. 'So how's that going to work?'

DCI Winter rolled his eyes. 'You need to get a move on. There'll be a space in this chair soon. If you pull your finger out, you could leapfrog him. Now get on with whatever it was you were doing.'

5

In the playground, Mari and Carly were talking loudly together, oblivious to Razia – the subject of their conversation – who was hovering nearby waiting to attract Mari's attention.

'But I'm back now,' Carly said. 'Surely you don't want to stay with that weirdo?'

'She's not weird. She's very nice. Besides, Mum's going to ask the priest if we can go to church tonight.'

'Well, I can come instead then. I've got to do a project too. Tell her... '

Razia stepped forward into Mari's eye line. Mari's mouth opened in horror. 'Oh Raz... '

'It's fine, Mari. I can join up with my other friends. Don't worry about it.'

'But I was going to ask you for tea and take you to my church and everything.'

Carly folded her arms and looked away.

'Another time perhaps,' Razia said. 'I would like that very much. I'll tell Mrs McCurdy about the new arrangements.'

'I'm so sorry... '

'I know.'

By the end of the school day, Mari was with Carly and had almost forgotten about Razia. They'd both settled back into their usual cliques. 'So you want to come to the church then?'

'Yes, of course,' Carly replied.

'I'll tell you all about the mosque then, on the way.'

'Do you have to?' Carly pouted.

'Yes, I do.' Mari was a little annoyed. 'It's meant to be both of us, you know that.'

Carly didn't reply and trudged alongside Mari to the church.

Mari wasn't sure she was listening to her but when Mari pushed the big wooden door open, Carly, at last, showed a bit of interest.

'I've never been to a Catholic church before. It's very colourful. What's that smell?'

'Incense.'

Mari herself now looked at the church with new understanding and wondered what Razia would have thought about the interior. She gazed at the stained-glass windows throwing colours on the worn stone floor. Wherever she looked there were paintings, statues, and images. And where there were none of these things, there were plaques in memory of important people, or maybe just very rich ones.

She genuflected and walked towards the candles. She especially liked the candles and often lit one for the father she never really knew. Scrabbling in her pocket she found some coins and threw them in the box.

'What's that for?' Carly watched as Mari lit a candle.

'To remember to say prayers for someone.'

Father George had seen the girls come in and waited until Mari had moved away from the candles to talk to her in his faint Irish lilt.

'Good evening, young Mari. Your mother told me you were coming. Who have you got with you and what can I do for you?'

'I'm Carly. We're doing a school project.'

'I'm Father George. At least that's what most people call me.' He shook Carly's hand. 'I am the priest here.'

'It's a project about important buildings in the area,' Mari explained. 'If it's good enough it'll be sent to the Mayor.'

'That sounds very important indeed,' he smiled. 'What do you want to know?'

'We want to know the history of this church.' Mari said.

'Well, that's a grand project. Let me start at the beginning. I believe we have a leaflet or two which will help.'

Father George walked the girls around the church pointing out particular things and explaining their significance; this bit was original, that area was destroyed by fire and rebuilt when this man, he pointed at a plaque, gave the church the money to rebuild it. He continued with his explanations as he walked them around the whole building. When they went downstairs to the crypt, Carly shivered. 'It's cold down here.'

Mari knew a fair amount about her religion but nothing about the history of the church so she found it very interesting. Mindful of her visit to the mosque there was a question burning in her mind. The priest noticed her expression.

'You want to ask me something, Mari?'

'Yes, Father.' She hesitated for a moment. Can Muslims go to heaven?'

Father George shook his head sadly. 'No, Mari. Only those who believe in Jesus Christ and our Lord can enter the kingdom of heaven. Muslims do revere the Virgin Mary and indeed Jesus Christ. But they do not believe that He was the son of God.'

'That's a bit unfair, isn't it? Muslims let anyone into their heaven; if they're good enough.'

'John Chapter fourteen verse six. I am the way and the truth and the life. No one comes to the Father except through me.'

'But supposing a Muslim did believe in Jesus Christ.'

Father George blinked hard as if it would provide him with an answer. He had been slow at realising what Mari was getting at. 'Anyone who finds Jesus Christ can go to heaven. Even Muslims.'

'Oh. So they can.' Mari was now confused. 'Do you think my father is there then? He would have known about Jesus from Mum.'

Father George smiled at her. 'I'm sure he is Mari. I know he was a very good man.'

Carly, who had been looking around with folded arms, piped up. 'Shouldn't we be getting home now?'

Mari was jarred from her thoughts; she looked at her watch. 'Yes. We should. Sorry. Thank you, Father. Thank you so much.'

'It was a pleasure. See you on Sunday, Mari?'

'Er,' Mari gave an unconvincing nod and hurried out of the church with Carly following.

They went to Mari's flat. But when Mari opened the door there was no welcoming smell of tea. Her mother was, as usual, still in her dressing gown watching TV. 'Mum? Carly's here. What's for tea?'

'Oh, I forgot.' Sinéad jumped up from the sofa and reached to get her handbag from the table. 'Hello, Carly. Are you better now?'

'Yes, thanks, Mrs Lone.'

Sinéad rummaged around in her bag, finally pulling out her purse from which she retrieved a five-pound note.

'Here. Treat yourselves. Get a burger or a pizza.'

Mari sighed but took the note anyway. At least she hadn't exposed Razia to this poor welcome. 'Thanks, Mum.'

'Result!' said Carly as they left the flat. 'My mum hardly ever lets me do that. We have to have proper meals, she says.'

'You're very lucky then. Razia's mother cooked us a lovely meal yesterday.'

'That foreign muck?'

Mari was shocked at her friend's remark. 'Curry and rice. It's Britain's favourite meal!'

'Yes, I s'pose,' came the grudging reply.

The girls skipped down the concrete steps and out of the estate to the burger bar. There were a couple of boys milling around outside and Carly gave them the eye, but they just mocked her.

'Go back to school, kid.'

They sat on a wall for a while, tucking into their burgers and talking about boys.

'Have you ever had a boyfriend?' Mari asked.

'Only when I was really little. But that didn't count. Mum says I can't go out with boys yet anyway. But I would if one asked me.'

'Me too,' Mari replied, thinking again of Saeed.

When she got home that evening Mari asked her mother the question again.

'You promised you'd tell me,' she pressed.

Sinéad was still not in the mood to answer. 'I didn't promise.'

'Yes, you did. You said... '

Sinéad snapped. 'It was all a long time ago. There was no other family. At least... ' she hesitated. 'No. No one. Haven't you got homework to do?'

With a dramatic sigh, Mari went to her bedroom where she began to assemble all the information she had accumulated for the project. She wished she had a laptop so she could do some research on the internet but her mother had told her she couldn't afford it.

As she worked, she thought about Carly. Experience had taught her that Carly would be of little use with the project and she wondered whether Razia would have been more willing to get involved. But soon, her creative enthusiasm took over and she got stuck into it. She would, of course, let Carly add her name as she always did but both girls would know the truth. Mari idly wondered if Mrs McCurdy would guess too.

6

Karen was done fuming about Harris's return. Even if she had engaged with boyfriend John on it, he would have been impartial and systematic in his analysis of the situation, and that was the last thing she needed that evening. Instead, she sat in the living room reading through something on her laptop with one ear on the TV. When the newsreader said something about three girls, she looked up.

'What was that about?' she turned to ask John, who was also doing something on his laptop.

'No idea. I wasn't watching and neither should you.'

Karen turned the volume up and listened to the rest of the story.

'Something about some girls going missing. I wonder what that's about.'

'Not your bag, I thought,' John ventured. 'Too recent.' He ducked to avoid the expected cushion; it didn't come. Karen had become somewhat notorious for solving some very old cold cases involving three little girls.

'If you mean the cold cases,' she answered in her most irritated-sounding voice, 'you know that that wasn't official business. I get lots of people contacting me about finding their children. I always redirect them. But this is different. I've just picked up an email from Macy. She told me that a Muslim woman rang in, very worried about her missing daughter. I just wondered if it might have been connected. That's all.'

John sighed. 'Do you know how many Muslims there are in the country?'

Karen shook her head. 'I don't even know how many there are in Hertfordshire.'

'Well, there are a lot,' John replied, for once not having an accurate number to quote. 'So it's not likely to be connected, is it?'

'I don't know,' Karen snapped. 'I didn't hear the details properly.'

John pointed the remote at the TV and pressed a button. 'Doesn't work,' he said.

'What doesn't?'

'Trying to rewind it.'

'Numpty. Anyway, it didn't sound recent. Probably something that happened a while ago. It does sound familiar.'

'Good. You talk about work far too much.'

'Go and make the tea. Or get me some wine. Just do something useful, why don't you?' she yelled as she finally grabbed the expected cushion. 'But that reminds me. It looks as though I'm going to be commuting soon. Placement in East London.'

'Cor blimey, Karen old gal … ' Now the cushion came and hit the target squarely in the face. 'About time,' he grinned.

***

The next morning, Karen caught Macy as she came in. 'That email... '

'Never mind that,' Macy replied. 'What got into you last night?' She hung up her coat.

'Oh, remind me of DI Harris again, why don't you?' Karen snarled. 'He's coming back.'

'Oh.' Macy sat at her desk. 'But why does that bother you?'

'Because I was under the illusion that when I finished my placement, I'd be coming back here.'

'Oh,' Macy's face fell. 'I see. Well, there's only one thing to do then.'

'What?' Karen frowned.'

'We'll have to organise the best leaving party ever!' Macy grinned.

Karen gave a weak smile in return. 'Just don't invite him.'

Emma Cadrose, the admin assistant, approached Macy's desk and looked at Karen. 'Why don't you like Detective Inspector Harris?' She asked bluntly.

'It's a very long story. All in the past, Emma. Don't you worry about it.'

'But it's not fair. You are a good person.'

Karen smiled at her. 'Unfortunately, not everyone agrees with you.'

'OK.' Emma walked away.

'Anyway, I've got some news too,' Macy said.

'Go on. Cheer me up.'

'I'm going to have some company soon.'

'Don't tell me... another '

'Another ethnic in the office,' Macy giggled. 'My little bro, Jamal. He's starting here as a Police Community Support Officer.'

'I thought your brothers made fun of you?'

'That was before I started on my sergeants' exams. When Jamal was seventeen he was a complete nightmare. Head all over the place, sighing over some girl or another, not knowing what he wanted to do with his life. Mum said all boys are difficult at that age.'

'So he changed?'

'Oh yes,' Macy nodded vigorously 'I think it might have been on his eighteenth birthday, he was suddenly all grown up. And, for the first time ever, he actually talked to me with something that was almost respect,' she snorted. 'Both my brothers think it's cool now, and Jamal decided he wanted to give it a go.'

'I'm really pleased for both of you,' Karen said. Now, about that email.'

Macy blinked. 'Oh, it's fine, false alarm. Apparently, she came home an hour after the woman rang me.'

'Good,' Karen said. 'There was something on the news about three missing girls, but I didn't catch the full story. I think it was old news.'

'I watched that. It was about those girls who ran off to Syria to join that terrorist group.'

'Of course!' Karen banged the side of her head with her hand. 'How could I forget that? And the guv mentioned terrorism in East London. They came from there too, didn't they?'

'Yes, Tower Hamlets,' Macy replied. 'Poor kids.'

'Poor?' Karen gaped. 'They wanted to go off and kill people didn't they?'

Macy shook her head. 'They were just kids. Indoctrinated. I doubt any of them had any idea what they were letting themselves in for.'

'At fifteen – or was it sixteen? I knew exactly what I was doing at that age.'

Macy frowned. Her face reflected her ticking brain. 'Karen, it was different for you. It must have been awful without your mother, and however wonderful your dad was, he was always busy. So… '

'So what?' Karen's hackles were rising.

'So you had to grow up fast. You had to manage on your own from an early age. We don't know anything about *those* girls, but I bet they came from a very sheltered background. They wouldn't have been streetwise. Not like you.'

Karen raised her head to speak but thought better of it. *She's probably right. Again.* 'I suppose,' she relented. 'But I guess it's something I'd better start taking an interest in if I'm going to be working there.'

'You mean you haven't already?' Macy feigned surprise. 'You're slacking.'

'And how is your revision coming along?' Karen shot back.

'Guilty,' Macy grinned.

'But you are right,' Karen replied. 'I really should have thought more about all this before accepting the assignment.'

'How do you mean?' Macy frowned. 'I'd have thought it was right up your street.'

'Oh, sure, it is. But it's different, isn't it? Bombings, knife attacks like that poor soldier a couple of years ago. You can't plan for it and how do you stop it? If they're not on any registers or anything. I think I'm going to enjoy getting stuck in.'

'Then again, it'll probably be all petty crime,' Macy speculated. 'Terrorist attacks don't happen that often, do they?'

'I can still do my research,' Karen smiled, then looked around. 'And how are our little lovebirds today? Emma seemed in good form.'

Macy snorted. 'Bradley is too. They're so sweet together. I bet he's going to propose soon. Which reminds me… '

'When hell freezes over,' Karen grunted.

'And does John realise that?'

'He bloody well ought to, by now.' Karen replied. 'I mean, can you actually imagine me with kids?'

'You're getting close to *that age*,' Macy laughed. 'I want kids one day.'

'And who with? Mr Right, or Mr Right Now?'

'We'll see,' Macy nodded. 'I'm still deciding.'

7

Far away in a warmer climate but still experiencing the cooler winter winds, Maryam pulled her shawl tightly around her shoulders as she made her way home from the market with her small basket of meat and vegetables. The dusty paths she trod each day seemed to be walked by fewer and fewer people. Her resolution to stay was wavering. *I will stay here as long as it is the will of my Lord.*

Inside her house, her pile of mending was gone and a stack of newly mended, neatly folded garments had taken their place. There would be no new orders. Everyone who was staying was already as prepared as they would ever be. She looked at the calendar pinned on her wall. The festival of St Nicholas had already passed nine days ago. There had been a reasonable attendance at the service held in his honour, but there had been no feasting that year. It was the fifteenth of December, just ten days to Christmas day and she wondered what it would be like. How many would be there?

When she next went to church she looked out for the missionaries who were attached to the village. She counted them in her head. *Yes. They are all here*. She listened to the service more distracted by her thoughts than usual. When it was over, she waited to catch the ear of the priest. They spoke in Aramaic.

'God bless you, Maryam. What can I do for you?'

'So many people have gone. I'm getting worried. And those that are left are preparing to leave also. They keep telling me I should go. What are your plans? Are you intending to stay here?'

He nodded. 'While we are needed here to do God's work, we will stay.'

'But your nephew, he is very young.'

'He is a fine young man and he is like a son to me now, since he lost his parents. Where would he go? He wants to stay with us too. The whole missionary team have decided to stay now. You will not be alone.'

'Thank you, Father. I will stay too.'

She left the church and walked home, ideas already forming in her mind. *The children*, she smiled to herself. *I must do something for them.*

Once inside, she went into her main room and began to look. Every cupboard and drawer was searched and emptied for all the little leftovers she saved from her work. Before too long she had a collection of bits and pieces that most people would have thrown away. But not Maryam. She nodded, more ideas coming as she studied the pile. There were scraps of material, large off-cuts of sheeting, strands of wool, buttons, clasps, and threads of every colour including silver and gold.

'Let me start with the dolls,' she said to herself. From an unsearched drawer, she took a well-worn cardboard cut-out in the shape of a simple child. 'Where are your bodies, little ones?' She smiled as she searched the pile for pieces of fabric big enough to cut from. The colour didn't matter, but the material had to be strong. 'And how many little girls will there be?' she sighed. The previous year she had made ten. This time, she guessed there would be two or three. 'I have enough for four, so I will make four,' she told herself. 'And maybe a lucky little girl will get more than one.'

As the pile depleted, so the little pile of dolls' bodies grew. With buttons for eyes and wool for hair, all she needed was some pretty material for their dresses. It was time for a break.

Over supper, she counted in her head the boys she knew who would need a new shirt and the girls who needed dresses. Just a handful. But the offcuts from the material she had, would make fine garments for her dolls. 'Ah.' She pulled out a large piece of blue fabric. 'That will make a nice shirt for the priest's nephew.'

She worked late into the night driven by her desire to make things that would bring happiness. When she had finished every scrap of fabric, she knitted woollen toys for the babies.

When all but the tiniest pieces had been deployed, she went to her bed satisfied with the pile of toys and clothes she had created.

Her reward, she knew, would come in heaven. The people for whom she worked had no money. But occasionally she would be invited to share the home of this family or that and take part in their Christmas festivities.

'And who will be there this year?' She looked up at the ceiling. 'God will look after me,' she concluded.

8

It was the last day of the school term and Mrs McCurdy's last history class of the year had begun. The projects had been marked and were being handed back to the teams of girls one by one, accompanied by a variety of comments. Most got a *good,* but a few were told to do some more work if they wanted to improve their grades.

Mrs McCurdy had left two of the workbooks on her desk, and by a process of elimination Mari and Razia realised that they must be their projects. They exchanged glances and grimaces; this could be praise or condemnation. Mrs McCurdy winked at them and they began to smile.

'Finally,' Mrs McCurdy announced. 'I will be submitting not one but two of the projects to the Mayor's office next year.' She looked at Mari as she spoke. 'Mari and Carly for their wonderful project on the church and the mosque in their area; well done you two.'

There was a faint round of applause from the other students.

She continued. ' And Razia, Sumi and Eva's project on Ikey Solomon. An extremely interesting find and very well researched. Very well done to all of you.'

Mari and Razia exchanged broad grins as Mrs McCurdy handed back their work. As she went back to her desk, Mari leaned towards Razia.

'Well done. Imagine if we'd both worked on each other's.'

Razia nodded. 'You too. Yes, I would so much have liked to see your church.'

'Who is Ikey Solomon?' They were interrupted.

'May I have your attention girls, please. We must get back to work,' Mrs McCurdy said with a clap of her hands.

In the maths class, Mari's hatred of the subject became apparent to everyone, especially the teacher, who told her off more than once. After the lesson ended, Razia came over to her desk. 'Ikey Solomon was a real-life crook and was the inspiration for Fagin in Oliver Twist.'

'Ah,' Mari nodded. 'That does sound interesting. Unlike maths.'

'It sounds like you don't like it.'

Mari grimaced. 'I just can't seem to *get* these equations however hard I try. What about you?'

'I'm not too bad with them now, but I did have some help.' She thought for a minute. 'I tell you what.' Mari looked interested. 'My brother is very good at maths. He's helped loads of people. He even helped me a few times, and he hates me. I'm sure he will help you if you'd like?'

'Oh!' Mari was startled and not at all sure how to reply. At the very mention of Saeed, his face had come into her mind and that wonderful smile. 'I wouldn't want to trouble him,' she said lamely.

'Let me ask him.'

'OK then,' Mari smiled. 'See what he says.' She panicked. 'Not now though. After Christmas.' She panicked again. 'Oh, I mean... '

Razia smiled. 'We celebrate Christmas a little too; well sort of. Jesus was one of our prophets and Mary is very much admired. But you know that already now, don't you?'

Carly had been loading up her school bag with things to take home with her and had been half watching the conversation. She came over and elbowed Mari.

'Earth to Mari. I'm still here, you know.'

Razia understood that this was her cue to leave. 'I'll see you next term,' she said, then hurried out of the classroom to catch up with her friends.

'I don't know what your problem is,' Mari said.

'They're different, aren't they?' Carly sneered.

'So are we.'

Carly misunderstood. 'Just because you're... '

Mari cut in, not wanting to see Carly get herself tied up in knots about her skin colour again. 'I don't mean that. I mean our religion. A few hundred years ago, Catholics and Protestants thought that too. Some still do in Northern Ireland.'

'That's different,' snapped Carly. 'And you know it.'

'Is it?' Mari gathered up her books. 'I'm not sure it is at all.'

'Don't get all snarky. It's Christmas, remember, and we both know what that means, don't we?'

'Presents,' Mari said although she wasn't expecting many.

'Exactly,' Carly grinned. 'I can't wait.

Mari was delighted when she got home. Her mother was properly dressed and the house looked clean and tidy.

'Your nana's coming soon,' Sinéad announced. 'Just for a few days.'

Mari's face broke out into a big smile.

'That's brill. Am I on the sofa again then?'

'I'm afraid so. Do you mind?'

'No. I love having her here. Why is she coming?'

'She wants to see us.'

***

The next morning, Mari woke to discover her mother had already gone out. When she returned, it was with a whole load of carrier bags.

'All for Nana?' Mari asked.

'You know what she's like,' Sinéad sighed. 'Help me unload.'

'When will she be here?'

'She rang early this morning as she got on the coach. We've got an hour or two yet.'

It was an impatient and fidgety Mari who waited with her mother at the coach stop. It was cold, too, so she kept stamping her feet and muttering about the boots her mother had supposedly promised her ages ago.

'Can I have a hot chocolate or something?'

'No. She'll be here soon. I hope she's got a decent suitcase this time.'

'Maybe you should buy her one for Christmas. And get her a mobile.'

'And you should mind your own business, young lady.'

'Look! Is that it?' A blue and white coach came into view. Mari strained to see whether her nana was on board. She peered then exclaimed. 'She's there! Nana's here at last!'

Niamh, a small round lady with curly grey hair and twinkling eyes, was waving frantically through the window. Someone inside helped her with her bag.

'Oh, bloody hell, ma,' Sinéad exclaimed as she saw the beaten old holdall emerge from the coach with her mother almost obscured by it. 'That's older than me.'

When they arrived home, it felt different to Mari. The sparse decorations her mother had put up helped, but it was her nana's presence that made the real difference.

While Sinéad put the kettle on, Niamh made Mari answer sums, before throwing her a clove rock sweet like a dog waiting for treats. Mari was pretty sure she got a few wrong too, but the sweets kept coming.

'Now, Missy. How are you getting on with the rest of your schooling?'

'I've done a project, Nana. It's being sent to the Mayor's office. I'm not sure whether they'll use it though.'

'Why, that's grand. What was it about?'

'Our local mosque. And our church. I met an imam and of course, Father George helped too.'

'Well, dear, that sounds very interesting,' Niamh replied, but there was an edge to her tone that Mari didn't quite understand.

After more talking and laughing Niamh declared it was time for tea and, as always, took over the kitchen. She began to cook one of Mari's favourite dishes – Lamb stew. There was always enough for a few days and it got tastier every day.

'It's at its best after a week,' she said, as usual. 'But it's too delicious to last that long. Now, me darlin', how would you like to come and spend Christmas with me?'

Mari whooped with delight. 'I'd love it,' she looked at her mother.

'Good.' Sinéad said. 'I've finally got myself a little job.'

'In Ireland?'

'No, here. Just a mail-order company but we need the money, Mari, and it's long and late hours. I can't leave you on your own. You're going tomorrow. Until school starts.'

Later that night, as Mari was tucked up on the sofa, she listened to what she could hear of the conversation in the kitchen.

Sinéad was speaking. 'So what about Jimmy and the bitch. Anything I should know about?'

'Your brother barely keeps in touch with me now, never mind you. He's taken against Kenny. Who, by the way, is finally moving in.'

Mari remembered Kenny, but *Brother?* She was shocked. *I have an uncle?*

9

24th December

Karen, a large carrier bag in hand, and John stood on the doorstep of Jack and Sal's house. They were the closest thing Karen had to family, and she had spent every Christmas that she could remember with them. This year was going to be different. The door opened and the well-rounded, blonde Sal, opened the door with a frown on her face.

'How could you do this, love? Your uncle, I mean Jack, he's beside himself.' She looked as if she was about to burst into tears.

Karen was horrified. 'I'm so sorry, Sal. I didn't realise he'd be upset.' She turned to glare at John. 'This is all your fault.'

John, who had seen the somewhat thinner, balding man, creep into the hall with his finger to his mouth, began to snigger. 'Ow!' he said as Karen elbowed him.

'You daft bat,' Jack, grinning broadly, said to her. 'We're not that sad. Now give us a kiss, love.'

'You two... ' Karen smiled as she obliged. 'I'd definitely rather be here tomorrow than,' she looked back at John, 'there.'

'Come on in and have a drink. It's only right that your lad here spends the day with you and his folk.'

'You haven't met them,' Karen said. 'I mean *her*. Big John's lovely. But Daphne... '

'Shush,' Sal stopped her, leading her into the sitting room. 'This evening's about us, not them. Now, what will you have?' She looked at John. 'I assume you're driving?'

John nodded. 'Orange juice for me.'

'Now, lad,' Jack said to him as he handed over the drink, 'I want an update on all this technology stuff. I'm thinking of doing a photography class.'

Sal took the opportunity to draw Karen into the kitchen. 'What's happening with you two? I thought I'd be buying a dress for your wedding by now.'

'Oh, Sal. You'll be waiting a long time for that. I'm going to be an Inspector now, remember?'

'Yes, clever girl. But you can do both. And I know he's keen.'

'I do love him. But the thought of having kids... ' she grimaced.

'And I'd have loved to have them,' Sal replied.

'I'm sorry,' Karen said. 'I didn't mean to... '

Sal put her palm up. 'Of course not, and it's none of my business. Now then, how about that Prosecco?'

'Please.'

They re-joined Jack and John in the sitting room where Jack had clearly reached the end of his understanding but John was still in full flow.

'John, love, give him a rest will you?' Sal grinned. 'He's a bit slow these days.'

Karen leapt in. 'Jack, what do you know about terrorism?'

Sal rolled her eyes. 'Well, that's a cheery subject for Christmas.'

'No, Sal, it's interesting.'

'Is this about your placement?' Jack asked.

Karen nodded. 'Apparently, I've spent too long in the suburbs and need to prepare myself for real life. You lived in London before settling here, didn't you?'

'That I did, love. I could tell you a few stories. It was all Libyans and IRA in those days. Sal could tell you a thing or two about that.'

'Karen turned to Sal. 'Really?' I didn't know you were in the police?'

Sal laughed. 'No, not my thing at all, love. But I was working in London when I was a teenager. In one of the big stores on Oxford Street.'

Karen frowned. 'And what's that got to do with the IRA?'

'They bombed Harrods,' Sal said, her face suddenly serious. 'I knew people who worked there. No one who died though. '

'People died?' Karen interrupted, suddenly horrified.

'Six.' Sal nodded. 'Seventeenth of December 1983. Just before Christmas.'

'Why didn't I know this?' Karen said.

'There was a long bombing campaign in London,' Jack replied. 'Went on for years.'

'How could I not know?' Karen said, looking at John.

'Because you never watch the news,' he said. 'Don't you remember 7/7?'

Karen frowned. 'The London bombings? I was at uni then.'

'I knew about them,' John said. But I had to be reminded,' he acknowledged.

Jack leant forward. 'That's because we move on. We have to. But their families will never ever forget. I suggest a toast to all those who lost their lives.'

'Yes.' Sal raised her glass. Karen and John followed suit.

'Now then,' Jack smiled. 'How about some present opening?'

'No, how about this?' Karen pulled a box out of her Waitrose bag for life.

'Cards Against Humanity?' Jack read the title on the box.

'Oh, God,' John wiped his brow with his hand. 'Karen?'

'Macy said it was good.' Karen replied.

'Just promise me you're not thinking of taking *that* to my parents' tomorrow.'

Karen grinned. 'What's it worth?'

10

Mari had slept well on the ferry, the long boring coach journey to Liverpool now forgotten. She charged onto the deck, leaned over the railings and watched until the glimmerings of sunrise began.

'Mari!' Niamh was shouting after her. 'Will you come and get some breakfast inside you?'

They just had time to grab a couple of muffins before the cafe closed. Then they went down to get their cases from the cabin. While Niamh managed to get someone to take pity on her and carry her bag for her, Mari ran upstairs to watch the ferry docking, fascinated as the seamen hauled the ferry into place by tying giant ropes around the mooring bollard.

'Mari!'

She ran to join her nana to disembark together. When they were on land, Mari could see her grandmother looking around anxiously. Then her face crinkled into a smile. Mari followed her gaze and saw a man wearing a flat cap, standing in the car park waving at them. He ambled up to them and took both their bags.

'Top of the morning to you, ladies. Your carriage awaits. Do you remember me, Miss Mari?'

'Yes, I do.'

'Then I've not got too old already.'

Mari laughed and followed him to his old pickup truck.

'Room for three little ones up front,' Kenny said as he put their bags in the back. Niamh pushed Mari up into the cabin and then waited for Kenny to do the same for her.

'How much have you been eating while you've been away?' Kenny joked as he manhandled Niamh into place.

'It's a dreadfully cold place, London, so it is. A woman's got to eat.'

Kenny, with a small grunt, climbed into the driver's seat and started the engine.

'Now don't tell your ma about this truck,' Niamh whispered to Mari. 'It doesn't have belts but Kenny is a very good driver.'

Mari giggled at the secret and relished the excitement of an illicit journey in such an unusual vehicle. It was a very bumpy ride but she enjoyed every second. With Dublin behind them, they came off the motorway and headed out into the countryside. Mari thought she recognised some of the names of the villages they went through. Then as they got close, she did remember the little old pub on the corner of the lane that led to her grandmother's house. 'We went there, didn't we, Nana?'

'I expect so,' Niamh winked. 'Tis the only pub for miles.'

Mari's eyes were glued to the windscreen, looking at the road ahead. When the pretty white-washed, thatched cottage came into view, she squeaked.

'That's it, it's just as I remembered it.'

Kenny pulled up outside and Mari climbed over the gear stick to get out his side she was so impatient.

'It's got smaller!' she exclaimed as Kenny helped Niamh down from the seat.

He took their bags to the front door.

Niamh laughed. 'No, dear, it's you who's got bigger.'

'I'll see you later then, ladies,' Kenny tipped his cap to them, climbed back in his truck, and drove off down the lane.

Mari ran to the door and waited for Niamh to open it.

'It's open,' she puffed as she walked up to Mari. 'We don't lock things out here. Suppose there was an emergency?'

'But in London... '

'We're not in London, thank the Lord.'

Mari opened the door and walked into the little hall.

'Nana! You're as untidy as me. What are all these boxes?' She remembered that the cottage always seemed cluttered, but now there was stuff all over the floor.

'Oh, sweet mother of heaven,' Niamh squeaked. 'I forgot. I've been clearing space for Kenny.' She scratched her head 'Where am I going to put it all? This is your mother's stuff and...' she tailed off. 'Did you know she kept things here after all these years? Such a hoarder.'

'Can I help?' Mari asked.

'No, you can't,' came the firm reply. 'Can you remember the room you were in?' Mari shook her head.

'Well, there's only the three of them and your bedroom's all pink. Be a good girl and get yourself up there. Unpack your stuff and get yourself sorted. I have to go and help Kenny pack. He's moving in today. But nothing's happening until we've had a nice cup of tea. I'm gasping, aren't you?'

Once she'd said it, Mari found that she was very thirsty. They sat and chatted over a cup of tea and a few biscuits then Niamh got up.

'That's better. Now, sweetie, are you all right if I leave you alone for a while? I'm only up the lane. When you've unpacked you can watch a bit of telly if you like. I won't be long, but Kenny, well he's a man who needs a lot of sorting out.'

'I'm fine, Nana. You go.'

Left on her own, Mari experienced a rush of relief, excitement, and pleasure. In the little bedroom, she looked out of the window and couldn't see another dwelling from that or any of the windows in the cottage. It was there she realised how much she loved the open spaces of the Irish countryside and how much it felt like home to her. *I'll live here when I'm older*, she decided as she went downstairs.

When she went to use the toilet she passed one of the large cardboard boxes. On the way back she couldn't resist the urge to look inside it. Feeling a little guilty, she knelt on the floor and took a closer look. It seemed to be full of old papers and letters.

She delved in with both hands and parted some of them, catching sight of the edge of a photo. She pulled it out to take a close look and gasped when she saw it properly. It was a very old photo of an Indian family. There were two parents and a boy standing outside a small, terraced house which looked very British. The boy looked strangely familiar but at first, she couldn't think why. Then it came to her in a rush. This was her father and his parents.

'So there is family,' she said out loud, dropping the photo. 'First an uncle, now this. What else didn't you tell me, Mum?'

11

'So you see, Maryam, we will not be moving away just yet.' Aram said.

'I'm sorry that your family in Turkey are not ready for you yet,' she replied. 'But I am glad of your company for a little longer.'

Raahel, Aram's wife, took Maryam's hands. 'And because of this, there is something else we would like to ask you.'

Maryam was filled with eager anticipation of the question she hoped they might ask, and fear that they would not. 'Ask away. I will always do what I can for you.'

Raahel's eyes twinkled. 'Baklava,' she said. 'Can you make us some of your wonderful baklava?'

Maryam disguised her disappointment well. 'Of course,' she replied. 'Any time.'

'Because,' Aram smiled at her, 'we would like you to enjoy it with us at our Christmas celebrations.'

'What?' Maryam's eyes widened. She had been caught out. 'That would be wonderful. Please let me know if there's any mending you need before the time comes. I would be honoured to do it for you.'

'We will,' Raahel said.

'And come soon,' Aram looked at the clock. 'We will be starting it all shortly.'

'And you must stay the night,' Raahel insisted.

Maryam politely refused. 'I will be locking my door tonight,' she said. 'Don't you worry about me. I will be listening for the sound of the bells.'

'We all do that,' Raahel laughed. 'And it's every night. Not just Christmas Eve.'

'I will see you later.' Maryam closed her door and went into the kitchen to begin preparations. When she emerged, it was to walk to Aram's house a few blocks away. He and Raahel lived in a traditional Syrian house with an inner courtyard. Maryam noted how sparse the house looked. *They've been packing up already,* she correctly surmised.

In the courtyard, a small bonfire had been constructed, ready to be ignited. Aram was in an animated conversation with a neighbour.

'The British have been bombing again,' the man told him. 'Two days running in Mosul. Maybe there is no need for you to go?'

Aram shook his head. 'We are determined we must go. But, my friend, I hope you are right.' He turned to greet Maryam. 'Welcome.'

'Is that true?' Maryam looked at the other man. 'Are they fighting for us?'

'They are certainly fighting Daesh,' he replied. 'And that is good for us.'

'Come,' Aram intervened. 'My son has an important job to do.'

Maryam's face, previously tense, broke into a smile. 'The reading.'

Aram nodded. 'His first time. He has been rehearsing. I must fetch him.'

The small gathering stood silently as Aram's youngest son, standing in front of the pile of branches and pieces of wood, began reciting the Nativity story in the courtyard. Maryam smiled and encouraged him as he stumbled over some of the words. 'Well done,' she beamed as he finished. She held him close to her as they watched his father.

'Now for the fire,' Aram stepped forward with a long, lit taper as Raahel passed around candles for the others to hold.

The bonfire, slow to light at first, suddenly burst into flame. 'It will be a good year,' the neighbour observed. 'Praise be to God.'

They recited psalms until the flames had subsided and the fire was dwindling. Aram seized the little boy and held him tightly. Now for the best bit,' he grinned. 'Are you ready? Have you made your wish?'

The boy gave a muffled response. The others watched as Aram first stepped back, then ran a few steps before leaping over the still-glowing embers. They cheered, then taking turns, began to leap the remnants of the fire as he had done.

'Your turn,' Aram urged Maryam.

'I am too old,' she resisted.

'Nonsense.' Aram took her arm and guided her towards the embers. She took in a deep breath and steadied herself, gathering up her dress so as not to catch any sparks from the fire. Feeling like a little girl again, she ran and leapt, clearing the fire with ease. She was greeted with cheers and applause from the others.

Later, when the others had gone and the children were in bed, she talked a little more with Aram and Raahel. 'Aram, I think you are right,' she said. 'I think next year will be a good year. '

Aram nodded. 'It's been quieter recently. We haven't heard so much from our enemies. Maybe their power is dwindling.'

'Let us hope so,' Raahel added. 'Maybe then we can stay. I love it here so much.'

'We all do,' Maryam replied. 'I must go home. See you in church tomorrow.'

12

By the time Niamh returned with Kenny and Laddie, the border collie, Mari had gone through the box very thoroughly. She had even read some of the letters her father had sent her mother while he was stationed in Iraq. They were real love letters full of *missing* and *wanting*. It was overwhelming. Ordinarily, she'd have been wanting to meet and fuss over the dog, but instead, Niamh came in to see her granddaughter sitting in the hall crying.

'Oh, sweetie. What's the matter?'

Without looking up, Mari handed her the photo she had first seen. Her words were punctuated with sobs and fast breathing. 'She said there was no family. Look, Nana. Are these my other grandparents? I overheard Mum talk about a brother. Now I've found this. Do I have other aunts and uncles? Pakistani ones?'

'Dear God in heaven,' Niamh muttered and blessed herself as her eyes took in the photo. 'Let's clear this away. Your mother will kill me for letting you see all this.'

'But it's my right to know! They are my family too.' Mari looked up, anger in her eyes. 'She should have told me the truth.'

Niamh looked round where Kenny stood as still as a statue. She gestured for him to go upstairs. 'Is the dog sorted?' Kenny nodded. 'Take your clothes up and start unpacking. I can trust you to do that, can't I?'

'Aye.'

Niamh put her arm around the girl gently encouraging her to stand up. She led her into the sitting room and sat her down in the chair.

'It's not as easy as all that,' she began. 'Do you think your ma would want to hurt you on purpose?'

'Then why did she keep all this from me?' Mari snapped.

'I'll put the kettle on.' Niamh went into the kitchen, returning with two mugs of tea and an even larger plate of chocolate biscuits. Miserable as she was, Mari could not resist them, and Niamh elicited the tiniest smile from her as she bit into one.

'Heavens now. Where shall I begin?' Niamh sighed. 'When your ma fell in love with Mo, well, we were all surprised. He was a soldier and he'd been stationed here to help keep the peace they called it. It was when the troubles were fading and things were getting a tiny bit more friendly. There were a few pubs that welcomed them and your ma was working in one of them.'

'So he was drinking? I thought it wasn't allowed.'

'He didn't seem to care much for his faith. I suppose that's partly why we took to him. He was just one of the lads. He proved to us how much he cared for her and he was such a charming young man. Your grandpa and I were very taken with him.'

'So what was the problem?'

'It's complicated, my dear. His family, well, they had their own way of doing things. I don't know if they knew he was drinking but they made it clear he'd have to marry one of their own.'

'But surely it was up to him?'

'Well, you and I think that to be sure, but not everybody thinks that way. Faith is important and some people think that you can have a stronger family if you're all from the same community.'

'So what happened?'

'Well, to be honest, I don't think they liked him being a soldier either. Maybe they had other ideas for him and didn't like him going away and fighting. Listen, love, it's beyond me, but he loved being a soldier and never had any doubts. So by the time he met your ma, he was already, how can I put it, estranged from his family.'

'So they disowned him? Is that what you're saying?'

'I suppose that'll be the top and bottom of it.'

'Did they know about me?'

'Ah, well, your ma did write to them when your daddy was killed. She wrote it when she was here with me. But they sent the letter back unopened. Our local postie would have known it was from here.'

Mari ran back to the hall and rummaged through the box pulling out the letter, still sealed. The address had been scrubbed out and Niamh's address scribbled over it. She looked at her nana for encouragement and got a nod in reply.

'You might as well see it now; the damage is already done.'

Mari pulled open the envelope and took out the contents. A small photo of her as a baby fell out as she did so. She read the letter out loud.

'Dear Mr and Mrs Lone. I have very sad news to tell you. Your son Mohammed was killed in action in Iraq. I don't know when precisely it happened as he was on special duties. All I know is that he was given an Islamic service as soon as possible. His dog tags were returned to me. I know he loved you both very much and I hope you can find it in your hearts to forgive him. He was a very brave and very loving man. We have a daughter, Mari. I've sent a photo. If you would like to come and meet her you would be very welcome.'

Mari and Niamh sat in silence. This time tears were slowly running down the old woman's face. 'Aye, that was a grand letter. So now you know.'

'What about Uncle Jimmy? Was it the same with him?'

The old lady's expression gave her away.

'But what have I ever done to him?' Mari's eyes were welling up.

Niamh hugged her tightly.

'It's like I say. Some people only want to stay with their own. Your ma and your nana love you more than anything. You know that, don't you?'

Mari nodded and looked up. 'Can I tell Mum I know?'

'No point in hiding it now, love. But no need to tell her straight away. We'll find the right moment when we get back. Now tidy up that box and I'll get Kenny to put it away in the loft when he comes down.'

Mari picked the letters up, making sure everything was put back as it was before; all except for one. The letter her mother had written and the envelope it was in. That, she kept back. And when she went back to her bedroom she put it in the pocket of her suitcase.

13

Christmas morning, Maryam, carrying a large linen bag, approached the church to attend Mass. She could see through the open doors of the small stone church that it was not well attended; there were even fewer people than there were at the previous evening's service. She counted only five children, but she was pleased to see that the missionaries had come.

She hurried to join the small congregation gathered inside. This year they all exchanged greetings and heartfelt hugs before settling in their pews. As usual, the church was lit by a small central bonfire and a multitude of candles, large and small, burning in every corner.

The priest came in; a figure of Jesus Christ clutched in his hands. He walked around the church while the congregation chanted hymns and prayers. Then setting the figure down, he reached to touch the hand of an old lady sitting in the front. 'I give you the touch of peace,' he said. She nodded and turned to her neighbour, doing the same. And so the touch of peace was passed around the church to everyone.

The hymn chanting that accompanied was loud and joyful and Maryam felt a great sense of identity and belonging.

When the service was over, Maryam took care to speak to every one of the congregation. She handed out her handmade toys and clothes to the children and wished everyone a happy Christmas with hope for a better new year. The priest's nephew stood with his father. She noticed how his eyes lit up when she handed him the shirt she had made for him.

At last, she had seen and spoken to everyone she could. Maryam hurried home to get ready for the rest of the day. She looked forward to Raahel's cooking – especially at this time of year. There was so much variety; dishes that there was no point in a solitary widow making for herself. And it made a nice change to have company. But she had her own contribution to make. Her speciality. Her baklava.

Putting on her best apron, she began the preparations. She always made her filo pastry and enjoyed the process of rolling, dusting, and stacking the layers before rolling again and again. Many years of practice meant that she made the perfect size for the baking tray without needing to trim. Spreading the crushed walnuts and sugar was the easy bit. Then covering the whole, she began to cut the diamond shapes. But with Maryam's baklava, each portion also contained a small cross. Before long, Maryam's house was filled with the wonderful aroma coming from her oven.

When Maryam arrived at Aram's house, she was warmly greeted by his whole family, especially his little daughter and young son.

'This is for you, Talitha.' Maryam handed her a small present wrapped in tissue paper. The girl hurriedly pulled off the paper to reveal a beautifully finished little doll. 'I love her,' the girl replied, hugging the doll tightly to her chest.

'And for you, Taley.' She handed the boy a flat present, also wrapped in tissue paper.

'A new shirt? Thank you, Maryam,' he replied.

'Come. Have some wine,' Aram said. 'Let us sit in wonder at these delicious smells coming from the kitchen.'

'I must first greet your hardworking wife,' Maryam replied, going into the kitchen.

'Raahel, may I help you?'

Raahel turned around from the oven. She waved her hand. 'It's all done. What will be will be. Maybe the Lord will keep us safe from my poor cooking.'

Maryam laughed. 'Your cooking is wonderful,' she exclaimed as she handed Raahel the wrapped packet of baklava.

'But not as good as yours,' Raahel replied, putting the parcel down, and hugging Maryam. 'Now, please sit and enjoy yourself.'

Maryam followed instructions and sat in the living area next to Aram. 'Have you heard any more news about our allies?'

Aram nodded. 'I have heard from my friend in Mosul that there have been more bombings there.'

Maryam crossed herself. 'May God forgive those who kill to help us.'

'Indeed,' Aram nodded. 'But please do not expect them to save us,' he added. 'I still believe you will be safer far away from this place.'

Maryam sipped at her wine. 'This is nice,' she said, and the conversation was ended.

Raahel appeared to summon them to the dining table.

'This looks wonderful, Raahel,' Maryam said.

'Sit and eat,' Raahel ordered. 'It is time for my glass of wine now,' she laughed.

They dined on mezze platters, followed by traditional chicken and lamb dishes, accompanied by sufficient, but not copious, amounts of wine.

'And now for your superb baklava,' Raahel announced, looking at Maryam.

'And how do you know it is superb?' Aram teased.

'Because somebody had to try it,' Raahel laughed. 'Thank you again, my dear friend. May we eat together again one day.' She raised her glass.

'May it be so,' Aram said.

'If God wills,' Maryam added.

Maryam enjoyed the day so much that, for a while, she forgot all her worries and basked in the warm, friendly company of her friends. *Maybe we will all be saved*.

But later, as she walked home, the cool air began to penetrate her body. She pulled her shawl around her shoulders and thought of the year ahead. *How many of us will there be then?*

14

On Christmas Eve, Mari went to her first ever Midnight Mass. It was something her mother rarely bothered about – not least because of their neighbourhood. Out in the countryside, though, it seemed magical to her. Kenny had driven them in the truck and as soon as she caught sight of the church lights, Mari had been transfixed. Best of all was the carol singing and she'd sung her heart out. As they drove home she was contemplative.

'How can there be so much anger and hatred if it's all about peace and love?'

'It's the people,' Niamh told her. 'We're all sinners and some are worse than others.'

'But didn't the Catholics and the protestants fight each other?'

'Ah, it's more complicated than that, and the British have a lot to answer for. Always meddling in other countries... '

'And our church here has an awful lot to answer for too,' Kenny interrupted. 'We're home and now's not the time.' He parked the truck and opened the front door for Niamh and Mari.

'How about a few stories?'

'Get away with you,' Niamh said.

'Please,' Mari looked at him.

'C'mon, Kenny ushered them into the living room and while Niamh resurrected the fire, he began.

Well then. 'There was this little fella called Sheamus... '

After a late night listening to some funny tales of elves and leprechauns, Mari went to sleep tired but very happy.

***

Christmas morning, Mari shivered in her nightie in the cold of the cottage but she was still in a good mood from the night before. Niamh had taught her how to light the fire and it made her feel very grown-up. Lighting some kindling, she held a sheet of newspaper covering the surround, leaving enough of a gap for the draft to fan the flame. When it was crackling away, she went into the kitchen, opened the door, and called Laddie in from his well-insulated kennel. She knew where his food was and forked out the contents of a tin into his bowl. Wrinkling her nose at the smell, she was feeling hungry herself. She took the lid off the bread bin and cut a thick slice off the locally baked bread. Then, taking her nana's big old toasting fork she sat in front of the fire toasting it. Laddie joined her when he'd emptied his bowl.

Even from downstairs, she could hear Niamh's snoring. She gazed at the little Christmas tree and knew there was a present for her underneath it but was happy enough to wait. Mari usually dreaded her nana's presents. It always seemed to be big bright jumpers which she could never wear at home. Here, however, she would have liked such a jumper, but Nana was being unusually strict. 'No presents until after lunch,' she'd said.

Kenny came downstairs first. He was meant to be sleeping in her uncle's old room. Mari neither knew nor cared whether he was; she knew her nana was happy and that was all that mattered. He saw Laddie. 'Shall we take him for a walk?' Mari nodded. 'Well then, you'd better get some clothes on you, Miss.'

Outside, it was cold and crisp, as if everything had been covered with sugar frosting. Kenny was good company and he kept Mari amused with tales about some of their neighbours.

By the time they got back, Niamh was up and the table was laid with full breakfasts for both of them. Mari noticed that the turkey was already in the oven. Laddie was allowed in and begged for scraps from their plates. When they'd finished eating, Kenny played his mouth organ while Laddie howled along. This made Mari laugh so much it hurt.

'Come on, we'll be late for mass,' Niamh scolded them.

'Another one?' said Mari as she was hustled out.

'Good for the soul,' Niamh nodded at her.

At lunchtime, Niamh poured Mari a small glass of sparkling wine as a special treat. Then, after an entire box of twelve crackers had been pulled, Kenny carved the enormous turkey while Niamh served the vegetables and gravy. Mari had never seen so much food on her plate before. She managed as well as she could but struggled when it came to the Christmas pudding – which Kenny insisted on setting fire to.

50

'Eat up now. How do you think I got this wonderful figure?' Niamh winked at Mari.

When they were all so full they could hardly move, it was finally time to open the presents. Yes, there was another jumper for Mari and Kenny was delighted with his new cap. Sinéad had bought her mother a pretty necklace from both of them and Niamh seemed to love it.

'Now for your other present, Mari,' Niamh announced.

'What?' Mari looked surprised.

Kenny held up his finger and went out into the lobby. He returned with a large, wrapped parcel.

Mari's mouth dropped open when she saw the size of it. Excitedly, she ripped off all the paper. Niamh, looking apprehensive, watched her until at last it was revealed.

'A laptop? That's amazing! How did you know?'

'A little bird told me it would help with your homework.'

Mari got up and hugged her tightly.

'It's wonderful,' she said. 'Just perfect.'

'And how are you getting on at school?'

'I'll be a lot better now,' Mari replied. 'Do you have the Internet here?'

'Aye. I've been working on that,' Kenny said. 'Give me a jiffy and I'll get you on it. Although I daresay we'll only get a signal when the moon's in the second quarter,' he winked at her.

A few hours later, when a harassed-looking Kenny finally emerged from the little dining room, he made an announcement. 'Well now, it's all yours,' he said to Mari. 'The hardest part is putting in this frisking password. Why they have to be so long, God only knows. Come, lass.' He tilted his head back to the dining room. 'Sit at the table and I'll start you off.'

It took him a while and a lot of suppressed swearing before the connection was established, but Mari, who'd used computers at school, was quick to pick it all up. When her nana had retired to her bedroom, Mari had already begun looking up names and addresses.

15

After their Christmas dinner, Karen and John were exchanging glances while his mother, Daphne, held court. Karen had history and she had only agreed to go to his parents for the day if they could escape to the pub as soon as dinner was finished. Big John had already escaped to say *hello* to a few of the neighbours, but Karen felt stranded. She had reached the end of her tether after forcing herself to be polite and smile sweetly all through dinner. She was sure she would burst if her torture lasted a moment longer. John seemed determined not to respond to her increasingly angry expressions.

'More tea, dear?' Daphne asked John.

'John?' Karen tried to hide the growl in her voice. 'There's somewhere we have to be. Remember?'

'Yes, my love,' John muttered. 'Just a tiny drop more, Mum.'

Daphne threw Karen a triumphant look.

Karen watched John take his last sip before getting up and nearly ripping his arm from its socket.

'Owwer. See you later, Mum. We'll bring Dad back with us.'

In the pub, Karen downed her glass of mulled wine in one before beginning her tirade.

'I'll get you another, ' John said, dashing to the bar. She let rip when he returned.

'She's just found out I've passed the first stage of my Inspector's exams and what does she buy me for Christmas? A make-up palette? For Christ's sake!'

'Shush. Dad's meeting us here, remember? Pipe down. You're the only person I know who could get angry over a Christmas present. She means well, you know that.'

'Does she? Or is it just her way of telling me to get more feminine like herself? I mean, where does she get off?'

'Can't you give it to someone? Macy?'

Karen laughed. It broke the tension. 'I don't think it would suit her skin tone, you moron. Emma, maybe.' She sipped at the fresh glass.

'Sorry, Pumpkin. It's over now. Dad'll be here any minute.'

Almost before he'd finished speaking, Big John Steele appeared through the doorway.

'He's here!' John gave Karen such a dig in the ribs she nearly spat out her wine.

Big John came over to join them. Karen liked *him* very much so she put on a smile and shuffled up to give him room to sit down.

'Dad? Pint?'

'Aye please.' John got up and his father turned to Karen. 'Now Karen, tell me all your news properly. What does it all mean? '

'Well, now I've passed my exams, they match candidates with suitable vacancies. Then the real test begins. I have to work as an Inspector on a temporary basis. That means I have to be assessed until they decide I'm ready to take a proper Inspector's job.'

'They move you? Where to?'

'East London. I don't know the exact details yet. I worked with The Met recently, so it would be nice to work for them again. The opportunities are much greater in London, and so are the challenges.'

'And you love challenges, don't you, Karen?'

Karen grinned as John joined them carrying his father's pint and *another* glass of mulled wine for Karen.

'How was Uncle Gary?' John asked. 'And why did you have to go and see him?'

'Because I wanted to get something very special, for a very special person. And I knew he'd be able to get it for me.'

Karen interrupted. 'Who's Uncle Gary?'

Big John answered for his son. 'He's a journalist of sorts now. Writes about military stuff. Freelance, I think.'

John frowned. 'But what on earth would he be able to get for Mum?'

'Silly lad,' Big John said as John handed him his pint. He took a big swig then put the glass down. Looking at Karen, he reached into his pocket, brought out a leather case and put it on the table.

'Glasses?' John guessed. 'Who needs glasses?'

'It's not glasses,' Karen said, staring at the case. 'I think I know what it is. But who's it for? Daphne wouldn't want one of those.'

Big John leant closer to Karen. 'I'm sorry about our Daph. She's not a bad woman, just a bit old-fashioned. In her day, women didn't leave the house without a full face of war paint. She still thinks you use it sometimes. She didn't mean any harm.'

Karen smiled. 'I suppose. Besides, there are the very *very* few occasions when I might need to dress up a bit.'

'You're a good lass,' Big John said. 'But I thought you deserved something a bit more… ' he paused. 'More useful.'

Karen smiled. 'Yes. Useful is always better.' She looked at him strangely. He was grinning like a Cheshire cat. She followed his gaze. He was looking at the case.

'No!' she said. 'For me?'

John shuffled in his chair. He stared at the object on the table then looked at his father. 'It's not, is it?'

Big John winked at his son then turned to Karen. 'Open it, lass. Let's all have a look.'

Karen took the case as if it was made of glass. She opened the clasp and tipped the shiny red object into the palm of her hand. 'It's beautiful,' she said. 'Thanks so much.' She leaned forward to kiss Big John on the cheek.

John took the Swiss army knife from her and began to study it. 'It's extraordinary,' he said. 'I've never seen one with all these functions before. Clever old Uncle Gary.'

'No telling her indoors, please.' Big John tapped his nose

'How did you think of this?' Karen said, her eyes shining.

'Because I used to have one and I loved it,' Big John replied. 'And I thought, what's a girl like Karen most likely to need?'

'It's perfect,' she said.

Big John looked at his son, who was still fondling the knife. 'I'll get you one next year,' he said. 'Matching set.'

John smiled, handing it back to Karen.

16

When Sinéad went to meet Mari at the coach stop, she immediately noticed a difference in her daughter. She was somehow more grown-up, more adult, but also strangely quiet. This was both good and bad. *She's not a bad child, but she's still got a devil in her. God help us if she meets a boy.*

Scooping the girl up in her arms, she gave Mari a big kiss, laughing when her daughter wriggled free of her hug.

'Did you have a good time, love?'

'Yes,' Mari answered without making eye contact.

'Did you not like your present?' she asked. 'Ma told me what she'd done. I told her off. She doesn't have that sort of money to throw around.'

Mari was politely enthusiastic. 'It was the best thing ever.'

When they arrived home, Sinéad watched her daughter closely, suddenly conscious that the tiny flat was no comparison to her mother's cosy cottage, especially as she had already taken down the Christmas decorations. 'I know it's not the same as Nana's,' she began.

'It's fine,' Mari said. 'It's a lot warmer.' She hauled her bags into her tiny bedroom, closing the door behind her.

Sinéad had been tipped off by Niamh about her daughter's discovery. After leaving time for Mari to unpack, she knocked on the door and went in. 'Do you have any questions for me, love?' Mari shook her head. 'Then how about I help you reorganise so we can set up your laptop?'

This brought a more positive response. 'Yes please.' Mari's face lit up for a moment. 'But we don't have the internet here, do we?' her face fell.

'We do now,' Sinéad smiled. 'And it's wireless. Come on. If we move this over there a bit, I reckon we can get a little desk in this space.'

'But I don't have a desk,' Mari said, looking at her mother, whose face was creasing into a smile.

'Will you check out the wardrobe?' Sinéad said. 'It'll take a bit of effort but I reckon we can do it between us.' She spoke as her daughter opened the wardrobe door

'Oh, Mum!' She pulled out a large, heavy cardboard box. It had a picture of a small desk on the side. 'It's perfect,' Mari said, giving her mother a big hug.

'Better make sure we can assemble it first,' Sinéad laughed.

An hour later, the desk was in place and Mari could reach it by sitting on the end of her bed. Sinéad set up the wires and fiddled with the settings until she got the connection established. 'I'll leave you to it now,' she kissed her daughter on the top of her head.

Sitting on the sofa, she was feeling more comfortable about things. Mari was soon going to be fifteen, an age at which Sinéad felt comfortable leaving her on her own while she was at work. *So far, so good,* she thought.

***

On her own again, Mari remembered that some of the girls at school were on Facebook. She signed up and immediately began to search. Carly wasn't there but Razia was. Tentatively she responded to a post and Razia replied almost straight away.

`Hello! Did you have a good Christmas?`

`I went to Ireland with my Nana. She bought me this laptop. You?`

`It was OK. Saeed says he'll help you with your maths.`

Mari sat back; she had completely forgotten about Razia's suggestion.

`BRILLIANT!`
she typed back.

`He says come round after school on Thursday.`

Tell him thanks.

See you Monday.

See you.

Mari felt strangely happy. She jumped when Sinéad stuck her head round the door.

'Are you OK, love? I'm just going out for a while.'

'I'm fine.'

Mari waited for the sound of the front door slamming. She took out the envelope she had taken from her mother's box in Ireland. She could still read the address underneath the scribbles. *Hornchurch, Essex*.

She typed in the postcode and brought up a map. It didn't look too complicated. She copied the map by hand into an old notebook and wrote the full address at the top to make sure she didn't get it wrong.

It made her think about Saeed again. She found a website which looked informative and began to read. But she didn't hear her mother come in. As Sinéad walked into her bedroom, Mari slammed the laptop lid down.

'Can't you knock?'

'What?'

'I'm not a kid anymore.'

'Sorry I spoke.' Sinéad shut the door behind her and went into the kitchen. 'It's starting,' she muttered to herself. 'Bloody teenagers.'

17

Wednesday 6th January

'It's come through!' Karen besieged John in the kitchen when she came home.

He jumped. 'That quickly?'

'Quickly? I was expecting to hear last year. It's brilliant news. Harris is back tomorrow. I've cleared my desk and I won't have to see his smarmy face ever again. What's for dinner, I'm starving.'

'It would help if you gave me some idea of when to expect you.'

Karen frowned. 'We can't all be nine-to-fivers. Some of us have to work all hours.'

'I do, too, when it's *essential*,' John countered. 'You do it out of choice. Anyway, I'm trying out a new recipe tonight, so you'll just have to be patient.'

'Again?' Karen clutched her stomach. 'I haven't recovered from yesterday's yet.'

'Hmm.' John pondered. You were in the bathroom a long time last night.'

'Exactly,' Karen said.

'Simple mix up with the Tabasco measurements. There's none in the pasta. I promise.'

'Don't you think it's about time we got a dog?' Karen asked.

John waved his wooden spoon with menace. 'And what has that got to do with anything?'

'So we can feed it everything you make instead of chucking it.' She ducked his pretend throw.

'I had actually thought of that for all the dinners you never come home to,' he replied.

Karen pouted. 'I haven't done that in ages.'

'But no doubt you will at the new place. Especially if you're commuting.'

'I can ring you when I'm on the train.'

John sighed. 'Just like an old married couple. Except, of course, we're not.'

'Not now, John.'

'OK. When do you start?'

'Tomorrow,' Karen beamed. 'Can't wait.'

After they had eaten and exchanged the obligatory *that was shite*, they sat watching the TV. Whilst the weekend was strictly for reality shows, mid-week TV, since they had been living together, always began with the news. There was another report of a terrorist attack in Paris.

'On the anniversary of the Charlie Hebdo attack,' John noted.

'Why France?' Karen said. 'Although there was the knife attack in Leytonstone last year.'

'Is that where you're going?' John asked.

'Close enough,' Karen replied.

'It's not a terrorist hotbed though, is it?' Karen shook her head. 'So why the connection?'

'Just following on from our conversation with Jack and Sal. Macy and I were talking about it recently too. About those girls who ran off to Syria. She had a false alarm with a runaway just before Christmas. I'm just wondering if it's going to be a *thing*.'

'I sincerely hope not,' John replied. 'But these kids are extremely vulnerable and easily led. And at that age, it's an adventure. The passion of youth. Having a cause.'

'Did you ever have a cause?' Karen wondered.

'I had a cycle,' John grinned.

***

Thursday 7th January

Karen's journey to her new station was much harder than she'd imagined. She'd rarely gone into London before and found the whole commuting experience complicated. Normally well-prepared, she'd had no idea about early morning ticket queues, incomprehensible machines, or the intimacy of the *crush* hour. She tumbled into her new station at a just about respectable eight-twenty-seven and was ushered straight into a grubby back office to meet her new boss, DCI Baron.

'So you're the famous DS Karen Thorpe?' the tall black man said as he stood to shake her hand. 'I expected someone older.'

'Why?' Karen mused out loud as she took his giant hand. She'd already seen his image online but he looked much bigger in the flesh. *And I expected someone smaller.*

'Because of your notoriety. You don't look,' his eyes lowered to read from an open file, 'twenty-nine. You've packed quite a bit in, haven't you? How come you've only just gone for the promotion? Please sit.'

'I've been busy,' Karen said as she settled down into the chair opposite him. 'And I didn't relish a desk job,' she couldn't help herself adding.

'Oh, you'll get your fair share of action here, I assure you. As I expect you know from your last assignment.'

'I wasn't sure if that was usual. But good. Although I expect to go back to *Home Counties* eventually. What do I call you, sir?'

'Call me Barry. It's not my name, well, not my first name. But given your status, I'm not going to get all formal. We're a friendly team here,' he narrowed his eyes. 'And I want it to stay that way.'

'Barry? Ah, Baron.' Karen replied.

'No, not that Barry,' he stood up and gyrated his hips a tiny bit. 'The walrus of lurve,' he mimicked in a deep voice.'

'Sure, Barry.' Karen gave him a look.

'As I thought. Too young,' Barry replied. 'Now, where were we?'

'Where do I start?'

'I've assigned DC Omar Malik to you. Nice man; very thorough. He should be in any minute. He'll give you the guided tour. Anything else you want to know?'

'Caseload,' Karen replied. 'Anything to tap into, or am I waiting for something to happen?'

'Oh, there's lots in the pipeline,' Barry replied. 'Don't you worry about that.'

A knock at the door was followed by the appearance of DC Malik. He gave Barry a quick nod and then turned to Karen who was getting to her feet. She guessed from his appearance that Omar was of Somali descent. He was tall, slender, and very smiley. *Oh, Macy would really like you.* Karen couldn't help smiling back.

'Welcome, DS Thorpe.'

Karen glanced at Barry for guidance but got none. She shook Omar's proffered hand. 'Thank you, Omar. I look forward to working with you.' If he was expecting her to say anything about her title, he didn't show it.

'Please. Let me show you around and get you a coffee.' He guided her out towards the kitchen area.

'Is it any good?' Karen asked out of habit.

'No, but I bring my own,' Omar smiled again.

The day was taken up with meeting people, settling into her new desk, finding the local eateries, and getting stuck into some recent case files. She navigated around all the systems and procedures with ease, thanking her luck that her last time with the Met had given her a head start on it all.

At the end of the day, Barry came over to her desk. 'So, how was your day?'

'Good,' Karen replied. 'When do I get my first case?'

'Let's see what we get tomorrow,' he replied. It's unpredictable. Get going before something turns up.'

'But I love things turning up,' Karen pouted.

'Tomorrow,' Barry smiled. 'See you tomorrow.'

Karen arrived home tired but happy.

'That good?' John asked.

'It was,' Karen replied. 'And the new boss seems OK. Much nicer than the guv. But John?'

'Yes, my love.'

Karen blinked. 'Do you know who the walrus of love was?'

'Why?'

'Something my boss said.'

'Was he big and black?' John gave a feeble hip gyration.

Karen's eyes popped open. 'How did you know?'

'I'll explain it all to you tonight. Actually, I'll give you a demonstration.'

18

Mari left the flat at the usual time but made her way to the station and not to school. She knew she was taking a risk, but depending on how things went, she could sneak back into school later on. Everything was always a bit chaotic the first days back after Christmas. Lots of kids skived off and she'd made a point of coughing. *And* this had been the first day her mother had left the flat before her.

Mari had been on the tube plenty of times before but never on her own. Now, as she got on the train, she felt both grown up and scared. The train was packed, but when a very drunken old man with bloodshot eyes got too close to her she panicked and moved away to get off at the next stop. Unfortunately, there were too many people trying to get on the carriage. She gave up and sat down on a bench where she studied her map instead.

She had better luck slipping on the next train as she was aligned with the opening doors, but she had to hold on tightly to the upright bars to avoid being pushed out by the people getting off. It was uncomfortably full at first but as they headed out of town, the carriage began to empty until she was able to grab a seat. She studied the floor until the train stopped at Hornchurch. That was the easy bit.

As soon as she exited the station she realised she couldn't work out where everything was in relation to her map. After two false starts and retracing her steps, a man handing out free newspapers asked her if she was lost. Relieved, she told him the road name and he pointed her in the right direction.

When she found the road, and began to get closer, she began to realise the significance of what she was doing. Her heart began to beat rapidly. What on earth was she doing here? Supposing they were angry? A woman in a niqab walked past, seemingly staring at Mari through the gap in her veil. She steadied herself and carried on down the road counting out the numbers on the doors.

'Thirty-three, thirty-five... here we are.' Mari stopped, dead still at the top of the small, paved path which led to a very ordinary-looking front door with a ridged glass panel. She tried to remember the photo she'd seen. Was it the same? Close enough.

She had a dreadful thought. Suppose they'd moved? How stupid was she not to check that? She breathed in deeply and decided that there was only one way to find out. She couldn't see a bell so she knocked at the door and waited. She saw movement through the glass. As the mass began to focus into the shape of a woman wearing green, she heard a muttered, 'I'm coming, I'm coming. Who could it be at this time?'

When the distorted shape filled the glass, Mari heard the sound of a safety chain being taken off. The door opened to reveal a small Pakistani-looking woman, wearing a richly embroidered tunic and pants suit. She looked much older than Sinéad.

'Hello. Can I help you?'

Mari stood open-mouthed. This was the woman in the photo; she was sure of it. 'Mrs Lone?'

'Yes, it is.'

What should she say? Mari hadn't even thought of this. 'I'm your granddaughter,' she spluttered. 'Mohammed was my father.'

Mari saw a flash of something – was it fear or recognition? – cross the woman's face. She stared at Mari as if she'd seen a ghost.

'Who is it?' a deeper, male voice came from the back somewhere.

The woman froze. She looked at Mari with sadness on her face. Mari stood there unable to move. Her feet were rooted to the ground.

The man, in a simple, long white shirt and loose trousers, appeared in the hall and approached the door. 'Who is this?' he asked.

'She says she is Mohammed's daughter,' the woman gasped. 'Our son's daughter.'

The man stood there almost as still as Mari but not for long.

'We have no son called Mohammed,' he said and reaching in front of the woman, he pushed the door shut.

Mari didn't move. Inside, she could hear the wailing of the woman, but through the glass, she heard the man say, 'Shut your noise, woman,' before both shapes moved away from the door.

Dazed, Mari followed her tracks back to the station and got onto the first train that came. Without even thinking about what she was doing when she arrived at her own station she began walking – not to school – but back home. It wasn't until she began to get a grip of where she was and more importantly, where she was meant to be, that she stopped. It was too late. She looked up to see her mother marching towards her.

'What the hell are you doing out here? Why aren't you at school?'

Mari couldn't hold it in any longer. She handed her mother the envelope with the address on it and burst into tears.

'You went to see your father's parents?'

Mari nodded.

Sinéad, overcome with long-suppressed rage, let it all out. 'How dare you do something like that? Going behind my back. It's prying for sure, you little witch. Now get home and go to your room. I'll ring the school before they ring me.'

Mari went home as ordered, flung herself on her bed and cried until she was so tired she fell asleep. She woke up a couple of hours later, somewhat disorientated. When she opened her bedroom door and looked around, there was no sign of her mother. But she was very hungry. She went into the kitchen and made herself a sandwich. She was still eating it when her mother returned, laden with shopping.

'Here. Help me with these,' Sinéad ordered. Mari took a bag from her mother and began to put things away. There was an uncomfortable silence for a few minutes until Sinéad finally spoke again.

'So? What happened?'

'They sent me away. The man said he didn't have a son called Mohammed but I know it was him; I recognised him from the photo.'

Sinéad let out an enormous sigh. 'Well, that's an end to it once and for all,' she declared. 'I've told the school you have a tummy ache but you'd better be there tomorrow, or I'll have your guts for garters, my girl.'

19

Karen remembered it was Omar's day off and once again, she was at the doorstep of the house of a missing child. But this was no cold case. It was clear from her frantic mother's pride in her daughter and pleas for help, that this was unwanted and unexpected. Her research had led her to think of terrorism, forced marriages, and suppressed education. She went in as tactfully as she could. She'd had some diversity training but hadn't had to call upon it much before.

'Was there any family pressure on her? I know that sometimes girls are found husbands.'

Mrs Ali looked up, now angry. 'Do you think we are from a village? Yes, we look after our girls and make sure they marry into a nice family. But it is their choice. We would never dream of forcing them to marry against their will.'

Karen took this on the chin. 'I'm sorry, Mrs Ali, we have to ask these things.'

'Actually, Selina was an exceptionally bright girl and had got very good exam results last autumn. She was getting on so well in the sixth form. We had expectations of Oxford.'

'Oh, I see. But I've read the post that she allegedly made on social media. That she was going to find paradise. Do you understand what she might have meant by that?'

'Knowing Selina, she was probably talking about a beach holiday.' Mrs Ali gave a little smile.

'You said beach holiday. Had she talked of going anywhere?'

Mrs Ali shook her head. 'I was joking. She would never have simply left school to go on holiday. She was such a good girl.'

'If I told you that similar phrases have been used by people seeking to cause,' she hesitated, 'trouble in the Muslim community, would that mean anything to you?'

The woman shook her head. 'She was always working on her computer. She studied hard. That was the way she wanted fulfilment in her life. Not by some sort of religious martyrdom.'

Karen nodded. 'May I take her computer? We can examine it to see if we can find anything to help us. And do you have a recent photo of her?'

'Of course.'

Karen looked around the room while Mrs Ali went upstairs. *Where's Macy when you need her. She's so much better than me at this sort of thing.* The room was decorated with photos and plaques of Islamic scripts which were beautiful but undecipherable to Karen's eyes. When Mrs Ali returned, they both sat down.

'Mrs Ali, can you tell me again your daughter's last movements? Think carefully. Any detail may be important.'

'I've told you everything. She took her passport. There is nothing more.'

'And a recent photo?'

Mrs Ali reached to the coffee table and handed Karen a school photograph. 'I have this for you.'

'I understand she was an only child. But are there any extended family members, cousins perhaps, who she might have spoken to? Or school friends?'

The woman looked away. Karen wondered if she was hiding tears. 'Thank you, Mrs Ali.' Karen stood up. 'I promise we'll do everything we can to find Selina.'

'Thank you, officer,' came the muffled reply. Karen saw herself out.

When she was back at the office, Karen spotted Omar at his desk. 'You're here?'

'Can't keep away,' he replied.

'Good!' Karen smiled appreciatively. 'Ordinarily, I'd just dump this on you, but we've got to work fast on this, if you're up for it?' He nodded.

She explained what had happened as she divided the list of airports and docks between them. 'You start, I'd better get the social media people on it.'

She picked up the phone and scrutinised a contact list. 'Here.' She rang a number. 'DS Thorpe here. Missing girl. Selina Ali,' she reeled off the address. 'She posted about going to paradise.'

'OK. We'll check it out.'

Karen and Omar talked while waiting for responses to their phone calls.

'She might have been kidnapped,' Omar suggested.

'But she had her passport. Would a kidnapper bother about that?'

'Fair point.'

'Where's paradise to you? The Caribbean? Or something more sinister.'

Omar shook his head. 'I fear it may be sinister. You know of the Caliphate?'

'A bit. Tell me what you know.'

'I have heard a great deal about it. It's based in Syria. It's basically a collection of violent extremists. A lot of Muslims are worried about it. Do you not remember the poor American journalist who was beheaded in Syria? It was all over the news.'

Karen pouted. *No I didn't watch the news much. I was always busy working*, she thought. She looked up at him. 'But of course, I remember that. Please don't tell me we're dealing with those,' she stopped herself from swearing, 'those evil men?'

'I truly hope not. I thought their time was coming to an end. But maybe not.'

Their phones began to ring. By the time the day had ended, there was no sign of Selina or where she might be. She had a feeling she'd be needing to use her training notes a great deal in this assignment.

Karen was just about to head home when Macy called her. 'Hi, Mace. What's up?

'The Crown. Seven o'clock. Be there.'

20

Mari arrived at school to find Razia crying in the playground. She ignored Carly's enquiring face and ran to talk to her. 'What's the matter?'

Carly tapped Mari on the shoulder and motioned for her to keep away, but Mari stayed where she was.

'Razia, what's happened?'

'My cousin Selina has run away.'

'Run away? Why? Where?'

'We don't know. But she's taken a suitcase and her passport. She posted a message on Facebook two days ago that she was going to paradise and there's been nothing since. My auntie is so upset she can't stop crying.'

'You don't think she's killed herself, do you?'

'We don't know what to think. We are all so worried.'

Mari put her arms around Razia; Carly turned her back in annoyance.

'If there's anything I can do.'

'Thank you,' Razia nodded, her eyes darting towards Carly. She whispered. 'They have called the police. I'm sure they'll find her. Oh.' she smiled. 'You're seeing my brother tonight aren't you?'

Mari blinked. 'I'd completely forgotten.'

'What was that about?' Carly pressed.

'Raz's brother is going to help me with my maths, that's all. I'd better tell Mum.'

'You'll be wearing one of those headdresses next,' Carly mocked.

'I will not,' Mari snapped. 'Come on, we'll be late.' The two girls went into the school building.

Mari was distracted all day and found it difficult to concentrate. There was so much *stuff* rushing around in her brain. By the time she got to the maths lesson, she was unable to do anything other than look mindlessly at the whiteboard.

'Mari? Are you with us?' asked the teacher.

'I've not been well, Miss.' She replied. 'I *am* writing it all down.'

When the lesson was over, Mari, with Carly almost clinging to her side, hesitated outside the school entrance. She wasn't sure what the arrangements were. She wondered whether Razia would come with her.

Carly was getting irritated. 'Are you coming or not?' she demanded.

'I'm not sure yet. I've got to phone Mum. You go on.'

Razia appeared just after Carly stomped off. 'There you are. I was looking for you inside. I thought you'd want to come with me.'

'Yes,' Mari agreed. 'That would be best.'

The two girls walked together. 'How was your Christmas?' Razia asked.

'It was really lovely,' Mari replied and told her all about it. They chatted happily all the way to Razia's house. When they arrived, Maria was waiting for them at the door.

'Welcome, Mari. I've cleared the table for you so that you can sit with Saeed. He'll be back soon. Would you like a drink?'

'Thank you. No, thank you. *Um,* a glass of water would be nice.'

'Of course. There, Razia, show Mari through.'

Mari followed Razia into the dining room, immediately noticing a sewing machine in the corner.

'Your mother sews?'

'Yes, she is so old-fashioned. Positively ancient.'

'I heard that Razia.' Maria swept in. The next time you want anything taken up I shall remind you of that.' She put a glass of water on the table. They all heard the noise of the front door being opened. Mari gaped as Saeed swaggered into the room. He seemed so much older and taller than she remembered. *Had it only been a couple of weeks ago?* His face was showing the beginnings of a beard and moustache.

'Hello,' she said sheepishly. 'This is very kind of you.'

Saeed smiled that smile again. 'Let's see if I am any use before you say that.'

'I'll leave you to it then,' Maria nodded at Razia and they left the room.

Mari was surprised at how well the lesson went. She was bright and Saeed had a real knack for explaining things to her. Once she had grasped a concept she was able to run with it.

'That's right,' Saeed praised her. 'You're doing fine.'

'It's the way you explain it,' Mari blushed. 'You make much more sense than our teacher.'

Maria poked her nose through the door. 'I heard that. There, Saeed! You were wondering what to do after school. Maybe you should be a teacher?'

Saeed stood up to reply. 'But I thought you wanted me to be a doctor.' He rolled his eyes. 'See how terrible my family are, Mari?'

Mari didn't see. 'Your family are lovely,' she said. Before he could argue, her eyes began to well up.

'What's the matter?'

'I'd better go. I forgot to tell Mum I was here.'

'Then ring her now.'

Mari nodded. She called her mother. 'There's no signal,' she said.'

'Then you'd better tell me all about it,' he said.

21

Mari did not have the maturity to know when to hold back. Instead, everything came pouring out in a long, garbled rush. At times, Saeed, who listened patiently, struggled to understand and made her slow down and repeat herself. When she told him about her grandparents, however, he was shocked.

'I'm so sorry that happened to you.' Saeed held her hand and she managed a little smile.

'In fact, there is a strong possibility that the whole world will realise what Islam can offer people. It's something very special. A relative of mine in Syria has been telling me all about it.'

'Oh? Tell me more,' Mari said.

Saeed shook his head. 'That is not for now. I need to find out more myself first. Now, how are you feeling?'

'Much better now. Thank you. Thank you for everything. I'd better be going home.' Mari took some tissues out of her bag, dried her eyes, and blew her nose. When she felt more composed she put her things away in her school bag.

Maria put her head round the door again. 'Are you not staying for tea, Mari?'

Mari looked at Saeed, who nodded at her. 'That would be lovely.'

'I'll walk you home afterwards.' Saeed said. 'It is dark and we can discuss Pythagoras's theorem.'

'I'd like that,' Mari beamed.

When the time came, Mari and Saeed walked and talked about all sorts of getting-to-know-you things. Saeed was very sporty and loved playing tennis but Mari wasn't and didn't. He liked some rock music but not One Direction. He said that his father was an accountant but that he wanted something better for him.

Mari then talked a little about her father and Saeed became very interested. 'So it was your father's parents you went to see. And you are nearly a Muslim.'

'I suppose so. That means we do have something in common.'

Saeed laughed and began to tell her what he loved about Islam. 'That is the real family,' he said. 'And one day everyone will feel Allah's love.'

When they said goodbye at her building, Mari was feeling much better. Razia's family were so friendly and Saeed, she sighed, had been so nice to her. But Sinéad was waiting at the door for her when she arrived home.

'Where the hell have you been this time? Your tea is stone cold.'

'I've been at Raz's. I rang you. I swear I did. Her brother's helping me with my maths.'

'No, you didn't.'

'I did!'

Sinéad's fury spilled over again. 'How dare you lie to me you little bitch. I don't know what's got into you, but I'm not putting up with your deceit any longer. And all this sneaking around.'

'But I need help with maths,' Mari wailed. 'And they are so nice to me.' She backed away, but Sinéad was ready for her and pulled Mari inside.

'Oh no you don't, young lady. They're not like us and they don't like us. They probably want to convert you. Get inside and I'll fix you something to eat.'

'I had something at Raz's.'

'Get to your room. I'm sick to death of you, I really am. Honest to God! I do everything I can to do the best for you and this is how you repay me? You're grounded, do you hear me? Grounded!'

Mari, without speaking, went into her bedroom and switched on her laptop. She looked on Facebook and found Saeed's account. They connected.

How's it going? he wrote.

Mum says I can't come to yours anymore. She hates me. She's being so horrible.

How so?

She doesn't believe that I tried to ring her. It's not just that, there's something else but I can't go into that now.

Mari I'm here for you always.

Thank you.

Later that evening, Mari heard the front door slam and guessed that her mother had gone out. There was half a bottle of wine in the kitchen and remembering what she had drunk with her grandmother, she poured herself just a little. This wine was bitter and she shook her head in disgust, then made herself a cup of hot chocolate. She tried to watch some TV but she couldn't concentrate. Instead, she went back to bed to daydream about Saeed and Ireland and maybe one day living in the countryside away from the horrible dull grey buildings of her London home.

22

John was already waiting with a sense of foreboding in The Crown when Karen walked in. He knew that above everything else, she hated surprises.

'What are you doing here?' she said. 'I thought this was something of Macy's.'

'Yes, well, it's all gone a bit pear-shaped, John admitted. 'We didn't manage to get the word around very well. But all your bessie mates are here.'

'Oh yes? Where? Karen, her hand to her eyes, peered sarcastically around the pub.

'That table over there,' John pointed.

Karen followed the direction of his finger and squinted. Then she began to smile. 'Oh, OK. That's fair enough.' She strolled over to where Emma and Bradley sat very close together. 'Where's Macy?'

'Hello, Sergeant,' Emma said, standing up to attention.

Bradley took over. 'Macy is coming as soon as she can get away. She said something about DI Harris keeping her working late. I'm sorry. We'd hoped more people would come.'

'More people? Why?'

'It's a leaving party,' John nudged her. 'It's what happens when people move on. Normal people.'

'OK. It is nice to see you all, but it hasn't exactly been that long, has it?'

'Davie sends his regards,' John said.'

'Scottish Davie?'

'Aye,' John bit his lip after speaking.

Karen sat at the table. 'It wouldn't make any difference to Davie if I was here or Timbuktu,' Karen said. 'Never mind. How have you all been in the last few days?'

'I've been very busy,' Emma piped up. 'DI Harris came back yesterday. I've already had to reorganise some of the files after he muddled them up.'

'Did you?' Karen said, trying to sound interested.

Bradley leaned forward. 'Nobody likes him now,' he said.

'That's not true,' Emma said. 'Everybody liked him because he used to bring cakes in. But I don't think that's a good enough reason to like someone.'

'I agree,' Karen nodded vigorously.

'But not many people like you either, Sergeant Thorpe.'

Karen laughed, a good hearty laugh. 'I know that, Emma, but thanks for reminding me. How's the guv?' She looked at Bradley.

'I don't know whether he likes you or not, but he's definitely missing you.'

'After one day?' Karen raised an eyebrow. 'I doubt that.'

'He muttered something about not liking to see an empty desk.'

'Moving on,' Karen said, 'What's everybody drinking?'

'Mine's a Scotch,' a familiar voice sounded. Everyone looked up to see the form of DI Harris approaching the table with Macy close behind. Macy caught Karen's eye with a shocked look on her face. Behind his back, she mimed *I didn't know he'd come*, with a shrug and gestures.

'Good evening, Detective Inspector Harris,' Emma said. 'I didn't think you liked Sergeant Thorpe.'

There was a stunned silence until Karen spoke. 'We go back a long way. As far back as the Cooper case. We were both detectives here. Although he took his exams before I did,' she explained. 'Let me get the drinks.'

John held his hand up. 'No, that's not right. I'll get them.' He jotted down their requests and left the note and the money at the bar.

Karen looked at Harris. 'And how are you after that attempted assassination? All mended?'

'I'm practically bionic,' Harris replied. 'I've got metal everywhere now.'

'Do you set off alarms?' Emma asked.

DI Harris frowned. 'Sometimes.'

The group sat in near silence until the drinks arrived. Harris downed his Scotch in one and stood up. 'Better be on my way. Tough call tomorrow.' He tapped his nose meaningfully.

'Goodnight,' Karen said, a little too quickly, adding, 'I bet it's nothing important,' when he was out of earshot.

The little group gave a collective sigh.

'I'm so sorry, Karen,' Macy said.

'S okay,' Karen replied, knocking back her wine. 'Thanks for doing this. Much appreciated. But I've got to get off too. See you all again soon.' She stood up and left.

John muttered embarrassed *sorrys* to Emma, Bradley, and Macy.

'What happened between them, John?' Macy asked.

'She won't ever talk about it,' John replied. 'I have tried.'

'I'm going to find the file for the Cooper Case.' Emma said.

Macy looked at Bradley. 'And we're going to find out what happened between them. I've always wanted to know too. And it's about bloody time.'

'Good luck,' John said. 'Better dash.' He charged out of the pub.

23

Karen was surprised to find a file on her desk, which had been meticulously tidied the previous Friday. It brought back a less-than-pleasant memory of when that had happened before. But this was no cold case. Fifteen-year-old twin Muslim girls had gone missing. She patted herself on the back for mugging up on her training before she knocked on the door of Barry's office.

'Come in, Karen. About the girls, yes?'

'Yes. I wondered why you wanted me to handle it personally. There's no problem... '

Barry interrupted her. 'The family had heard of you. And after I thought about it, I decided it would be very good local experience for you. And it's a possible fit with Selina Ali.'

'I've heard no more from Mrs Ali,' Karen said. 'From my experience, that's unusual. My colleague in Herts. had a similar situation. I'd better check it out. No point wasting resources on a false report.'

'Agreed,' Barry nodded.

Back at her desk, Karen rang Mrs Ali, who spoke before she'd had time to ask the question.

'Oh, I should have rung you. Everything is fine. She's been offered a job in P R. And that suits her very well.'

Karen frowned. 'And when did you find this out, Mrs Ali?'

'It was very late last night,' Mrs Ali replied.

'And where is she?' The line went dead.

There was no sign of Omar in the office so Karen headed out alone. She was frustrated to discover that there was no pool car available. Reluctantly, she took the tube. Always happy to have an actual case to work on, she knew it would probably amount to nothing. Missing girls almost always turned up and twins were especially hard to hide. She wasn't completely convinced about Selina Ali, though.

Half an hour later, Karen found herself on the doorstep of a little terraced house. The door opened and Mrs Khan, clearly distressed, beckoned her in. 'Please come in, officer.'

They stood in the hall.

'Thank you, Mrs Khan. Can you tell me what happened, as far as you know? When did you last see them?'

'It was yesterday morning when they went to school.'

'And how did they seem then?'

'They were fine.'

Karen wondered about the brevity of Mrs Khan's responses. It didn't chime with situations she'd seen before. 'And they never came home?' Karen queried. 'When did you realise that they were missing?'

'They used to stay on at school with their friends sometimes. That's what I thought they had done.'

Karen tried not to frown. Something didn't feel right. 'But they were happy to go to school? There was no sign of bullying or anything like that?'

'Of course, they were happy. I had told them the night before that we were finding good boys for them to marry.'

Karen didn't blink. 'But Mrs Khan, they're only fifteen.'

'I know that. They wouldn't be married straight away. We know the law.'

'And do you think that this has anything to do with why they ran away?'

'No, of course not. That is our custom. These are our ways. They know what is expected of them.'

Karen continued the interview calmly and efficiently until she had gathered all the relevant facts. As she left, she was already convinced that the girls had fled their impending marriage arrangements, but she kept it to herself.

When she got back to the station she saw Omar sitting at his desk. He jumped to attention when he saw her.

'Sorry, Sergeant, I was finishing something off.'

Karen held up her hand. 'That's fine. Now let me run through what we've got.'

She relayed the facts and then finished by tentatively voicing her concern. 'It sounds to me like they might have run away rather than be married off.'

To her relief, Omar nodded. 'That's not unusual but thankfully getting rarer.'

'Can you check out all the refuges and local community organisations first, please? My guess is they won't have gone too far. And another thing.'

'Yes, Sergeant,'

Karen looked at him; it didn't feel right, especially with *Barry* as a boss. 'Call me Karen for now,' she said. 'Back to about Selina Ali. Her mother says she knows where she is, but I'm not convinced. I want us to keep an eye on it, just in case.'

'Right, Sarge.... I mean Karen,' he smiled. 'I'll be right on it.'

Before the end of the day, the girls had been traced to a refuge. When Karen got home she talked to John about it.

'So you were right?'

'Yes. This time. But don't worry; I know I can't jump to conclusions without the full facts. But in this case, their mother had form. It seems that her elder daughter was packed off to Pakistan a couple of years ago, so the girls were terrified it would happen to them. Thanks to the school, there were notices up about forced marriages so the girls were brave enough to speak out.'

'What happens now?'

Karen sighed. 'It's very complicated. They're now in the care of Social Services. But ultimately, the objective is to try to bring families back together if possible. It will mean counselling for all of them I suppose.'

'And what's the likelihood of it all working out?'

'Bloody hell, John, give me a chance. I've only just started, you know. And another thing.'

'What?'

'I don't like this commuting nonsense.'

24

It was Mari's fifteenth birthday and her mother left for work without speaking to her. At school, Carly gave her a card and a couple of the other girls wished her a happy birthday but it didn't cheer her up.

Razia caught up with her during the day and gave her a handmade card. 'I'm sorry, I only found out today or I would have bought one.'

Mari smiled. 'It's lovely. Thanks.'

By the time she got home from school, Sinéad, too, had relented.

'Here,' she handed Mari a card. 'I didn't have time to get you anything. Anyway, I don't know what you even want these days.'

'Thanks,' Mari muttered. Sinéad didn't wait to see her reaction to the ten-pound note.

Mari put the money in her purse and went into her bedroom to get on her laptop. *Even Nana hasn't sent me a card.* She heard the phone ring followed by her mother banging on the door. 'It's for you. I'm off to work.'

Mari opened the door and took the phone from Sinéad. She was startled by the noise at the other end of the receiver.

'Happy birthday to you,' her nana sang down the phone. Mari couldn't stop laughing at the tuneless offering.

'Thanks, Nana.'

'And what are you doing tonight?'

'Nothing. Mum's gone out.'

'Oh, that's not good, but she's got her work.'

'I know but she's been horrible to me recently.' Mari commenced a long rant about Sinéad.

'Cheer up now, my darlin'. It'll pass. Teenagers and parents always hate each other. That's why you need nanas. Think of your Easter holidays. It's not long now and you can come and stay with me and Kenny if you like.'

'Thanks, Nana, I would like that. See you soon.''

Mari hung up. She did like the idea, but today she wanted to do something more fun than talking to Nana. Talking online to Saeed had become an important part of her daily routine.

Happy Birthday! My sister told me.

After exchanging their normal banter, Mari asked something she'd been curious about.

Has your cousin been found yet?

Yes, I think so. I also have an idea about where she has gone.

Mari was surprised.

Where?

I can't tell you. I'm not really sure. But I'm hoping she'll message me soon.

Shouldn't you tell the police?

If she's where I think, she'll be very safe and well. I might go and see her.

What?!

That place I told you about.

Where?

Mum is calling me. I'd better go. Talk tomorrow, yes?

Yes.

As Saeed signed off, Mari heard a loud knocking on the front door. She wasn't expecting anybody so she put the door chain on and opened it a little. It was her friend; she was holding something behind her back.

'Carly? What have you got there?' She shut the door to release the chain then opened it to reveal Carly grinning at her.

'Is the coast clear?'

'If you mean Mum, yes, she's out.'

Carly held out a litre bottle of supermarket-brand cider. 'Look what I've got.'

'Cider? I don't know.' Mari hesitated.

'You'll love it, I promise.'

Mari looked around. The coast was clear. 'Quick, come in before someone sees.'

Carly waited for Mari to shut the door then she sang Happy Birthday at the top of her voice.

Mari began to laugh. 'I'll get the glasses.'

'Hurry up then. I'll just have some to try.' Carly opened the top of the bottle and took a swig. It wasn't her first, as Mari realised when she returned. She knew from her mother's example that her increasingly slurred speech meant that her friend had been drinking.

'My turn,' Mari took the bottle and poured out two glasses. Carly watched her as she took her first sip. She'd tried cider before but it was bitter and flat. This was sweet and fizzy, more like lemonade.

'Oh, it's nice.' She swallowed some more.

'We need music!' Carly yelled and turned on her phone. She began wriggling around to the beat.

The more cider Mari drank, the funnier she found her friend. When the music stopped, Carly started prowling around.

'What's your mum's bedroom like?'

Mari laughed. 'Don't go in there. I'm not allowed.'

'But she didn't say *I* couldn't,' Carly grinned. 'I must!' She went into the room and began looking around. 'Not very tidy is she?'

'No,' Mari agreed, giggling.

Carly's eyes rested on a tiny bit of pink lace sticking out of one of the drawers. She pulled it open. 'Has she got a boyfriend?'

'No. Carly, you're so bad.'

'She'll never know. Now, what have we got here?'

Carly came back into the living room holding Sinéad's vibrator. Mari was snorting with laughter. 'It looks like a willy.'

'It is! It's one of those things you put up you.' Carly was almost bent double with laughter.

Mari squirmed. 'Why would you do that?'

'Because it's sex. Have some more cider.'

Mari drank while Carly waved the vibrator around, pretending to stab Mari with it. She waved it at Mari's groin. 'Go on, try it.'

'I don't feel very well,' Mari said out of nowhere. 'I'm going to be sick.'

At the exact moment she threw up, the door opened and her mother walked in. Sinéad stood still for a moment before her temper began to grow.

She turned on Carly. 'Put that thing down and get out of my house, you little tramp.'

'You're the tramp,' Carly spat back. She stumbled towards the front door. Sinéad opened it quickly and pushed her outside.

When she shut the door behind her, Carly shouted through the letterbox. 'TRAMP!'

Sinéad, her back to the front door, waited for Mari to recover a little. When Mari was able to look at her mother, Sinéad slapped her hard across the face. She looked at the mess of vomit on the carpet, then at the vibrator, then sat on the floor and wept. 'Mo!' she wailed. 'What did I do to deserve this?'

Mari was shocked out of her drunkenness. Without speaking she went into her room and slammed the door behind her.

25

Saeed stood outside the mosque waiting for the imam's son. Nadeem, like Mari, had sought his help with his maths. Their conversation had strayed over the past few months. Saeed had begun to find the Mosque a little boring but Nadeem talked of an Islam that was exciting and dynamic. They had learned of the caliphate. It would be full of wonderful rewards both spiritual and actual, but it would have to be fought for. Only dedicated souls whom Allah chose could go there. Their job was to reinforce and expand the caliphate which would then be opened to the whole world of believers living in peace and harmony.

Saeed was no fool. He had listened to the news, heard the debates – he'd even watched the videos. He hadn't listened only to Nadeem; he'd had long discussions online with his cousin Ahmed in Pakistan.

He didn't have much in common with his cousin; Saeed was lively and physically fit and also susceptible to new ideas. Ahmed couldn't have been more different. He was scrawny and, by his own admission, useless at sports. But he was a studious boy who thought very deeply about everything. His dream was to become a philosopher, the sort of person he believed to be vital to his country's future. 'I aspire to become part of a moral authority which will weed out corruption and deceit,' was his mantra.

Saeed had let something slip of what the imam's son had told him about a new society and Ahmed had shocked him with his reply. 'Yes, sure, I have been thinking along the very same lines myself.'

Tentatively Saeed had explored Ahmed's point of view and there he found a great deal of agreement. When Saeed outlined his vision, Ahmed was quick to join in. From then on it looked easy, especially to Saeed; what better cover for his intended travel than to meet with his cousin?

He had summoned up all his courage to press Nadeem to let him join and now the moment had come. His heart pounded as

Nadeem approached. 'I have made my decision. I am ready to join the caliphate.'

Nadeem smiled. 'I thought you might say that. But saying it and meaning it are very different things. What preparation have you made?'

'I am going to Pakistan soon. My cousin wants to come too,' he explained. 'Surely we can go from there?'

'I'm not sure,' Nadeem replied. 'I don't think you are ready for it yet. You're too Western.'

'I can change,' Saeed implored. 'And my cousin will help me. He has never lived here.'

Nadeem shook his head and began to walk away.

Saeed grabbed his arm. 'Please, I beg of you. This is what I want to do. I am willing to give my life for this.'

Nadeem turned to face him. 'And is your cousin as committed as you?'

'He is,' Saeed declared.

Nadeem stared at him, his face, at first blank, broke into a wide smile. 'Then it shall be. When do you leave?'

'The twelfth of February.'

'Good. I will make arrangements. I will tell you everything you need to know.'

* * *

Sinéad walked Mari to school, lecturing her as they walked. 'No more seeing anyone after school. You'll stay in on your own until you've learned how to behave.'

'How could you have such a disgusting thing?' Mari had shouted back.

'It's nothing to do with me. A woman at work bought it as a joke once. I should've thrown it away ages ago.'

'I don't believe you,' Mari had replied. 'Why would you hide it in your bedroom?'

Sinéad snapped. 'None of your business young lady. And you are grounded. Give me your key now!'

'Then how will I get in after school?'

'I'll be here. I'll make sure I am. And then I'm locking you in.'

'Hello there!'

They both looked ahead to see Carly's mother approaching, with her daughter in tow.

'It seems like the girls got up to some mischief last night.'

'Aye, they did.' Sinéad replied, eyeing the woman suspiciously.

'I don't care what you get up to, but you should watch your daughter better. She shouldn't be buying alcohol at her age.'

'You what?' Sinéad countered. 'It was your scally of a daughter that did that.'

Mari threw Carly a look. She turned away.

'Don't you dare accuse my Carly of anything, you dirty cow!'

Sinéad grabbed Mari's arm and dragged her onwards towards the school. 'From now on, you're having nothing to do with that little bitch. D'ye hear?'

'Oh, she won't, don't you worry. She doesn't want friends whose mothers are on the game,' Carly's mother shouted.

Sinéad stopped in her tracks, then thought better of it. She shoved Mari forwards and marched her to school.

When she was settled in class, Mrs McCurdy gave Mari the news that the project she'd worked on initially with Razia had not been selected. In the break, Mari sat on her own in the cloakroom and cried. She had no friends at all now, and she was getting depressed. The only person she felt she could talk to at all was Saeed. But she wasn't allowed to see him, so instead, she messaged him that night. Then he told her his news.

Dad wants me to go to Pakistan for half term.

She typed back.

But you are my only friend, Saeed. I hoped I could spend some time with you. She can't keep me locked in forever.

We'll think of something.

26

Sinéad was feeling isolated. She'd reluctantly given up her job to make sure her daughter was safe. Now she was already short of money and bereft of company. She rang her mother to tell her how Mari had lost her way and she didn't know what to do.

'Send her here for the holidays,' Niamh said. 'I'll sort her out.'

'You'll spoil her,' Sinéad replied. But she knew that with the half-term coming up, she couldn't keep Mari locked up forever.

With a sigh, she knocked on Mari's bedroom door. 'Can I come in?'

'If you must.'

Sinéad walked into the room and sat on Mari's bed. 'OK. How about a truce?'

Mari turned around. 'I can go out again?'

'I need to earn money for both of us. And the pub is on at me to go back. But can I trust you?'

'You can. Carly doesn't speak to me anymore, thanks to you. So you don't need to worry about her.'

'Have you no other friends, love?'

Mari pouted, thinking. 'No.'

'Well then,' Sinéad nodded at her. 'How about you have a wee holiday to put you to rights?'

'A holiday? We never have holidays.'

'Och, just a wee trip to see your nana.'

Mari smiled, taking in the importance of her mother's proposal. 'I'd love it.'

'Go on with you.' Sinéad smiled, pleased at seeing her daughter's face happy again. 'So that's a yes then, is it?'

'Yes, please,' Mari replied.

'I'll go and ring her now.' Sinéad looked her daughter in the eye. 'If you're sure that you can promise to behave yourself.'

'Of course.'

Sinéad left her daughter to go and ring Niamh.

'Ah, that'll be grand. It'll be lovely to see the lass again. Kenny and Laddie will be thrilled. There's just one thing.'

'What's that, Ma?'

'I'm not going to come all that way and spend all that money coming over just to take her over here. She's fifteen now, is she not?'

'She is, but... '

'No buts. She's old enough to come on her own. She's seen the route and she can come on the day ferry. We'll be in touch by phone the whole way.'

Sinéad sighed. 'That's a tough one, Ma. I'm not even letting her out on her own after school. How can I suddenly decide she can travel all that way on her own?'

'Oh, you'll have to admit you were wrong. It'll be good for you and even better for Mari. Try it.'

'I suppose you're right. And it saves a lot of money too.'

'Exactly,' Niamh replied. 'Sure it'll be fine. I'll ring the ferry company and make sure they keep an eye out for her like I did when I sent her home last time. They're very good if you get the right person.'

'OK, I'll tell her the good news then. Bye, Ma.'

Sinéad knocked on Mari's door again but didn't wait for a response. 'It's all set, young lady. But there's something important to tell you.'

'What?' Mari's face was full of puzzlement.

'You're fifteen now and a young woman. You've done the journey back on your own before. Can I trust you to go on your own this time? I'll put you on the coach. All you have to do is find your way to the ferry again. Do you think you can do that?'

'Of course I can do that.'

'Well then, I'll ring Nana and we'll sort out a date.'

**

Mari waited for Sinéad to leave her room before she messaged Saeed.

Mum says I can go to Ireland for the holidays. I still won't be able to see you, but I think she's calming down. When are you coming back?

She watched her screen wondering if he was online. He was.

Mari, can I trust you with something?

Of course. Anything.

I'm not coming back. Once I've seen my family, I'm going to leave them and go to Syria to help the people there. You know there is a war there? I want to do something useful with my life.

But that's dangerous. You can't go. You might get killed.

No silly. I won't be fighting, just helping people. Distributing aid, that sort of thing.

Oh. That sounds good.

You could come too if you like. It's a beautiful country and I will be with people who will be better than the best family.

I'd like that. But Mum will never let me go abroad. I'm too young to travel on my own.

There are people you can travel with. I can arrange it.

I'll think about it.

I thought you wanted to be with me?

Mari read his words and at that moment in time, she couldn't think of anything she wanted more.

I want to. Mum is sending me to Ireland. Maybe I can come with you instead?

There was a long pause before Saeed replied.

We cannot go together. I will contact you and you must follow the instructions. What is the route you will take?

I catch a coach to Liverpool. Then the ferry to Dublin.

I will look into it. There will be a way.

Yes. Saeed, please keep safe until I can see you again.

I will. I will tell Razia that we are no longer friends. I'm going to set up a new account. Look out for me. But remember, no one must know where I am. Promise me.

I promise.

27

Saeed had finished his packing. His instructions were to delete everything on his laptop and destroy it. He deleted everything he could but couldn't rationalise why he needed to destroy that too. Who would be suspicious about him when he was just going to Pakistan? Instead, he slipped it into his case.

Saeed's mother came with him on the underground to the airport. It was too noisy on the train to talk much, but when they arrived at the terminal, Maria began to look sad.

'I will miss you so much, Saeed. Your sister will miss you too. She wanted to come, but she has school. You know how fond she is of you.'

'I'm only going for a week. Tell her I'll bring some fancy clothes back for her. It will give her something to look forward to.' For a moment he almost believed that he would, then he steeled himself and got in the check-in queue.

'You go now, Mum. Don't waste your time here. I know you have sewing to do.'

'No, those damned curtains can wait. And...' she looked around. 'Ah, here he is!'

Saeed turned to see his father hurrying up to them. 'Just in time,' he puffed. Ibrahim hugged his son tightly.

'Hi, Dad,' Saeed smiled. 'I'm glad you came.'

'Be a good boy and don't trouble your auntie and uncle too much,' Ibrahim said.

Saeed kissed his mother goodbye. 'I won't. And I'll be back before you know it.'

'Don't get carried away,' she said. 'You mustn't stay too long. There is a reservation for your flight back home on the eighteenth. You can extend it a little but remember you have a university place waiting for you.'

'Only if I pass the final exams.'

'I have faith. But you must be back home to study. OK?'

'Of course. Mum,' He was called forward by the woman at the check-in desk. 'I'd better go.'

Maria gave him a long hug. 'Send my love to your Auntie Laila and Uncle Jafar; tell them I will come out there to see them again one day.' She turned to Ibrahim. 'Should we have organised a chaperone?'

Ibrahim looked thoughtful. 'He's a good, sensible boy. It's a straight flight. He'll be fine.' They waved him off as he went through the security barriers.

Saeed waved back and went through the gates. Now relieved of the pressure of keeping up his pretence, he relaxed as he stood in the security queue. By the time he had followed the signs to the gate, he was beginning to get excited. He had never journeyed on his own before.

He settled down in his seat on the plane and played computer games all the way to Islamabad. When the plane descended and he disembarked, the smell, the heat, and the noise hit him instantly. He was shocked at how crowded and backward the airport looked compared to the shiny new terminal in Heathrow. It seemed to take ages to get past aggressive security checks and everything looked dirty. When at last he got through to the main hall, he felt exhausted.

His uncle and aunt spotted him straight away. 'Saeed!' Jafar shouted. 'Over here.'

Saeed made his way towards the smiling couple. His uncle patted his back. 'My, what a fine young man you have become. How was your flight?'

'The flight was OK, but this airport is awful.'

Jafar nodded. 'The worst airport in the world, so they say. A sad tribute to Benazir Bhutto. But they are building a new one already.'

His aunt hugged him tightly. 'You look so grown up. You will need a wife soon.'

Saeed laughed. 'No, Auntie, I have to go to university first.'

'You are going to be a doctor?'

'No. A mathematician. And then I'll see.'

'Very good, I suppose. Doctor is better,' she tweaked his cheeks. 'I'm joking,' she laughed.

93

'Hurry,' Jafar said. 'We must get to the short-term car park before my ticket runs out.'

Saeed enjoyed the drive from the airport, remembering how he'd first marvelled at the Margalla Hills.

The family home was a block-shaped building two stories high, with a balcony on the top floor. It was modest but comfortable. His aunt apologised to Saeed that he would have to share Ahmed's bedroom as the spare room was now full of Ahmed's books and Jafar's unfinished projects.

This suited both boys well. They would be able to plan their adventure together without the family overhearing them and getting suspicious.

After they had all eaten dinner, Saeed and Ahmed retired to Ahmed's room. They talked late into the night. At first, the differences between their aims didn't matter. Their excitement and enthusiasm were enough for each to overlook the shortcomings of the other, and there was so much to talk about.

13th February

After breakfast, Saeed, as agreed, put their proposition to Jafar.

'Dear Uncle, we want to go travelling for a few days. Ahmed here wants to show me some of your beautiful countryside and I want to see more of the hills. I have money; enough for two.'

Jafar laughed. 'Go then, go and make men of yourselves but Saeed, don't tell your mother I let you go.'

His aunt was not so happy when he told her. 'They are still so young. And how can they get in touch if something goes wrong?'

'They have telephones these days,' he mocked gently. 'We can't expect them to stay with old people like us.' He said to her. 'It's what I would have done, given a chance. I was working full-time and travelling everywhere when I was years younger than them. It will be good for them. Pack them a good lunch and let us wave them off. Besides, I bet they will be bored and come back in a day.'

Saeed was a little ashamed about how easy it was to fool his uncle but more excited about what was about to happen. They took their rucksacks with small tents and sleeping bags but few clothes. Saeed had been assured by Nadeem that everything would be provided for them.

Jafar and Laila waved them off as they walked away from the house and out of sight. Ahmed first led Saeed to a nearby road and walked up to a house. Saaed looked puzzled.

'My friend. He will look after our things and send messages to my parents for us. They will worry.'

'But we're not coming back?' Saeed queried. 'Can't we explain when we get there?'

Ahmed shook his head. 'There is no guarantee we will stay, and until we decide, we must let our parents think we are safe here, in the mountains somewhere. Come, he lives here,' he knocked on the door.

A boy answered the door. 'So, you're really doing it?' he said.

Ahmed handed the boy his phone. 'Every other day,' he said. He and Saeed began to unpack the camping items.

The boy nodded. 'But what if they ask something?'

'You're inventive. You'll think of something,' Ahmed grinned. He turned to Saeed. 'We must go.'

Ahmed led Saeed to a busy street where they hailed a taxi to the airport.

'What does your contact look like?' Ahmed asked when they arrived.

'I have no idea,' Saeed began. I was told we should wait near this entrance,' he pointed. Almost as soon as they reached it, a tall, smiling man with a very long beard walked towards them.

'Saeed and Ahmed?' They nodded. 'Here are your tickets. You will be met when you arrive. Speak to no one about this until you are safely there. You are going to this college,' he handed them both a leaflet, 'to study Arabic. Do you understand?'

'Yes. Thank you.' Saeed put the leaflet in his pocket while Ahmed studied his.

'May Allah look after you on your journey.'

They made their way to the check-in, neither of them daring to speak. When they got to the passport control desk, Saeed went first.

'Why are you going to Iraq?'

'My uncle recommended this college in Erbil. My cousin is coming too.' He showed the leaflet to the man at the desk. It was taken, glanced at, then handed back with disinterest. Saeed was waved through and the man did not bother to ask Ahmed the same question.

The flight was nearly nine hours long. Saeed soon began to tire of Ahmed and his thoughts. Instead, he began to play games and listen to music while Ahmed read. *I hope there will be others more like me at the camp*, he thought to himself.

Both boys managed to get some sleep on the plane. And by the time they disembarked, their enthusiasm was back again. They were met by a jovial young man with a fledgling beard who bounded towards them.

'Welcome, my brothers! I am Yousef. It is good to see you. I am your guide. Come; I have a car waiting.'

28

Saeed and Ahmed exchanged excited glances after Yousef's greeting; this sounded like a holiday.

'What happens next?' Ahmed asked.

'First, we have to settle you in. Give you good and thorough training. It is important that you learn everything you need to know. There is no turning back now. You understand? You saw the guards?'

Ahmed nodded; Saeed gulped. 'We're ready,' he said.

'Follow me,' Yousef ordered, striding ahead of them. 'We have a long journey ahead.'

The boys were taken to an old off-roader vehicle which was waiting for them in the car park. Yousef opened a back door and waited for them to sit down before slamming the doors and getting in the driving seat. He pulled out without another word.

Saeed and Ahmed dared not speak. Instead, they looked out of the windows, taking in the changing scenery. Gradually the urban sprawl of Erbil thinned into a few houses and out-buildings until all that was ahead was open space. They gazed as they meandered through grassy plains unfolding ahead of them. In the distance, they saw a faint blue backdrop of mountain ranges. Saeed had no idea where they were going but he worked out from their position relative to the sun that they were heading west. While they travelled, Saeed remembered his cousin.

'I have been wondering about my cousin Selina. Do you know her?'

'A British woman?'

Saeed nodded.

'Maybe. I will ask around. Is she in Raqqa?'

'I don't know. But she told me she was going to be making posts of encouragement for others to join.'

'I will find her.'

'May I take pictures?'

'You will have much time to see this wonderful land,' Yousef replied.

'No, it's for my girlfriend. Mari. I want her to come here. She loves the countryside above everything. If only I could show her how lovely it is.'

'I see,' Yousef applied the brakes. 'Then we must encourage her. Now, brother, how will this do?' He pulled over. 'Go ahead.'

Saeed got out of the truck and gazed at the scenery. 'She will love it.' Saeed took some photos. 'I know she will come now,' he said as he got back in.

'Good,' Yousef nodded as he set off again.

Saeed was the first to spot their destination. His searching eyes picked out the hard lines of fencing in the distance. 'Look there!' he said to Ahmed, unable to contain his excitement.

'Yes,' Yousef said. 'That is our destination.'

As they approached the training camp it was clear that guards were waiting for them at the entrance. The guards looked at and grinned at him. One of them waved the vehicle in.

They carried along the rough road which got bumpier as they progressed until they arrived outside a dilapidated building. Saeed thought it looked like an old school. As they got closer, he saw tents scattered around and behind the building. Guards were patrolling everywhere.

'To keep you safe,' Yousef smiled.

'Can I get a message to my girlfriend?'

'In time,' he replied. 'First, we must get you some new clothes. Come this way.'

The boys were taken into the building where two guards looked them over. One asked for their names and wrote them down. 'Bags here.' He patted the counter.

'Get changed,' the other ordered.

The first guard threw their rucksacks into a corner. The other took out two bundles of tunics and trousers from a cupboard. 'Here,' he said, throwing the clothes to each of them in turn. He watched them dress. 'You have an early start in the morning but we must feed you first. Follow me.'

He took them back to the tent area where Yousef was waiting.

'You will sleep in there,' he said. He pointed to a large tent. 'Wait here. Food is coming.' He looked at Saeed. 'Do you trust this girl?'

'I do.'

'Then come with me and I will make the necessary arrangements. You,' he pointed to Ahmed. 'Wait here.'

Saeed gave Ahmed a little wave as he followed Yousef into the building.

***

Ahmed sat on the ground outside the tent and waited until a small woman wearing a burqa appeared from the building. She came up to him carrying two plates of barbecued chicken and rice. She looked around, confused.

'My friend is coming back. Thank you,' Ahmed said. The girl put the food down. She turned away without speaking and disappeared back into the building. Just as Saeed appeared, she returned with two bottles of cola.

'What's your name?' Ahmed asked but the girl once again left without talking. 'Not bad,' he said as he began to eat.

'I'm so hungry I'd eat anything,' Saeed said, smiling as he began to chew. The food was demolished quickly.

'So you're bringing your girlfriend here?'

Saeed nodded. 'Yes. She is having a hard time in London. It will be much better for her here.'

'And they gave you access to the Internet?'

Saeed shook his head. 'They've taken my laptop now. And it's too secret. Yousef contacted her on my behalf. I told him what to write to reassure her it was me. And he sent my picture to her.'

'And do you really think they will bring her here?'

'Of course!' Saeed stood up. 'But now I need a shit.' He stood up and looked around. He walked over to the building but a guard stopped him from going in. He made a squatting motion and pointed him over to another tent behind the building.

'Shit!' Saeed said without irony when he came back. 'It was a hole dug in the ground.'

'Well, what did you expect?' Ahmed sneered. 'It's not London, you know.'

'I wonder if the girls have to do this too?' Saeed replied.

'Your girlfriend? She'll have to manage,' Ahmed said, getting up. 'Like I will.' He went to the tent, coming back holding his nose. 'You should've told me to wait,' he laughed. 'What do we do now?'

Saeed yawned. 'We sleep. I'm exhausted.'

'Me too.'

The boys went into the tent finding two empty metal-framed beds close together.

Saeed shrugged. 'I'll take this one.' He began to strip off. Ahmed went to the other and did the same. The boys got into bed, pulling the simple sheets over their bodies.

'Night,' said Ahmed.

'See you in the morning,' Saeed replied.

29

15th February

Mari had been waiting anxiously to hear from Saeed. She only had a small window in which to make her escape and that was today. In the early morning, when she checked, there was a new message from someone with a familiar face, called Batal.

`Mari it is me.`

`Are you all right?`

`It is a wonderful place here. And it hardly ever rains. Not like Ireland. Here they will treat you like a princess. I promise.`

Mari smiled at that.

`What do I have to do? It's today I'm getting the coach to Liverpool.`

`There is a coach which goes via Birmingham airport. Make sure you get that one.`

`I will.`

`And Mari, you must delete all our conversations on here. And bring your laptop with you.`

`I will.`

'Time to go,' her mother called. They set off for the coach station together. Mari's heart was thumping so hard she thought it might burst through her chest.

When the time came to get on the coach, Sinéad made the driver promise to look out for her until they got to Liverpool.

Mari was worried. Supposing this one didn't go to Birmingham? But an old woman sitting at the front had heard the conversation. As Mari went past, the woman touched her arm. 'I'll look out for you, too, dear,' she said. 'At least as far as Birmingham.'

Mari was relieved. This was going to be much easier than she had thought. There was no snoozing for her this time. She was wide awake, her case on her lap, and the most excited she had ever been in her life.

When the coach arrived at Birmingham, she was the last to get off. She'd kept her head down as she walked up the bus in case the driver saw her, but he wasn't in his seat. She quickly passed the old woman in her haste to find her contact. The woman began to speak but was jostled by someone behind her.

Mari began to run, anxious to get away before the woman said anything. A woman in a hijab began walking alongside her. She took Mari's arm and talked as she walked.

'You're Mari?'

'Yes.'

'And you're going to see Saeed?'

'I am,' Mari smiled.

'You are so lucky to be going there. I wish I could. I have to stay here a bit longer but I will take you on the first stage of your journey.'

'Where's that?'

'Turkey. We're flying to Turkey in two hours. '

Before they reached the doors of the airport terminal the woman whisked her to a dark corner.

'Here,' she said. Put this on. Your skin is quite pale and your hair not so dark; it will help disguise you.' She wrapped a shawl around Mari's head and shoulders then dabbed eyebrow pencil on her eyebrows.

'Your eyes are brown. I think you will pass.' She handed Mari a passport opened at the photo page. Mari gasped. 'It's almost me.'

'Our people are very skilled these days. It is my daughter's passport but she is in Turkey. Young girls with brown skin look very similar to white men's eyes, especially under the hijab.'

She was proved right. As they checked in, Mari drew no more than a cursory glance from the passport control officer. When they got on the plane, the woman accompanying her took another seat far from Mari. She was left on her own, a bit scared but also tingling with the excitement of it all. She braced herself for take-off and was in the sky. *They won't even know yet. I'm safe,'* she thought. She began to daydream about what a wonderful life she would have with Saeed.

When the plane began its descent, Mari hugged herself with anticipation. She was too excited about the prospect of seeing Saeed again to think about her family. The woman who had left her reappeared to take her arm. This time, Mari overheard the officer at passport control call her Fatima, but they were waved through the barriers without question.

'What happens now, Fatima?'

Fatima frowned at Mari's use of her name. She put her finger to her lips. 'You must tell no one my name or they will kill me.'

Mari gasped but nodded.

'I must make arrangements. We must stay until they are ready to take you.'

Mari, her skin reacting to the relative heat of Adana, followed Fatima outside where she waved her arm at a taxi and whispered to the driver when he pulled up.

***

Unbeknown to Mari, there had been a change of plan. Kenny had needed to visit Liverpool himself, so had decided to surprise Mari at the coach stop in Liverpool. He was pacing furiously in between repeatedly asking the attendant there what had happened to the coach.

'It'll be traffic,' was the consistent reply he received.

When the coach eventually arrived, he waited at the door. There was no Mari. He rang Niamh. 'Are you sure this is the right bus?'

'It must be you, you auld fool.'

'Well, she's not on board.'

'Ask the driver.'

The driver had already clocked off and was nowhere to be found. Kenny was worried. He rang Niamh back to tell her.

'I'll call Sinéad. Check what time she got on.'

Sinéad had not hesitated to celebrate her freedom. She was out with her friends, drinking heavily, relieved to be free of her daughter for a few days.

'I swear I'd have killed her if it had been one more day.'

'Teenagers. Drive you mad,' her friend agreed.

Neither of them heard Sinéad's phone ring. By the time she got home, there were ten missed calls on her display. She sobered up immediately and rang her mother.

'What's the matter?'

'There's no sign of Mari. She's gone missing.'

'Oh no!' Sinéad crumpled into a heap on the floor. 'What have I done? Ow, my head. Coffee.'

When she'd drunk a large mug of coffee, Sinéad steeled herself to talk to the police.

'My daughter's gone missing!' she shouted down the phone.

'Please calm down, Mrs…?'

'Lone.'

'Mrs Lone, when did your daughter go missing?'

'I put her on a coach to Liverpool at ten this morning. She should have arrived at around half past two. But she wasn't on the coach.'

'And have you contacted the coach company?'

'My mother has. We've tried everything. No one knows what happened to her.'

'How old is your daughter?'

'Fifteen.'

There was a pause at the other end. 'Has she ever done anything like this before?'

'No, of course not. What are you saying?'

'Nothing. Mrs Lone. Let me have a few more details and we'll get on it.'

30

15th February

To Saeed it seemed like they had been in bed for seconds before he and Ahmed were woken up by one of the guards and taken to the shower complex.

'You must be clean before you take religious instruction.'

'It's five o'clock!' Saeed exclaimed, looking at his watch.

The guard grinned. 'Your time is ours now.'

After washing, they were escorted to a room in the building where a black-robed man waited to begin their lesson.

'Today you will be taught alone. When you have been assessed, we will teach you with others of your understanding. Now let the lessons begin.'

'But I am well-schooled,' Ahmed said.

'Shush,' Saeed nudged him. 'You're drawing attention to yourself.'

Ahmed bit his lip.

Their first session was devoted to finding out how much they knew of their religion and their capacity to challenge sections of it. It was intense and lasted for several hours. The teacher was reasonable and friendly and tested their knowledge thoroughly. Where there were gaps in Saeed's knowledge, he would smile at him and say things like 'Your western society has been rather handy with the scissors and snipped out the most important bits.'

The next session was different. The teacher went on to introduce some old texts that neither boy had come across before.

'That's not what I was taught,' Ahmed said.

'These are the original ancient texts,' the teacher explained. 'It is because of Western society that these things have been hidden from you. These are the proper texts. You must learn the truth so you can become closer to Allah.'

'But I know all the proper texts,' Ahmed persisted.

Saeed glared at him. 'Please shut up. Do you really think you know more than our teacher?'

Ahmed looked down.

When the session finished, the boys were given a small meal of bread and water. Yousef came to join them.

He spoke to Saeed. 'I have heard news of your girl, Mari.' Saeed nodded. 'We have been successful. She has been located in Turkey and is on her way.'

'That's brilliant news,' Saeed said. 'When will she be here?'

Yousef shook his head. 'I cannot say that her path will lead her here. But you will no doubt meet her again in time.'

'What do you mean?' Saeed's face fell. 'I promised her she would be with me.'

Yousef ruffled his hair. 'You are so young. It is not for you to decide what is best for the girl. She will be placed where she can be of most benefit to our caliphate. And you must play your part too. Look, your next lesson is about to begin. Your duty is to be the most useful person you can be. May Allah be praised.'

Saeed grimaced, but he took the words to heart. *This is bigger than both of us*, he decided. *I must do what is wanted of me*.

After a few minutes, the next teacher arrived. This man was stern. The first thing he did was to test them on some of the new scripts that they had been taught earlier, but he put much greater emphasis on certain passages. Saeed could tell that Ahmed felt uncomfortable. This time every challenge he made was met with a decisive put-down.

'This is the truth and you must learn it,' was the repeated response.

Saeed was getting irritated with his cousin. In a rare moment when the teacher paused to look up a specific text, he hissed at him. 'Why do you keep arguing? He speaks the truth. Don't you want to get on here? I do, and you're making me look bad.'

'OK. For you, I'll keep quiet.'

After that, Ahmed put on such a show of acquiescence even Saeed was impressed. The teacher was delighted.

'You have done well. You are now ready to join the rest of the class. We will teach you Arabic; the proper language of Islam, and then you will begin your journey to learn how to be a soldier for Allah.'

'See?' Saeed smiled. 'We're on our way now.'

Ahmed gave a weak smile in response. 'I know Arabic well, ' he said. 'But I can always improve.'

Their reward was a decent-sized meal of chicken and bread with a glass of cola. When they were left alone together, Saeed spoke to Ahmed. 'So you agree with the teaching now? I was sure you would. It all makes sense to me.'

Ahmed shook his head. 'No, no *no*. It is all wrong. Don't you see? I don't believe all he told us. I just *pretended* to keep you happy. I think it is a corruption. I have heard of some of these things before but they are not true or are of unsafe origin.'

Saeed's eyes nearly popped out of his head. 'What? Are you mad? It is clearly the truth, Ahmed. Don't play games with me.'

'Calm down, Saeed, you must keep a clear head and use your logic. Can't you see what is happening? They are brainwashing you.'

Saeed was furious. 'I have been told for a while now that there are texts which were hidden in order to trick Muslims into behaving like Westerners. It's all beginning to fall into place. If you are not with me then you should just go.'

'I will listen again tomorrow before I make my decision.'

'What decision? You mean you are actually thinking of it?'

'We'll see how things progress. Are you so sure of what you have heard?'

'Yes. I am absolutely positive. And you are an idiot if you cannot see it too.'

That night Saeed slept soundly unaware that Ahmed had been tossing and turning all night.

31

Karen arrived at the station where the staff were discussing Mari's disappearance. She grabbed a hot chocolate from the machine and was about to curse the train service for her late train when she tuned in to the gossip.

'If I had a pound for every time a teenage girl ran off... ' an older PC was saying.

'A missing girl?' Karen asked. 'Who's on it?'

'PC Malik was first in, again.'

Karen walked into the main office area and zoomed in on Omar, who was talking on the phone. He finished his conversation and turned to Karen.

'Mari Lone. Meant to be on the ferry to Dublin yesterday, but never arrived. She boarded the coach in the morning. They didn't check where she got off. They have CCTV on most of their coaches but, of course, not on that one, or at least it wasn't working. And before you ask, yes the coach stopped at several places.'

'Good work. Who reported her missing? Her mother?' Omar nodded. 'Anyone been to see her yet?'

'Not yet boss. Guv. I mean Karen.'

'I'll go. I'm good at this sort of thing. I'll see if I can get more information, a photo at least. We can show it around all the stops; see if anybody remembers her getting off. You check passenger lists; they'll have mobile numbers for some of them. Someone will surely remember a teenage girl getting off the bus.'

'Yes, Karen.'

Karen gulped down her drink as fast as she could, beckoning her fingers at Omar. He correctly assumed she wanted the address and wrote it down on a sticky note for her. *He's good*, she decided as she hurried out of the office.

As always, Karen preferred to be out doing things rather than being stuck at her desk, but she was finding that getting a pool car wasn't always easy. Today, she was lucky and managed to get to Sinéad Lone's flat in fifteen minutes. She briefly wondered about the safety of the car as she parked it on the estate. Then shrugged before scaling the concrete steps up to Sinéad's flat.

She knocked on the door which was opened quickly by a woman even paler than Karen herself. She had panda eyes, looking as if she hadn't slept in ages.

'Mrs Lone?' Sinéad nodded. 'Detective Sergeant Thorpe. I'm here about your missing daughter Mari; I assume she hasn't made contact?'

Sinéad pulled the door back to let her in. 'Nothing. It's like she's disappeared off the map.' Sinéad led the way into her flat and waved her hand for Karen to sit down.

Mrs Lone, we've done some initial investigating, but can you tell me why she was on a coach to Liverpool?'

'She was going to stay with my ma in Ireland. She's done the journey before. We knew it'd be safe.'

'But she was fifteen?' Karen queried.

'My ma's friend Kenny went to meet her off the bus. Except that she wasn't there.' Sinéad's head drooped.

'And Mari wanted to go to Ireland?'

'Oh Lordy, yes. She loves going there and she loves staying with her nana. She was talking about nothing else.'

Karen frowned, perplexed. 'Can you think of any reason at all why she would get off the bus at the wrong stop?'

Sinéad's response was immediate. 'None whatsoever. She's done the route before and the coach people are very good at looking out for her.'

'Mrs Lone, teenagers sometimes make arrangements without their parents' knowledge. Is it possible that she went somewhere else entirely?'

'No! Mari wasn't like that.'

'And how is your relationship with your daughter?'

Karen caught Sinéad's expression. *Now we're getting somewhere.*

'It's a typical mother-teenager relationship. They're never easy.'

'Had you argued at all?'

Sinéad gave a hollow laugh. 'All the bloody time. But that's why she was so pleased to be going away.'

'*Um*. Is she on social media? Facebook or something like that? It may be she told someone what she was doing?'

Sinéad shook her head. 'Not that I know. She had a laptop that she used for her homework but that's all.'

'May I see it?'

'She's taken it with her.'

'And there were no boys or girls on the scene?'

Sinéad shook her head.

Karen was stumped. 'We're looking at all the options, Mrs Lone. May I have a photograph of Mari, please? So that we can get her picture out there?'

'Of course.' Sinéad went to the shelf unit and took out an album. 'Her last school photo. Will that do?'

Karen started a little when she saw the picture. Sinéad, used to the reaction explained. 'Her dad was Pakistani.'

'Thank you, Mrs Lone. I promise you we will do everything we can to find Mari. Try not to worry. In my experience, it's very rare that something bad has happened. It's more likely to be a spur-of-the-moment thing. She could have got off at the wrong stop and got lost, something like that.'

'I hope to God you're right.' Sinéad flopped down on the sofa, her head in her hands.

'We have your phone number. I promise I'll be in touch as soon as we have any news.' Sinéad looked up at Karen but didn't reply. 'I'll see myself out.'

32

Today was different again for Ahmed and Saeed; their military training was beginning. In the morning they were first marched and drilled. Later, they were pushed through challenging assault courses.

Saeed loved every second but when he finished the last course, he found Ahmed still at the starting position. He was puffing heavily, and having fallen off a raised platform, was examining his foot.

'Come on, Ahmed! You're turning into a joke,' Saeed sneered. Ahmed didn't respond. He limped over to the side of the course and slumped on the ground, rubbing his ankle. There he was exposed to the ridicule of all the others who went past him. There was no sympathy for him.

Saeed saw the trainer go up to him. 'On your feet and walk,' the man said. Ahmed limped in obeyance. 'If you can walk that far you can finish the course,' the man ordered.

Saeed watched as Ahmed struggled on again until the entire run had been completed. 'That was hopeless,' the trainer concluded. 'We will start tomorrow morning with this course again. And I expect you to complete it perfectly.'

'Hopeless,' Saeed repeated to Ahmed.

After a brief break for food and another wash, the religious instruction began again. Ahmed looked at Saeed. 'I must correct him if he tells untruths,' he said.

'Don't be so stupid, Ahmed. Do you believe you know more than a scholar?'

'Yes, I believe I do,' Ahmed replied.

'Then you're stupid. Hopeless at sport, useless at school,' Saeed snapped.

The teacher that day was a very large and imposing figure with a face that looked as if it could never smile. Saeed watched as the scrawny Ahmed challenged almost everything the man said. Every counter-argument Ahmed put forward was flattened not with reason but with anger and forcefulness.

Saeed was embarrassed. He moved his desk away from Ahmed in an attempt to show the tutor he was dissociating himself.

Halfway through the lesson, the teacher, infuriated at another intervention, loomed over Ahmed and roared at him. 'I think that Allah does not want you if you are not prepared to believe in his word. Are you an infidel, boy? You know what happens to infidels. Speak now!'

Ahmed caved. 'I'm sorry, sir, I was just trying to explore the arguments.'

Saeed turned his head away. The lesson continued. When it was time for lunch, Saeed sat with the other boys leaving Ahmed on his own.

The afternoon was spent learning Arabic and there were no arguments from Ahmed. When the day drew to a close, Saeed approached him.

'So, have you changed your mind now?'

Ahmed frowned. 'No, Saeed. I can never be with you and the people here. Everything I have heard now outrages my senses. I am going to leave. You should come with me and save your soul.'

Saeed snapped. 'I can't believe you, Ahmed. For the first time ever you get to hear the proper teachings of Islam and you reject them. He is right; you are no more than an infidel.'

'Are you so taken in already?'

Saeed could feel the temperature rise on his face. 'I never liked you, Ahmed, but I thought this might make a man of you. You're weak in body and now I see you're weak in the head too. Why can't you see that they're telling us the truth?'

'There is no truth. There are distortions, lies, even, but no truth.'

Saeed raised his hand to hit Ahmed but dropped it. Then he turned his anger on himself for being unable to see the action through. Finally, he turned on Ahmed. 'You are despicable. Allah will never want you for a soldier.'

Ahmed shook his head sadly. 'What will be will be.'

***

When Saeed was asleep, Ahmed gathered his few possessions together. He had no money; it had all been taken by the guards. He was worried for Saeed but he was determined to leave. *I can help him better from the outside*, he decided.

He crept out of the tent and walked slowly to the edge of the complex following the road they had come in by as closely as he could while remaining as far out of view as possible. Ahead of him lay a checkpoint patrolled with guards. He looked around frantically at the wire fences surrounding the compound. He had seen them but not realised their extent before. There was no way he could climb them and he couldn't see any way through.

One of the guards spotted him. 'You!' he shouted. Ahmed walked over to him trying to smile. 'What are you doing?' asked the guard.

'I need to go home for a short while. I forgot my glasses.' This was the best he could think of and it was not going down well.

'You cannot leave without permission.'

'But I must go,' Ahmed insisted, his heart beating rapidly. 'I will come back soon, I promise.'

For a second it looked as though the guard was changing his mind. He smiled at Ahmed. 'Go on then, boy. Hurry back.'

Ahmed ran past the checkpoint, his heart stopping as he heard the sound of rifles being cocked.

***

Saeed was woken from his sleep by the sound of gunfire. He looked around and saw that Ahmed's bed was empty.

'Ahmed?!' he shouted. 'Are you in the toilet?'

He got up and looked outside the tent. Ahead of him, he could see some guards approaching. They were dragging something behind them. What was it? *A body?* He stood, mesmerised in the firelight of the camp torches as the convoy came closer. His blood began to run cold as he thought he recognised the clothes on the body. When the guards got close enough, he saw the dead face of his cousin. 'Ahmed?'

One of the guards laughed. 'That was your friend, huh? We'll find you a proper one tomorrow.'

Saeed went back inside the tent unable to decipher the emotions he was now feeling. To be honest, he hadn't liked Ahmed that much. He had become increasingly irritating.

But to be killed? For that? It was too much.

Then he thought about how Ahmed had challenged everything the teachers had said. Even when he didn't speak out, Saeed knew from Ahmed's facial expressions that he didn't believe what he was being told.

And what happens to unbelievers?

Even Saeed knew that. What was more, in some countries, even Pakistan, death, whether according to the law or not, was often the penalty.

Why didn't he just believe? Saeed thought. *Even if he had told me what he was doing, I could have stopped him. What will my uncle think of me? But what could I have done?* Saeed lay on the bed, fighting back tears, trying to think everything through. But he was certain that whatever his fate was, it would be with the Caliphate.

33

Karen and Omar had drawn blanks from all their investigations of Mari's disappearance. None of the passengers they had contacted remembered Mari at all. The driver said that he'd been on the coach the whole time, except for taking a comfort break at Birmingham. There was no available CCTV inside or outside the coach.

'What's next?' Omar asked.

'Something's bugging me, Karen replied. 'I can't help thinking about Selina Ali. But neither can I remotely see a connection there, other than they both disappeared. But Selina's mother is cool, whereas Mrs Lone is chewing her fingers off.'

'They both lived in the same vicinity,' Omar said.

'Not that close.'

Karen sensed a presence. She turned round to see Barry appear through his door. 'The boss,' she replied, before going to his office.

'We're not getting very far,' she explained. 'But there's definitely something suspicious about it. We'll have to get her photo out there.'

'Family? What's her ethnicity?'

'She's mixed race. Bad relations with her white Irish mother but very good with her grandmother in Ireland. And she was on her way there to stay with her when she went missing.'

'So not just a stroppy teenager running off?'

'No. She sounds stroppy enough, but I'd be far more worried about it being abduction. I've had recent experience of that.'

'Get on it then.'

'I'm going for the papers in the Midlands, nationwide social media, and the regional evening news.'

'OK.'

Before long, the station was buzzing with reports of potential sightings. Karen yearned to have Macy and Bradley at her side again, it made her appreciate them even more. Emma, too, formerly, would have been a great help in eliminating false sightings. Not so much now, Karen sighed.

'Sarge?' A young female officer came up to her desk. 'Can I help? PC Jones. Precious. My shift's ended but I've got spare time.'

Karen looked up at the woman who reminded her a little of Macy but without the style. 'Of course. That's good of you.'

'She's the same age as my little sis,' Precious explained. 'I'd hate it if anything happened to her.'

'That's a very good reason, Precious. It might help if you can think about what your sister might have got up to. Maybe something we've overlooked.'

'Like a gig or something?'

'Exactly that. See Omar over there. He'll set you up.'

Karen seized on the idea and rang Sinéad. 'Mrs Lone, we're exploring all options. Did she have a favourite band? Or can you think of anyone she'd want to see without you knowing?'

Sinéad sighed. 'You're clutching at straws. One Direction. But they're not touring anymore.'

'I'm sorry, Mrs Lone. We are trying everything, I promise you.' Sinéad hung up

Karen went to Omar's desk. 'How's it going?'

'We're being thorough but no leads at all. We've had the usual hoax calls but most were easily eliminated due to being in the wrong area or timeframe.'

'OK.' Karen hated the lack of results but knew it was to be expected. 'Are we missing anything?'

She and Omar went through all the guidance line by line. When they'd ticked off all possible options, she called in on Barry.

'Sorry, Barry. We're getting nowhere fast. Can we get national TV coverage? While memories are still fresh.'

'How long's she been missing?' Barry grunted.

'Over thirty-four hours.'

'Tomorrow morning. Get something properly prepared. It's no good rushing it. My guess is she'll either be back home by then or found partying in Birmingham.'

'Thanks.'

Karen, Omar, and Precious worked late into the evening, taking and following up calls until they began to slow to very few. There was still no news.

'I'm putting a media pack together,' Karen announced. 'Go home. It'll be even busier tomorrow.'

When they'd gone, Karen rang Macy.

'I saw the coverage. No news, I take it.'

'Nothing Mace. It's beginning to get to me.'

'Remember Emma?' Macy said. 'It was days before we got close to finding her, but she was OK. I'm sure Mari will be fine.'

'But there was a reason for someone taking Emma. There's nothing here.'

'Yes, but we didn't know that at the time,' Macy replied. 'There'll be a reason, we just don't know what it is yet. I think she's another runaway.'

'To Syria?' Karen said. 'But there's no connection there at all.'

'She's a brown girl in East London,' Macy said. 'Maybe that's enough? Maybe someone's got to her and she wants a different sort of life.'

'Thanks, Macy. She's part Pakistani heritage. You might be onto something there.'

34

17th February

Mari woke up on the floor of the tiny ground-floor apartment Fatima had taken them to two nights before. Fatima had taken the only bed and all Mari had for comfort was a blanket. As a result, she was tired and aching all over. She could hear Fatima talking on the phone but couldn't understand what she was saying. She guessed she was making the next arrangements.

When the talking stopped, Fatima came to her with a piece of pitta bread. 'Here. You have a long journey ahead of you. You must eat. Do you drink coffee?'

Mari shook her head. 'You know I don't.'

'Water then.'

Fatima's phone rang and she hurried to answer it. She nodded and turned to Mari. 'It is not good. We have to wait.'

'What's wrong?' Mari asked.

'I am going out. Stay here. Get yourself ready, I will be back soon.'

Mari sat on a small wooden chair and began to chew at the bread. She watched Fatima leave and then heard the sound of a lock clicking. Jumping up, she tried the door. *Definitely locked.* Looking around, she saw that the windows were old and wouldn't open when she tried them. *Why am I worrying? This has to be secret. It'll be all right. Saeed promised.*

When she'd finished the bread she went into the tiny kitchen area and found an unopened bottle of water. When she'd drunk most of it, she went into the bathroom area and this time, found a flannel provided in the sink. She wiped her face with it. For the second time, she began to think how nice her own home was in comparison. She'd only packed a few clothes and no toiletries in case it gave the game away.

Then she waited. And waited. She had nothing to do except stare at the walls. Her laptop was there but there was nothing she could plug it into. There was no signal on her phone and the battery was low so she didn't dare play any games. Eventually, she went into the bedroom and tried to sleep.

Late in the afternoon, Mari heard the noise of the lock opening and Fatima reappeared. She scowled at her as if she was being a nuisance.

'Always the same. They don't look after me,' Fatima moaned.

'So why do you do it? Is it because you believe in the new state?'

Fatima made a spitting gesture. 'I do it because I have to.' Her phone rang and she began hurriedly speaking into it.

Finally, her face broke into a smile. 'All is going well. The car will be coming for you tomorrow. It's not ideal, but it is the best we can do. Then you will begin the next stage of your journey. For now, you must sleep.'

'But I can't sleep,' Mari said.

'This will help.'

Before she could react, Fatima had plunged a needle into her arm. The room began to spin and Mari fell into a deep sleep.

Mari woke to Fatima's pulling at her. 'Get up, they will be here soon.'

Mari stood up and stretched herself. 'What happened to me? I don't remember,' she plonked herself on the little chair.

'Hurry. We have to get ready to leave.'

'But I'm really hungry now,' Mari said. 'I need to eat.'

'I only have bread,' Fatima said. 'That will have to do. The soldiers will have food for you when they come.'

'The soldiers?' Mari looked scared. 'Are you not coming with me?'

Fatima shook her head. 'You will be safe, I promise you.' Her eyes fell upon Mari's laptop. 'Not allowed,' she snapped, taking the laptop, and putting it in a cupboard. 'Phone?'

Mari, shocked at losing her laptop, didn't want to lose her phone, but Fatima seized her case and took the phone out. 'Not allowed,' she repeated. Now we must walk. We must hurry to the border.'

'I'm hungry,' Mari repeated.

Fatima took the last of the bread from the kitchen and handed it to Mari. 'You will get more food soon enough. Come, we must go.'

Mari took her case and followed Fatima along the dusty road. But as she began to walk, Mari's legs began to ache. She also realised that something was wrong. Fatima was on her phone. Mari couldn't understand what she said, but she seemed to be getting angrier with every exchange.

She turned around and snarled at Mari. 'You have to walk faster,' she hissed. 'I have to get back. I cannot be found here. It will be dangerous for me.'

'Will Saeed be there?' Mari asked.

'Who?'

Mari concentrated. 'Batal?'

Fatima walked on. Mari tried to speed up but her legs hurt so much and her case, only small, felt so heavy.

'Are you really that stupid?' Fatima sneered.

'What?' Mari asked. 'What do you mean by that?' She stopped to look where they were. Ahead of her, she could see what looked like a crossing point. There were lines of wire fencing and she could see men dressed in combat gear holding rifles.

As they got closer, Fatima went ahead and spoke to one of them. Mari saw something passed to him and assumed it was money. When she got there she was pushed through. Fatima turned to walk back without another word.

'Wait!' she shouted. 'What happens now?'

35

Maria stared at the telephone, willing it to ring. 'Ibra? I'm going to try again!' she shouted to her husband.

Ibrahim appeared through the living room door. 'You rang them only yesterday, Maria. 'They're fine.'

'Because it's a foreign country to him. I want to be sure. He's meant to be coming home tomorrow. We can't let him mess up his studies. This was meant to be a short break.'

'It's an open ticket,' Ibrahim replied. 'Another day or two won't matter. Let him have his fun.'

Maria ignored him and reached for the phone. As usual, it took several attempts before she got through. Her brother-in-law, Jafar, answered.

'Any news?'

'Yes, Maria. Ahmed messaged me again today. They're fine. You must not worry. Boys will be boys.'

'But the ticket. And he must study.'

'The planes are not full. There will be space for him.'

'And I thought I could trust him with your son,' she replied angrily.

'Of course you can. Ahmed is a good boy.'

'I think you should tell them to come back now.'

Jafar didn't reply straight away. 'Is something wrong?' Maria pressed. 'What does my brother think?'

'He thinks the same as you that a day or two won't matter. I am worried. Jafar, I will not forgive you if anything goes wrong.'

'OK, OK. I'll send him a message. We will speak soon.'

Maria heard the phone click off. She turned to her husband. 'I should contact the police here,' she said. 'He is a British subject.'

Ibrahim shrugged his shoulders. 'And do you think they will do anything? He's gone on holiday. I'm sure it will be fine.'

Maria's eyes began to water. 'Ibra, I have this feeling inside. Something's wrong. Do you not remember that Selina, too, has disappeared somewhere?'

Ibrahim came close to Maria and held her in his arms. 'They had nothing in common,' Ibrahim said. 'Selina is a difficult child. Always fighting against her culture. I expect she has run away with a white boy or something. Saeed is a good boy. He regularly goes to prayers and he loves his faith. It's not the same at all.'

'Are you so sure of that?' Maria looked at him.

Everything's fine,' he said. 'I remember how I was at that age. It's all part of growing up. And Ahmed is a very sensible young man. They'll be fine. I promise.'

'I'm going to talk to Razia,' Maria said defiantly. 'Do you remember that Saeed did meet Selina? At that wedding.'

'That was two years ago. He was far too young.'

'But they may have kept in touch. Now I remember. Razia was very concerned when she went missing. She was on that Facebook thing. Where is she?' Maria shouted up the stairs. 'Razia? Are you there?'

Razia came bounding down. 'Is there any news of Mari?'

'No, I'm sorry. Sit down, Razia. We are worried that your brother has also disappeared.'

'Saeed can look after himself.' Razia scoffed.

'This is serious. He is your brother. Don't joke about such things. Did he keep in touch with Mari at all?'

'No. He was angry with her. He didn't tell me the details, just that he wasn't going to teach her anymore. I know he unfriended her because I saw it on Facebook.'

Maria huffed. 'I suppose it was some teenage thing or other. I thought she was a nice girl, but Saeed is very picky.'

'And he's getting all religious,' Razia said. 'She wouldn't be suitable for him now.'

'Maybe he might think that. What about Selina?'

'She was on Facebook. But I'm sure they weren't friends.'

'Are you positive, Razia? This could be important.'

Razia shook her head. 'I don't know for sure.'

'If we don't hear anything tomorrow, I'm ringing the police,' Maria said.

36

Mari was relieving herself behind a shrub at the side of the road. The journey had been horrendous from the beginning. They'd stopped for the night and the men, thankfully, had left her alone to try to sleep in the jeep. She'd eaten nothing since the bread the day before and managed on one bottle of water. Her stomach had ached as much as her legs and arms but they wouldn't stop the car for her to relieve herself so she'd squatted where she was. They were so angry with her that one of them had slapped her. This time, they'd let her go. Not far, but just enough to preserve what little dignity she had left.

Mari still believed that she would be reunited with Saeed. 'Batal?' she said as one of them approached her. 'Am I going to see Batal?'

The man grabbed her arm and dragged her to the truck.

'Why won't you tell me?'

It's fine, she said to herself. *Saeed said it would all be fine. That they would treat me like a princess*.

As she was bundled into the back seat, the vehicle took off before she had even been able to sit down properly. She hurt herself as she tried to sit up. 'Ow!'

'Silence,' came the reply.

They drove off as fast as they could in the dusty terrain. Mari sat holding tightly to the door handle to help stop the jostling around. She tried to stay calm, but the bumping of the vehicle was making her feel ill.

'I'm going to be sick!' she yelled. But the men either didn't understand or ignored her.

Too late. She bumped her head on the seat as she threw up. It was only dried bread and stomach acid, but it burned her throat. One of the men shouted something but they didn't stop.

Mari sat in uncomfortable misery. Deprived of her laptop and phone, she had lost all track of time. She was tired, hungry, and now she was beginning to be scared. *Saeed will be waiting for me*, she decided. *It will be all right soon.*

She noticed that the terrain was gradually changing. There were small houses dotted around. The houses increased and she saw ahead of her they were approaching the outskirts of a city. Which city she had no idea, but she could tell from the tone of the conversation the men were having, that they were getting closer to their destination.

When they arrived at a security point, the guards peered into the jeep and looked at her. A few words were exchanged, but they were waved through.

'What's going on?' she asked boldly. 'I came here to see Batal.'

The men still did not answer. They looked this way and that, trying to find their bearings. They pulled up outside an impressive-looking building and immediately a guard dressed in black appeared from the front entrance.

More words were exchanged but this time Mari sensed that they were talking about her. One of the men got out of the jeep and opened the back door. He stared at the remnants of vomit and grabbed Mari, pulling her out of the back. He slapped her on the face and she howled in pain.

The man grabbed her arm with one hand and took her case from the jeep with the other. Mari was dragged to a small house opposite the building. At the door stood a woman in a burqa. She took Mari's arm and case.

'I am with Batal!' Mari screamed. The woman laughed as she pulled her through the door.

Mari went inside. The woman passed over her case and then went out, slamming the door behind her.

Mari grimaced a little at the state of the place. It was dusty and looked somewhat basic. She walked into the tiny courtyard and looked up amazed to see the open sky.

Suddenly, things didn't seem so bad. *This is better. Much better*. It was already nicer than her old flat. She tried each door in turn. A small kitchen here, a room with a television there. Upstairs, a bedroom and a small bathroom.

This is quite nice, she decided as she stripped off and ran the shower. The water wasn't very warm but she didn't care, she was beginning to feel normal again.

When she was dressed in clean clothes, she went into the kitchen. There she found some bread and cheese and began to eat as if she'd never eaten before. *Maybe it will all be all right.*

But as soon as she'd had her fill, the exhaustion overcame her. She went upstairs to the bedroom. I'll just rest here for a moment, she decided.

37

Saeed had drifted off into a troubled sleep. His first thoughts when he woke were that it had all been a bad dream. But a glance at Ahmed's unoccupied bed jolted him back to reality. He got dressed and stuck his head out of the tent. Yousef was walking towards him.

'I'm sorry about your friend, Ahmed,' he said. 'How do you feel about it all?' Yousef peered at him.

Saeed understood what was happening and knew how he had to respond or he might meet the same fate. 'He wasn't my friend. He didn't believe. He deserved to die.'

Yousef smiled broadly. 'Good. That is correct. Come look. See what we do to unbelievers.'

Saeed followed him to the training area where others were beginning to gather. He saw their faces before he saw what they were looking at. Some were grinning, and a few looked terrified. Most stood with blank expressions.

He turned to look at what they saw. Ahmed's body had been strung up by his feet, his lifeless eyes open and staring into an upside-down blank space. His body was covered in dirt and blood.

Saeed knew he was being tested again. He swallowed down the vomit hitting the back of his mouth.

'This is what we do to infidels!' roared a man in fine black robes. He walked in front of the body, looking each of the gathered young men in the face.

Saeed looked up and studied the man. His outfit was tailored and very ornate, decorated with embroidered emblems. To Saeed, he looked like an ancient warrior. He had such stature, such power in his voice, such majesty; this man could do anything. Saeed was awestruck.

At that moment, Saeed decided he could not think of anything better than to be like this man. He was the camp leader and a true leader of men, and Saeed could not wait to follow in his footsteps.

'He is a great hero and a magnificent leader,' Saeed felt Yousef's hand on his shoulder.

'He truly is,' Saeed answered. 'I will be like him one day.'

'If Allah wills it,' Yousef gave a small laugh, 'it will be. Come Batal. Come with me and we will test you further. I believe that you may have the strength and ability to become one of our elite fighters. How does that sound?'

'It's what I want,' Saeed acknowledged. 'I will work as hard as I can to merit that distinction.'

'Today you may have your chance.'

Yousef led Saeed to the training compound where Saeed saw around forty young men standing or sitting on the ground.

'I will be watching you and if I believe you are worthy, I will recommend that you be chosen. I believe you have great strength in you, Batal, May Allah bless you today.'

Saeed took in a deep breath and strode purposefully over to the gathered group. They eyed him with suspicion. One, a teenager about the same age as himself, stood and faced him, speaking in Urdu. 'You're new. Why are you here?'

Saeed replied as best as he could. 'Because I'm the best man here.'

The lad spat in the sand. 'They want you because you are a Westerner.'

'I'm still the best,' Saeed replied.

'We will see.'

When the training began, Saeed showed that he was a very fast learner and his physical strength soon helped him stand out from the others. At the end of the session, Yousef came over to him, a big smile on his face.

'Batal, you have passed my test. Our leader is impressed. So much so that this evening you will be sent to the caliphate to become a soldier. I have high hopes for you, Batal.'

The others looked to Yousef. 'What about us?' one asked.

Yousef grinned again. 'You, you and you,' he pointed. 'You will come also.'

127

Saeed noticed that the lad who had first challenged him had not been chosen. He looked him in the face and saw in his eyes that he had made an enemy. 'See you in Raqqa,' he said. 'Maybe one day,' he added.

38

Mari's disappearance was headline news on all the local TV stations. At the police station, as expected, the volume of calls increased. Karen glanced over to Omar's desk. He was taking a call and she could tell from his demeanour and intense expression it was an important one. She got up and went over to his desk.

'Thank you, Madam. Can you tell me your name? Do you mind if I put you on the speaker?'

'Oh, no, that's fine. It's Mrs Goldman. Ruth Goldman. I'm so sorry I didn't ring before. I've been away for a few days and I've only just got your message.'

Karen's ears pricked up. Omar nodded at her. 'Can you tell me what information you have?'

'Yes, about the girl. She got off at Birmingham. I know that for a fact because I saw her pass me even though when she got on, I heard her mother tell the driver quite clearly she was going to Liverpool.'

'Thank you, Mrs Goldman.' Omar gave a tiny fist pump. 'May I take your details in case we need to contact you again?'

'Of course.'

Smiling broadly, Karen was distracted by an animated Precious, holding her phone in one hand and waving at her with the other.

Precious put her hand over the receiver. 'We've got a missing boy now. A possible connection to Mari.'

Karen's eyes widened. 'Who's that?' she asked.

'His mother. Do you want to talk to her?'

Karen nodded and took the receiver. She paced as she spoke. 'Good morning, Mrs... '

'Rahman. Maria Rahman. I've just heard the news about Mari Lone.'

'Yes...'

'She was a friend of my son, Saeed. And I think he, too, has gone missing.'

'I see.' Karen wriggled her bottom onto Precious's desk and made a *writing* gesture to her. She spoke, repeating what Maria said to her.

'So he left for Pakistan on the 12th of February. And you say he's gone missing from there?'

'And his name is Saeed. S A E E D. He's seventeen.'

'So he was helping her with her maths homework. Were they in a relationship?'

'I don't think so.'

'And he hadn't been in contact with any other family members.'

'Yes, may I take your number? I'll come to talk to you as soon as possible if that's OK with you?'

'Good.'

Karen repeated the number and thanked Maria for the call. She got off the desk and turned to Precious. 'Did you get all that?'

'I did.'

'It may be nothing, but it may just be connected. It's too much of a coincidence not to be. Now, where's Omar?'

***

'So, are you up for a trip to Birmingham?' Karen asked.

Omar grinned broadly. 'I'd prefer Blackpool, but yes, OK.'

Karen visibly relaxed. 'That's great. We're going to have to go up there.'

'What, now?'

'No time like the present. I'll drive.' Karen saw his expression change. 'What's wrong?'

Omar stuttered. 'Oh, nothing. It's just that my wife… ' he tailed off.

Karen narrowed her eyes. 'Do you know, I was just about to think you had a problem with women drivers.'

'No, boss, Sarge, Karen.' Omar replied. 'I'm cool with that.'

'It'll be a late night, I expect.'

Omar gave a faint smile but Karen had already hurtled towards the door. He had to chase after her to get to the car park by which time his face was red.

130

'Get in.' She clicked the doors open and took off before he had time to put on his safety belt.

Karen talked non-stop about the case all the way there. 'So we've got two missing girls. One Muslim Asian, Selina Ali and one mixed-race Catholic.'

'But we don't know if the other girl, Selina, went to Birmingham. And we did check that at the time.'

'Yes, we did. But we had no leads then and I've got a hunch about this one.'

Omar gave an involuntary shudder. 'I don't believe in hunches. I prefer fact-checking, ticking boxes, and telephoning people. That's the policing that works in my opinion.'

'That too,' Karen brushed aside his observation. 'Have we looked for a connection, Omar? Could there be one? Think.'

'They are about the same age. Selina Ali is two years older.'

'Family?'

'She was an only child.'

'Extended family?'

'I can't remember without my notes.'

Karen passed her phone to Omar. 'Macy,' she said. 'It's on speaker.'

Omar, frowning, tapped into her phone.

'Hi, Karen.' Macy's voice responded.

'Macy. Missing girl, a good few months back. Any links to Birmingham airport?'

'No actual links to her, she supposedly reappeared, remember? Not that I believed that.'

'Didn't you check it out?'

'Not a priority,' Macy replied. 'But we did uncover a potential terrorist route from Turkey to Iraq, via Birmingham. It's very vague though.'

'Thanks, Mace. Can you let me have anything you have on it? It might be useful.'

'Sure.' The call ended.

'See? I knew there was a possible connection.'

'But that wasn't Selina. And why a mixed-race Catholic girl?'

'I don't know yet, Omar, but religion's a funny thing. Some people find God then they move on to others. Fills a need I suppose. Not a need I've ever had,' she added.

'I don't doubt that,' Omar commented.

'Who have we got back at the station?'

'Precious might be there still.'

'Ring her. Get her to check Selina's extended family. Every detail. Mosques, schools, social networks; anywhere where there might be a connection. Macy thought there might be one, and she's really good.'

'OK.'

Ten minutes later, Karen had a moment of enlightenment. 'Sorry, can you ring John for me?'

'John?' Omar's mouth fell open.

'He's my partner. Don't worry, he's a professional too. Forensics.'

Omar, clutching the phone with embarrassment, tapped the contact.

'Hello, Bunnykins. What's up?'

'Sorry, John,' Karen yelled. 'Been called away. Back late. That's all.' She looked at Omar. 'Anything from Precious yet?'

Omar sighed and rang her on his phone. 'OK, thanks.' He ended the call. 'She's researching it now. She'll ring if she gets anything.'

'Damn,' Karen said. 'Can you ring her back? Get her to fax photos of Mari and Selina to the head of security together with the dates of disappearance. Oh, and tell them we're on our way.'

39

Yousef clapped his hands. 'Follow me.' He led the chosen ones out of the compound to the entrance of the camp where a truck was waiting for them. A pile of black garments lay on the ground next to the truck. 'Put those on and get in,' he urged. 'You are special men. You are going to the very heart of the caliphate.' He sat next to the driver while the lads climbed into the back of the open truck.

There was no conversation in the back, not least because it was a bumpy, uncomfortable ride which was broken only by the driver's occasional need to urinate. They were given bottles of water but no food.

Saeed estimated they had been travelling for nearly four hours when gradually, buildings began to appear ahead of them. Yousef put his head through the back of the cab to make an announcement. 'We're in Al Raqqa now.'

Saeed gulped. It was suddenly all becoming real and he was a little scared.

At the city entrance, they were waved through by the guards. 'It is very easy to get in,' he told them. 'but impossible to get out unless you are a soldier.'

They arrived in the main square to be greeted by other young men all similarly dressed in black fighter tunics. There was much back-slapping and shouts of encouragement to the new recruits but the noise died down when a much older man appeared dressed in a white Jubba with a black overcoat and simple cap. He walked to the middle of the square. The fighters moved a respectable distance away from him, pushing the recruits to the front.

'Welcome. I am the Mudhir. I am the man in charge of all of you.'

The recruits bowed to show respect.

'I wish you an illustrious career fighting for our caliphate. You have all been highly trained and specially chosen and there is still much more for you to learn. You will be shown to your new homes and in time you will be given instructions for your military training. I will meet all of you in time. But first I want to speak to Batal. Step forward.'

Saeed was mesmerised and did not recognise that he was being summoned until Yousef pushed him forward.

'Batal. You are very important to us. As a British man, you can help spread the message.' He paused and Saeed realised that this was an order, not a request.

'I would be honoured,' he said.

'Do you not yet have a wife?'

Saeed shook his head. 'There is someone... '

'Yousef?' He stepped forward. 'We wish Batal to feel at home here. First show him to his house then arrange to bring this woman over here for him.'

The Mudhir, with a small nod of his head, walked away leaving Saeed bemused.

Yousef slapped him on the back. 'He has picked you out for special treatment. Do not fail him.'

'What? '

'Come with me.'

He led Saeed to the little house down the road and opened the door. 'Here, Batal. Your house.'

Saeed was astounded. 'This is mine?' He entered the villa and looked around, first taking in the small courtyard in the middle. Then he walked around it, looking at the little garden and up at the sun.

Yousef stayed by the entrance. 'Yes, brother. Good fighters are given good homes. There is food and drink in the fridge. The electricity is, well, shall we say, intermittent. There are plenty of kebab shops and food places for men without wives. Oh, which reminds me. Your pay.' He took out a wad of notes and handed them to Saeed.

Saeed's eyes widened as he took the money. 'About the wives. the Mudhir said... '

'Yes. Let us sit.' Yousef waved his arm towards the sofas in the main living area. When they were both seated, Yousef looked serious. 'Your wife will be chosen for you. This is something you must accept as part of your duty to our state.'

'But... ' Saeed began.

134

Yousef hushed him. 'It is our way,' he explained. 'But as you deserve a treat, I have good news for you. Tomorrow you begin your military training. But tonight you have a surprise. I believe you will find something upstairs. Now I must depart. I have other duties to attend to.

'Of course. Saeed saw Yousef out. *Did I hear something?* Saeed looked up, then tentatively walked up the stairs and into the little bedroom. There he saw a young woman curled up on the bed, her back towards him.

'Mari?' he said as he walked towards her. He touched her face. 'Mari? Is it really you?'

Mari stirred at his touch. She blinked as she looked at him. 'Saeed? You're here?' She stood up and they embraced, neither of them wanting to be the first to let go.

At last, Saeed broke the silence. 'Tell me how you are. How was the journey? Have you seen the countryside yet?'

Mari smiled. 'One thing at a time. Let me look at you. You look different. Older.'

Saeed touched his growing beard. 'It's customary,' he laughed. 'You will have to get the right costume too.'

Mari pouted. 'I'm not looking forward to that,' she said. Then smiling, asked, 'Have you eaten? There's some food downstairs.'

'I'm starving,' he replied.

'Come with me.' She led him downstairs into the kitchen and made up a plate of bread and cheese for him.

While he ate, Saeed thought about what Yousef had said to him. Surely they would not have left Mari with him if they were going to take her away again? So far everything had gone to plan and here she was, as promised. He resolved that they should both keep their heads down and trust that they would be allowed to stay together. And that would mean she would have to take the faith and they would get married. He was sure.

After they had finished eating, they sat on the sofa in the living area and talked.

'Are you happy now?' he asked.

'I am now that I'm with you.'

'Me too.' Tentatively, he leaned towards her to kiss her. She responded.

135

'I don't know what to do next?' he laughed. 'Should we go upstairs?'

Mari blushed. 'I think so.'

In the bedroom they stood and kissed again, their bodies pressed close together. Saeed took off his shirt and Mari stroked his naked chest.

'I've never done this before,' she said as he helped her take off her top.

'Neither have I,' he giggled as she untied his trousers.

'I'm tingling all over,' she said as they stood together naked. He gently manoeuvred her to the bed.

'So am I.'

40

Karen and Omar headed straight to the airport security section. After waving her ID, Karen was directed to a specific parking area and with a display of both their IDs, they gained entry to the security complex. Once inside Karen scanned the area and made for the office marked 'Head of Security'. She walked in with Omar right behind her.

'DS Thorpe and DC Malik. Have you got anything?'

The head of security looked up and sighed loudly in an attempt to express his distaste at her manners. 'And I am Don Catchemall. Pleased to meet you.'

Karen missed the joke. He carried on. 'Are you sure she was getting on a plane?'

'No. But why would you go to the airport? It's an obvious thing to check.'

'I've got people working on it. We've found this.' He tapped his keyboard and called up an image of a girl with a woman.

'It's the right date; 15th February, and it's for a flight to Turkey.'

Bloody hell, you're quite efficient, Karen conceded as she glanced at the screen.

'Travelling with a woman purporting to be her mother,' Don added.

Karen peered at the image. It was too indistinct. 'It could be,' she said. 'But who's the woman? What do you think?'

Omar took a printed image from his in-tray. 'Here's the one you sent me.'

Karen looked from one to the other. 'I'm not sure. I've done lots of facial recognition and I don't think this is good enough. The headscarf hides too much and the image is distorted too. Can you email this to our lab?'

'Yes,' Don replied. 'What's the address?'

Karen looked at Omar. 'He'll tell you.'

'Did I ever tell you that I have a photographic memory for numbers and addresses?' Omar muttered. 'That's as good as having hunches,' he added very quietly. While he leaned over

Don's keyboard to type the address his phone rang. He saw it was Precious and handed the phone to Karen.

'Precious? What have you got?'

'A connection of sorts. Selina's cousin goes to the same school as Mari.'

'Perfect,' Karen chirped. 'Now we're getting somewhere.' She turned to look at Don, who was studying his screen.

'This has just come in,' Don told her. 'The day the other girl, Selina Ali, went missing.'

Karen looked at the two images and nodded. 'It could be Selina. Can you send these too?'

'Already sent with the other one while you were talking,' Don replied.

'Well done. Thanks.'

'It is our job,' Don squirmed.

'Now, what about the older woman? Do we have anything on her?'

Don shook his head. 'Whoever it was, they were very clever. Managed to avoid the camera. All I can show you is this.' He pulled up the image of a woman walking towards the desk, head bowed, and the hijab obscuring most of her face.

'Was she seen anywhere with the second girl, Selina? Have you cross-checked flights to see if someone travelled on both?'

Don shook his head in irritation. 'We haven't got that far yet but we will. It'll take a while.'

'OK. Send the image anyway, it might help. It may be that she wasn't so clever with the cameras back then. And if you get her, and find a name, check all the other flights too. My colleague has got a potentially similar case, a few months earlier. I'll get you the details.'

Karen turned to Omar. 'Anything else you can think of?' Omar shook his head. 'OK. Let's get back home. We can't do any more from here now.' They walked to the car together.

'Any chance you could drop me off boss? I have a date with a gang of card players.'

'At the tube station?' Karen replied.

'That's fine. By the way,' Omar was testing the water. 'Did we need to be there? Couldn't we have just asked them?'

138

'Omar, you have to apply pressure. A phone call is not pressure. It's an *add-it-to-the-list* thing. If you're there in person, it's a *let's-do-this-and-get-rid-of-them-as-soon-as-possible* thing.'

'Yes, Karen,' Omar gulped.

Karen and Omar arrived back at the station to find Precious anxiously waiting for them.

'I think I have a connection at last.'

'You do? Shoot,' Karen said.

'He was a relative of Selina Ali. They were cousins.'

'Well done! Two missing girls and a boy in the same area. And Mari is half Pakistani *and* she knew Saeed. Could they be connected?' Karen exclaimed. 'That's the best progress we've made all day,' she added to Omar's obvious dismay. 'I'm going to find Mari if it kills me. Or you,' she smiled at him. 'And we are going to see her mother.'

'What, now?' Omar looked at his watch.

Karen sighed, thinking of John's dinner. 'OK. Tomorrow.'

41

Karen waited in the car until her watch showed 9 am precisely. 'Dad always told me if it's not a matter of life or death, nothing before nine,' she explained to Omar. She knocked on Maria Rahman's door. When the door opened, Maria looked pleased to see them.

'DS Thorpe,' Karen introduced herself and held up her ID.

'And Detective Constable Malik.'

'How very good of you to come,' Maria replied, standing back to let Karen walk in. 'Now I am only sorry that I may have called you unnecessarily.'

'Why? Has he turned up?' Omar asked hopefully.

'No, not at all. But as my husband keeps reminding me, his cousin has kept in touch by phone. Please come in.'

Maria guided them into the sitting room Karen sat on a chair and waited for Maria to sit. Omar remained standing. He looked around the room.

Just like Macy, Karen thought. 'Mrs Rahman. I won't beat about the bush. We're not here just for Saeed. We are investigating several disappearances and we think there may be a connection.' She pulled out a photo of Mari. 'So, your son, Saeed, knew this girl?'

'Yes, this is Mari. Poor girl. She goes to the same school as my daughter. We were so worried when we saw she had gone missing. Her poor mother. Have you found her?'

'No, Mrs Rahman. But as I said, we think there may be a connection. How well did Saeed know her?'

'She came here once. No twice. She was doing a school project with my daughter Razia, and Saeed offered to help her with her maths homework. But I think that was only the once. A few weeks ago.'

'And they've had no contact since?'

'No. Why should there be? What do you think has happened to her?'

'We don't know Mrs Rahman. But we think she may have left the country to go to Syria. Are you also aware that Selina Ali has disappeared?'

Maria put her hand to her mouth. 'Yes. Please don't tell me he may be with her. Such a difficult child.'

'We don't know, Mrs Rahman. That's what we're here to find out. Where is your son meant to be? Does he often go away without you knowing where he is?'

Maria's face lit up. 'He's a lovely boy. Respectful, truthful, and very caring. Except he has felt a bit distant recently. He's in Pakistan with my husband's brother. But he's meant to be coming home today and I haven't heard from him.'

Karen looked at her notes. 'He's seventeen, isn't he? I've been told that that can be a very difficult age for a young man.'

Maria nodded. 'That is probably true too.'

'What about your daughter? Would she know anything?'

'I've already asked her and she says not.'

'May we speak to her?'

'Of course.' Maria stood at the door to call Razia. 'Come quickly; the police are here.'

Razia came into the room looking worried. 'What is it?'

'Razia, do you know if Saeed had any contact with Selina?'

Razia looked embarrassed. 'I don't know for sure. But he did say something about her once. I think he knew she was going away.'

'Razia! Why did you not tell me this?'

Karen interjected. 'It's fine, Razia. What do you think he knew?'

'Just that she was going to live in a new country or something. But he didn't know what happened to her; at least he said he didn't.'

'And you think he might have been lying?'

'I don't know. I think he thought her mother was interested in him... ' She stopped and looked at her mother.

'No,' Maria shook her head. 'We'd never agree unless it was what he wanted. Besides, he's too young and they knew that,' Maria said firmly.

Karen looked at Omar. 'Marriage,' he mouthed.

Karen turned to look at Razia. 'And Mari Lone. Was she a friend of yours?'

'Not really. But I liked her. We haven't spoken in weeks. Since Saeed... '

'And did she keep in touch with Saeed at all?'

'No. He did speak to her on Facebook, just to help her with her homework, he said. Then he unfriended her. But... '

Karen leaned forward. 'What Razia? Please tell me anything you know. It might be important.'

'I think they, you know, liked each other.'

Karen sat back and clicked things into place in her head. 'Thanks, Razia. Now, does anyone else know anything? Who were her friends at school? Who did she hang around with?'

'Carly. But something happened there too. I don't think they were speaking.'

'Carly? What is her second name?'

'Carly Morgan.'

'Thank you, Razia.'

'What will you do now?' Maria asked.

'First, may I have a photo of Saeed, please?'

Maria jumped up. 'Of course.' She went to a sideboard unit and took a school photo from the drawer. 'But he has tried to grow a beard recently,' she smiled at the picture.'

Karen took the photo from her. 'Thank you. We'll talk to everyone we can. We have a possible lead in Birmingham.'

'Birmingham? Why there?'

'We don't know yet. Mari may have gone to Turkey. Where did Saeed fly from?'

'Saeed went to Pakistan from Heathrow. Why would they go to Turkey?'

Karen looked at Omar, who gave a little shake of his head.

'Sorry, Mrs Rahman. It's just a theory. Thank you. Thank you, too, Razia. And please let me know if you hear anything or remember anything.' She handed her card to both of them. 'And I'll be in touch as soon as we have anything to tell you.'

'Thank you, officers,' Maria stood up to show them to the door.

Razia spoke again. 'There was something else. I'm not sure if it's important.'

'Go on,' Karen nodded.

'Mari did come to the mosque with me once. She seemed very interested.'

'And what does that mean?' Maria glared at her.

'Nothing. I just thought it might help.' Razia replied.

Karen and Omar left the house but when they got to the car, Karen asked him, 'What was that look for?'

'Because they probably know that people are going to Turkey to join the fighting. They are scared of being terrorist suspects and all the shit that goes with it. It's better not to even hint at it until we know what's going on.'

'Ah. OK. I'll find this Carly Morgan. Can you go to the mosque?'

'Of course. I can walk from here.'

'Good. See you back at the office.'

42

Mari was bored almost as soon as Saeed had left. She sat trying to draw a plant in the courtyard for the umpteenth time and was just tearing up this new effort when she heard a knock at the door. She guessed it was too early for Saeed's return but anything would be a welcome distraction. She ran to the door and saw a woman in a burqa, holding a bag.

'Hi. I'm Selina. Saeed's cousin?'

'Hi. Come in. I've been so bored.'

Selina walked in. She commented as she removed her burqa 'You can always clean.'

Mari didn't know how to react; cleaning was never her forte. She laughed instead. 'Yes, when it gets that bad, I will.'

'Or read the Quran.'

Now Mari knew she was being disapproved of but she had an answer for that. 'I can't read Arabic.'

'Then you must learn,' Selina retorted. 'How are you going to be a good wife to my cousin? Are you even a wife?'

'He loves me how I am,' Mari shot back. 'And it's none of your business.'

Selina, seeming to realise she had upset Mari, began to adopt a more conciliatory tone. 'I'm sorry, Mari. You've come a long way into a strange land. It is different, but you will get used to it.'

Mari smiled. 'Yes, and it's a very beautiful land. I want to go and see the river and look at the mountains. I don't want to just stay stuck in here.'

'You draw?' Selina said, looking at the pad of paper on the table.

'Don't tell me that is not allowed?' Mari was exasperated.

Selina looked thoughtful. 'Just don't draw people,' she declared eventually.

'What do you do here?' Mari asked.

Selina's eyes lit up. 'They are training me for media duties. I will be the female face of the new caliphate. We need more brides for our fighters. I will tell the world how good it is for women here and Saeed... ' she hesitated.

'Saeed what?'

'Nothing. I must be getting back. I just wanted to see what sort of girl you are. And to bring you this. You must wear it at all times outside the house.' She handed Mari the bag.

Mari took it from her and saw at once that it was a black burqa. She grimaced.

'I'll come and see you again if you like,' Selina said.

Mari decided anyone's company was better than no one's. 'Yes please.' Then she added, 'Do I really have to stay here all day? What will happen if I go out on my own?'

Selina's eyes glistened as her hands reached for her burqa. 'You shouldn't. You might get told off and escorted home.'

'OK,' said Mari, thinking that didn't sound too bad. 'But you were on your own.'

'I'm special,' Selina said as she covered up. 'You have a lot to learn.'

After Selina had gone, Mari's brain went into overdrive. *Selina was on her own. What's the worst that can happen? How would they know who I was? I'm about the same height as Selina...*

She picked up the burqa and already hated it. Not today, she decided.

***

In Eastern Syria, Aram was getting even more worried. He had been waiting for the news from his family in Turkey that his own family could join them. But there had been a change of plan. A new baby on the way meant that they no longer had room. He felt betrayed. He had heard the news. The terrorists were on the road again. Rumour was that they were being beaten by the Western forces and were ransacking villages for food supplies and killing people who resisted, especially Christians. There was no time left. He decided that they would first flee to a refugee camp in Turkey. From there, he hoped, his relatives in America might take pity on them. They were all packed up and ready to go but he could not leave without trying one more time to help his fellow churchgoers.

Aram ran to the church where he found the priest, the missionaries and their aides praying inside. 'They are coming,' he shouted at them. 'Please leave. I beseech you. Save yourselves.'

The senior missionary listened politely but shook his head. 'Our director also told us to go. But our work is here. We must stay to look after the people left behind. It is Christ's will that we do so. So many need help and healing. How can we desert them?'

'But you will all be killed!' Aram shouted. 'Who will you be able to save then?'

'We will stay. It is what God wants.'

'What about the boy? He's so young.' He pointed to the priest's nephew. The boy stood up and addressed him confidently.

'My place is here.'

'Why are you so stubborn?' Aram left, cursing them under his breath. He was Christian but not so strong as he wanted to lose his life. His thoughts soon turned to another stubborn woman, his friend Maryam. He hurried to her house and walked in through her always-open front door.

'Maryam, my dearest friend. They are coming soon. They have already taken the next town,' he said. 'Please, please leave. You can travel with us.'

Maryam coughed. 'We have had this conversation many, many times, Aram. You know my views. Besides, I thought you had already gone.'

'I would never leave without telling you. But this time it's for real. We're leaving as soon as the taxi comes.'

Maryam coughed again. 'I am too ill to travel. I wouldn't want to pass this cold on to you and your family. You must go. Please go safely. I will be fine here.'

Aram knew that this was an excuse. 'I tried,' he said, looking up. 'You know that I tried.'

'God knows you have tried, Aram. I hope He will keep you safe on your journey. Maybe we will meet again, God willing.'

'I pray for that too. Goodbye.'

Maryam smiled at him. 'Goodbye, Aram.' She looked down at her machine and carried on sewing.

43

Karen was beginning to piece things together in her head. She wasn't sure what information she could expect to get from Carly Morgan, but even she, as a child, had friends she'd confided in at school. Then, even the ones who weren't friends seemed to know whatever was going on with other girls. *Was it still like that?* She rang the office to get Carly's address then punched the details in her Satnav. As she expected, it wasn't far away and she arrived there a few minutes later. She couldn't help noticing the difference between this house on a nice little road and Mari's tower block flat.

'Good morning. DS Thorpe,' she said, holding up her ID as Mrs Morgan opened the door.

'What is it? What's happened?'

'I'm sorry, Mrs Morgan. I didn't want to alarm you. I just wanted to talk to your daughter Carly about something. Is she here?'

Mrs Morgan looked relieved. 'I'm sorry, Carly's gone on holiday for half term. She's with her aunt and uncle. Can I help?'

'It's about Mari Lone.'

'Oh, yes, that poor girl. I saw it on the news last night. What must her mother be going through? Mind you, it was a troubled home.'

'Why do you say that?'

'Well, single mother, going a bit off the rails, Carly said. She rang me up and gave me quite a mouthful a few weeks back. Told her she didn't want Carly spending time with her precious daughter.'

'Oh?' Karen was intrigued. 'What happened to bring that on?'

'Well, my Carly. I admit she can be a bit of a handful, but Mari's mum shouted at her. All she'd done was make a bit of a mess; at least, that's what Carly said. Oh, and bought some cider. They were both drunk, she reckons. I mean, who hasn't done that at fifteen? But my Carly was fine when she got home. I suspect it was Mari.'

'So you think things were not good between Mari and her mother?'

'Not from what Carly said. She told me she'd hit her more than once.'

'Thank you, Mrs Morgan; that's very helpful. Do you happen to know anything about a boy called Saeed?'

Mrs Morgan shook her head. 'Not that I recall. I know there were a couple of Muslim girls at the school, but no boys.'

Karen mused as she went back to her car. *So troubled teenager falls for young boy with dreams of a wonderful foreign land somewhere. And terrorism. Maybe it's time I spoke to the experts.* She picked up her phone and rang the Counter Terrorism Command.

'Sure,' said a cheerful voice. 'Come over. Always happy to help.

Half an hour later, Karen was holed up with one of the team. 'It's just an inkling. I don't want to alarm the parents yet but I've got these missing kids.'

'Names?'

Karen was startled. 'Can't I just ask on a no-names business?'

'Are you serious? No such thing in this game. Names.'

'Saeed Rahman.'

The officer tapped into his PC. 'Nope.'

'Selina Ali.'

'Oh, yes, she's on our radar. We haven't pinpointed her location yet but she's been on Twitter under an alias. Quite the little recruiting sergeant.'

'Bloody hell! Do her parents know?'

'Not yet. They're under surveillance. And you can't tell them.'

'Saeed Rahman is a cousin of hers.'

'Ah. Who else are you looking for?'

'Mari Lone. She knew Saeed. We've got her at or around Birmingham airport on the fifteenth of this month. There was another girl a few weeks earlier who disappeared but was traced to Birmingham airport. It's possibly Selina Rahman.'

The officer tapped into his keyboard and called up a picture of a woman. It was a bit obscured but the size and shape of her corresponded to the image of the woman Karen had seen before.

'That looks like the woman Birmingham Security found with Mari. Who is she?'

'We don't know yet. When did she go?'

'Selina, about six weeks ago.'

'OK. We're watching this woman now.'

'What? Why?'

'We think she might be an escort for would-be jihadists.'

'Shit. What do I tell the parents?'

'Absolutely nothing yet. And don't jump to conclusions, at least not until I tell you. We don't know anything for sure. It might be completely innocent.'

'Actually, Selina's mother called off our search. I'm only following it because of the relationship. She told me Selina was fine.'

'Sounds like she's aware then, if not actually involved. As for Mari, we'll see if we can track her down. I'll get on to our contacts now.'

44

Saeed had begun the day feeling deliriously happy. He was looking forward to his training, but most of all, he was looking forward to seeing Mari when the day was over. He, and the others selected, were taken by truck to a remote area which was already set out like a military training ground.

The first lesson was on the use of guns; how to load them, aim them, and fire them. After extensive target practice, the young men were taught how to strip the guns down and maintain them. It felt professional and Saeed was impressed. Unfortunately, he was clumsy with the weaponry and his eye was not as good as others at hitting targets. He'd noticed two of the trainers look at him as they talked.

The rest of the day was taken up with being drilled and shouted at. He liked this a great deal less, but he saw that his fellow recruits felt the same. This helped them gel as a team. Now he had friends. Other lads he could talk to and share banter with. It felt good.

At the end of the day, when he wasn't chosen to serve on the battlefield, he was upset. But he realised it made their army more professional. He resolved to train harder every day until he could be called up for active service.

He was dropped off near his house and was desperate to see Mari. But as he got out of the truck, he saw a woman waiting for him. She was dressed in a burqa but additionally wearing a headband bearing an emblem. He recognised it from his internet searches. It was the emblem of the female Islamic police.

The woman grabbed his arm and led him to a house in the next alley. He was confused. Was this Mari? Had she already obtained the clothing? She opened the door and went inside.

'What's going on?' he said as he followed her in.

Once the door was closed, Selina pulled off her burqa.

Saeed stood open-mouthed at the slender woman in a tight T-shirt top and jeggings. 'Selina! I wondered if I would see you here. How are things?'

'Good,' she confirmed as she settled on the sofa. 'Very good. Because I'm British they are treating me very well and I've got high status here. Drink?'

Saeed shook his head. 'Surely that isn't allowed?'

'It is for us guards,' Selina replied. 'We can do anything we like. I even get to torture other women.'

Saeed didn't know how to react. 'Really? Does your mother know you're here?'

Selina laughed. 'She does now. She's very proud of me and wants to come out herself. She's dying to meet the husband they found me. He's a brave fighter and I'm sure I'll learn to love him. He's quite cute and he seems to love me already. How was your training?'

'It is good so far, although my shooting is rubbish. And I'm now Batal.'

'So, I heard,' Selina nodded. 'And I also heard you have a girl here. Is she a Muslim?'

'No. She's Catholic, I think.'

'Then you know that you will not be able to keep her, don't you?'

'What?'

'Do you not realise she's just a hooker? To keep you happy? They will make sure you have a wife whom they can trust to behave properly and not remind you of home and forbidden things.'

Saeed frowned. This reminded him of what Yousef had said. 'Then why did they say I should call her over here?'

'Because when she converts, assuming she is not stupid, she will become a beacon for other would-be converts. That is why they like British men and women coming here. We can talk their language and make them understand why they should join us out here. It is our duty.'

'Yes, I see that.' Saeed replied. 'But it will be different for me. They promised me...'

Selina laughed. 'Maybe you're right. What do I know? I know they have plans for you. I will look out for her. Make sure she is guided in the right direction.'

'Thank you. And what about you? What are you doing?'

151

'I've had media training. Can you believe that? I'm getting to be quite a star on Twitter. I'm planning on having a whole new career when I go home. You should look out for me.'

'Ah, I don't have my laptop anymore. They took it away at the training camp. Did you hear about my other cousin?'

Selina shook her head. 'Should I?'

'I expect you met him at our big gathering a few years back. My father's brother's son.'

'Oh. And what happened to him?'

'He didn't make it past the camp.'

Selina slapped him on the arm. 'Not everyone does. You've done so well, Saeed -— I mean Batal. Now I have to get my beauty sleep before the first audition tomorrow. Enjoy your training. You will make a good soldier eventually, I'm sure.'

45

19th February

Karen was pacing around the office until Omar appeared. 'How did you get on at the mosque?' she asked him as she sat at her desk.

'Ah, that's a long story.'

'Tell me.' She nodded towards the visitor's chair and he sat down.

'When I arrived there was no one in, but I heard some shouting coming from the back. I went and had a look and saw the imam, the old boy, shouting at someone. I know a bit of Urdu. It sounds like this young chap is a bit of a troublemaker. The imam was telling him off. I'm sure I picked up something about going to fight in Syria. Unfortunately, they saw me before I heard it all. The boy ran off and the imam hurried after him.'

'You know Urdu? Karen gaped. 'I can hardly manage French.'

'It helps with the job,' Omar replied.

That's dedication, Karen was impressed. 'Can you find out who he is and what he said? How old was he?'

'About seventeen or eighteen. Difficult to tell when they have all this face fuzz.'

'Can't you ask the imam?'

'I'll see if he's got a contact number.'

'Good. I've found out something interesting about Selina. And I need to speak to Mari's mother again. I'll ring her now.'

She rang Sinéad and asked if she could come round. 'No news, I'm afraid,' she added hurriedly. 'I just want to get a better picture of things.'

'OK,' said a weary-sounding Sinéad. 'Any time.'

When the call had been made, Omar came back over to Karen's desk. 'It was the imam's son. He was thrown out of school last year.'

'What's his name?'

'Nadeem. Nadeem Khan.'

'Thanks, Omar. Find out what you can about him; see if there's anything to connect him to Selina or Saeed.'

'Of course.'

'I'm off to see Mrs Lone.'

***

Sinéad's door was opened by a much older woman, Karen correctly assumed it was her mother.

'Come in, come in.'

Karen went into the living room where Sinéad sat on the sofa. She looked around. Something was different; she noticed a wedding photo on the shelf unit. Sinéad caught her looking at it.

'Mari knocked it over and broke it. I've just put it in a new frame. I shouted at her. I'm so sorry… ' she broke off into floods of tears.'

'Hindsight's easy enough,' Niamh said, sitting next to Sinéad and putting her arms around her. 'Mari is a high-spirited girl.' She turned to Karen. 'I'm her nana. She was meant to be coming to see me, you know.'

'Yes, Mrs Lone told me. Do you have any idea why she would run away?'

'Because I was so horrible to her,' Sinéad blubbed. 'I'm so sorry; I'd do anything to get her home now.'

'They'd had a row or two for sure,' Niamh said. 'But who hasn't with their daughter? We've had a few barneys over the years, haven't we, love?' Sinéad nodded but didn't speak.

'As for Mari, she loved Ireland, the countryside, more than anything. And she knew there was no threat from me. I'm a pushover.'

'So, do you have any ideas?'

'She mentioned she'd done a project at school. Won an award or something; it was about a mosque and a church.'

Karen's ears pricked up at the word, remembering what Razia had told her. 'I heard she was interested in Islam.'

'A little, what with her father and all that.'

'He was a Muslim?' Karen said.

Sinéad sat up. 'Not relevant. She hardly knew him.'

154

'Probably not,' Karen agreed. 'But it would help to know her state of mind.'

'Then I'd better tell you the whole story,' Niamh began. 'When Mo and Sinéad got married, his family wouldn't have anything to do with him. They refused to come to the wedding.'

'Was it before Mari was born?' Karen asked.

'Yes. They were married first,' Niamh said.

'Was there no reconciliation? Even when he was killed?'

'No. Sadly, no, and he was a lovely chap. Mari came to stay with me last Christmas. She found out all about it. It was my stupid fault for leaving all those old boxes all over the place.'

Sinéad sat up and looked at Karen. 'But she went to see them. Mo's parents. They pushed her away, she told me. So it's not as though she was looking to find her heritage, or if she did, she got short shrift. You wouldn't want to have rellies like that, would you?'

'But do you know that for sure?' Karen asked. 'Teenagers are a difficult species. She may have been more determined to find out for herself.'

'That's true enough,' agreed Niamh, looking at Sinéad. '*She* led me a right merry dance. Especially when she was courting.'

Sinéad smiled. 'He was so handsome in his uniform.'

'Do you have a picture of him?'

'Yes, of course. Why?'

'No specific reason. It just builds up a picture.'

Sinéad went to the cabinet and took down the photo. Karen's eyes widened but she said nothing. She could just about make out the emblem on his beret and filed the information in the cabinet in her head.

'Thank you, Mrs Lone. That's been very helpful. I'll be going now.'

Karen went back to the office feeling a bit better but she didn't know why. When she arrived there was another surprise waiting for her.

Omar looked up as she came in. 'I've had a call from Mrs Lone. Mari's paternal grandmother. She wants to talk to you.'

'Really? I've just been hearing about her. Now *that* could be very interesting indeed. When can I see her?'

'She wants to come here. Between ten and noon tomorrow.'
'Saturday? Yes. Tell her I'll be here.'

***

Karen went home comparatively early that night. John had just started cooking and poured her a glass of red wine.

'Good day?' He kissed her on the mouth.

'Bad. No, worse than bad; uneventful. Let me sit down, I'm worn out.'

'So you're not getting anywhere with the missing girls?'

'No, not really. They may just have been mixing in bad company. There are teenagers all over the world flocking out to join this weird cult. They're terrorists but they're not just living in caves, these guys are taking over whole towns and cities.'

'I do know about them, Karen. There have been some very unpleasant stories in the news recently if you care to read or watch them.'

'I'm too busy catching criminals,' Karen snapped.

'Actually, they've suffered a lot of losses recently. I was hoping they were on the wane. I wonder if they're using new initiatives to persuade more kids to go out there?'

'That would certainly fit with what I know.'

'So, you think your missing kids might have gone out there?'

Karen nodded. 'I hope not. A week ago I'd have bet on them just running off together somewhere. But we've got one of them definitely out there and we've traced Mari to Birmingham Airport. The day she disappeared, a woman – who looks like a woman who was being watched by the Counter Terrorism Command – took a girl, who might be Mari, to Turkey. And the CTC think this woman is working for them as some sort of escort.'

'But it might not be,' John added, thoughtfully. Which girl is definitely out there?'

'The older girl. Well, at least she is on Twitter singing the praises of the terrorists. Encouraging others to go out there. And she's a cousin of the boy. *And* it looks like Mari was very fond of him.'

'So you think he persuaded her to go out there?'

156

'Could be. Maybe she's still in Turkey. Bloody hell, she might still be in Birmingham. We just don't know.'

'Have your drink and chill. You need to unwind a bit.'

'You're right.' And she drank her glass and another and another, but Karen did not unwind.

46

Saeed and Mari argued about her wearing the burqa. 'You cannot go out without it,' he insisted. 'Or on your own. You will be safe then from prying eyes and nobody will take any interest in us.'

'But I'm not Muslim. I don't have to wear it.'

'You must here or you may be punished. It's safer. And I will teach you all about Islam. You will wear it happily when you understand.'

'Let's not argue already. Can we go somewhere?'

'Not today,' Saeed had tried to keep things from Mari. He was trying to protect her, he thought, but this he *had* to tell her. 'Today I am going on my first mission. They have put me in the special forces unit. It is not a battle; we are just expanding our territory, so don't be worried about me. But I may be gone a few days.'

'What?' Mari was shocked. 'But I'm so bored. There's no electricity. I can't even watch their rubbish TV. I want to go and see some of the beautiful places you showed me.'

'When I get back, I promise. Do some drawing. You're so good at that. And don't forget, you must stay indoors.'

Mari kissed Saeed goodbye. 'Be safe and don't be too long.'

'It is in Allah's hands now.'

Saeed sat in the back of the army truck, full of emotion. Proud that he had finally been on his first mission, he was also a little afraid. He sensed he was being tested; he certainly hadn't excelled in his training. His colleagues had made fun of him. His Arabic was getting better but he still didn't understand the subtleties of what they were saying. All he knew was that they were visiting a small settlement to take supplies and establish a base. When they pulled up just outside the small town, the captain of their unit instructed them.

'This is a village in which there are many infidels. We come to give them Islam and if they will not take it, we will take their money and their possessions and anything else they are unwilling to give us.'

Most of the men laughed at that, apparently knowing what it meant, but Saeed was unsure.

They all took their rifles and followed the captain in a disorderly group and marched towards the village. The captain came to a stop just outside.

'Go to every house,' He commanded. 'Take out anyone you find there and bring them to the square in the village. I will wait there for you.'

The men dispersed. Saeed followed their lead. Each man took a house in turn, going in room by room. Most of them were empty.

'Here!,' a fighter shouted, another joined him.

'Mercy. I am Muslim. We are Muslim,' said the man. His wife and children were hiding behind him.

'Speak then, from the Quran.'

The man replied and the fighter was satisfied. 'Wait there,' he ordered, pointing to the outside wall of the house. The man and his family stood there; the younger children were trembling.

'Please don't take our house, sir,' the man begged; the fighter was silent.

House by house they went taking it in turns until they came to the very last one. It was Maryam's and it was Saeed's turn.

Saeed stood outside for a moment before going inside. He tried to look brave, mean even, and he strutted in waving his rifle. But when he saw Maryam sitting defiantly behind her sewing machine, something clicked in his brain. This wasn't some infidel sitting there; he looked hard at her and all he saw was his mother, just as she would have been in England sewing his shirts or taking up his jeans.

Maryam stared back at him, seeing something in his eyes but not understanding what it was.

Saeed saw the silver crucifix around her neck. Was she an infidel? Surely she was a simple woman, a woman just like his mother. He had to think fast.

'What is your name?'

Maryam tried to speak but couldn't. She coughed and pointed to her throat.

Saeed, realising her condition, nodded at her. 'Take that off,' he pointed to his neck. Maryam shook her head. He went closer, leaned forward, and grabbed at it, pulling it off and throwing it to the ground. She winced at the pain but kept still.

'Put that on.' He grabbed a piece of cloth and tried to get her to cover her head. She shook her head again. Another fighter appeared.

'Do you need help?'

'No. She's just putting on her hijab.'

'Hurry up and take her!' he yelled.

Saeed looked at Maryam, and there was an understanding between them. She got up from behind her table and took the cloth, fashioning it around her head like a shawl. Then she allowed him to march her out of the house and down to the village square.

47

In the village square, a small group of people, most wearing crosses, were being held by some of the fighters. Maryam stared at them; among them were the missionaries and she realised that there was nothing she could do. She caught sight of Tayley, who was wearing the shirt she had made him. He smiled at her and her eyes moistened a little.

On the other side of the square, there were several Muslim families. They looked on, frightened but not seemingly threatened. Saeed pushed Maryam towards them. Her height made her stand out from all of them.

'You have a choice,' the Captain shouted at the Christians. 'Turn to Allah and you shall be spared.'

The priest spoke up, his nephew at his side. 'We will never renounce Christ. He is the way, the truth, and the light.'

'I give you one last chance.' This time, the captain took out his sword.

'Never!' Man and boy said together.

The captain stepped forward and without another word, slashed the man across the chest, swiftly doing the same to the boy.

'Then you will meet your Christ soon,' he said. He turned round where two of the fighters had retrieved from the truck, two large crosses fashioned from wood and iron bars. They leaned them against building walls and hammered them into the ground. The boy had died instantly but the priest was still alive and singing a hymn as loudly as he could as he was carried to one of the crosses. When his hands had been nailed securely to it, the leader hit him in the face.

'Stop your wailing. It offends my ears.'

'Jesus is the way, the truth and the light.'

The captain raised his sword and slashed across the man's mouth causing a stream of blood to run down his body. 'Now you will be silent.' He turned to his men. 'Take the others. We will see if we can't convince them.'

The Muslim families watched, horrified, their children beginning to cry.

An older boy pointed to Maryam. 'She is a Christian!' he shouted. His mother tried to say no, but it was too late.

'Is this true?' He looked at the woman. She was too afraid to defy him. She nodded.

'You should have said before,' He slapped her across the face. 'Next time I come here I will test you on the Quran myself.'

He grabbed Maryam and pushed her onto the truck. She looked at the woman and smiled as if to forgive her; the woman shook her head and looked down.

There were nine taken in all. Three men and six women, including Maryam. Their hands were tied and they were bundled onto the truck.

'Where are you taking us?' one of the women asked. She instantly received a slap round the head.

The truck moved off in the direction of the nearby town, which had been taken a week earlier. They drove straight into the town square where people soon began to gather. The prisoners were pushed and pulled off the truck and made to stand in a line in front of the now jeering crowd.

'I ask you again,' said the captain. 'Will you denounce Christ and turn to Allah?'

The woman who had asked the question spoke again. 'Why are you doing this to us? All we are doing is sharing the love of Jesus. We have done nothing to hurt you Muslims. We live in peace.'

'Take the women and teach them a lesson.' The captain shouted. He pulled forward six fighters, including Saeed.

Saeed watched, trying to hide his horror as the other five threw two women to the ground and began tearing off their clothes. Even as they began raping them, the women sang hymns and promised them forgiveness. This only served to make their assailants angrier and the women were beaten.

While everyone was watching the others, Saeed moved towards Maryam. He looked at her, and all he could see were his mother's eyes. He willed her to obey him and he pushed her not so roughly to the ground but he did not tear at her clothes.

162

Instead, he pretended to listen to her, then stood up and shouted.

'She repents!' he shouted. 'Allah has taken her voice in punishment for what she was, but she is now turning to him. Allah be praised. She is a seamstress and she will work doing Allah's will.'

The captain turned to acknowledge what he said and gestured to Saeed to take her to the truck. There both Maryam and Saeed watched as others came to rape the woman who still sang hymns. After what seemed to Saeed and Maryam like hours, the captain finally put up his hand.

'Bring them here.' He pointed to an area in the centre of the square. 'Line them up with the men.'

The women were dragged and made to kneel on the ground. The men were put next to them, and once again they were asked. 'Do you repent?'

'We will never defy Christ!' one said. 'He is our Lord,' said another and the singing recommenced.

Maryam looked in horror as, one by one they were beheaded and the singing ceased. She saw the lips of a dead woman's head form the name Jesus as it lay on the ground.

I will serve Christ, my lord, she said to herself. *You have chosen me for a different path; I will not let you down.*

When the massacre was over and the bodies put on display, they were adorned with signs saying *Infidels*. The fighters assembled back to the trucks for the journey home.

The captain came up to Saeed. 'You have saved this woman. I will hold you responsible for her now. 'You,' he turned to Maryam, 'are now a servant of the army of the caliphate and you will serve it with every breath of your body, or you will have the same fate as those women back there.'

Maryam coughed a long, catarrh-filled cough and found her voice. 'I have no sewing machine now,' she whispered. 'How can I sew without the right tools.'

The leader smashed the back of his hand against her face. 'Stupid woman. Do you think we do not have machines?'

Saeed sat and watched the exchange dispassionately. What was a blow to the face compared to a severed head? He hoped the woman would behave, or that if she didn't, he would never hear about her fate. He turned his thoughts to Mari and worried for her. She was so young and unaware of this new country. He willed the truck to go faster so that he could get home to keep her safe.

48

With Selina's words ringing in her ears, Mari put on the burqa. She stood at the door and looked out. *Surely, if Selina can go out, I can too?* It wasn't until she stepped outside she realised she didn't have a clue where she was or where she wanted to go. She'd tried to put the door on the latch, but it seemed to shut on its own. *No choice now, I might as well go for it.*

Tentatively, she took a few steps outside. The streets seemed to be empty. She hardly saw anyone around. *This isn't too bad. Now, which way?*

She looked up and down the street. Looking left seemed less built up and she saw hills in the distance, so she walked that way. She passed another street, and she became aware of footsteps behind her. Before she could react, an arm appeared around her neck, almost throwing her off her feet.

The guard shouted something at her, but she couldn't understand it.

'I am Batal's wife!' She screamed.

The guard turned her around. She saw in his eyes he knew that name. Holding both her arms behind her back, he marched her to the council building where the Mudhir's office was. He muttered something to the duty guard and was waved inside. Going straight to the leader's office, he knocked on the door and was summoned in. He spoke to the Mudhir, who said something in reply. The guard lifted Mari's burqa, throwing it over her head.

Mari stood there as steadily as she could while the Mudhir peered at her. Her blood ran cold.

'You are Batal's woman?'

Mari was relieved to hear English being spoken again but did not pick up the severity of the tone in his voice.

'I'm sorry, sir, I got lost. Can I go home now? I think I know where it is from here.'

'Foolish child. Did you not know you may not walk out without a male relative? It is forbidden.'

'No, I didn't know. I'm sorry. Selina said that … '

'You will have to be punished for this.'

'What? It was a simple mistake!'

'There is no such thing. Are you a Muslim?' Mari shook her head. 'Then we cannot allow you to stay with Batal.'

Mari's face fell. 'But why? Why can't I stay with him? He's promised to teach me.'

'Batal is a soldier now. He doesn't have time to spend with you. Guard? Take her to the prison. I'll decide what to do with her later.'

'Please, sir. Let me speak to Selina!' Mari wailed.

The Mudhir waved his hand dismissively.

Now the guard knew her fate, he was even rougher with her. He manhandled her out of the office and around the corner until they reached a set of stairs leading to the basement. He spoke to a guard at the entrance and handed Mari over. There she was taken to a small, dirty room with no windows and locked in behind big, reinforced doors. She began to cry.

***

Maryam and Batal sat quietly in the back of the truck in stark contrast to the other soldiers who were still punch-drunk and celebrating their experiences.

When they arrived back in Raqqa, both were taken to the Mudhir's office where the captain explained what had happened. Saeed tried hard to follow the conversation but the captain spoke quickly. He was sure he heard something about him not being a good soldier. When he had heard what the captain had to say, the Mudhir discharged him and turned to speak to Saeed. The guard outside came in as the captain left.

'So you saved this woman from the sword. She will be company for your woman from Britain.'

'She can stay with us?' Saeed said, surprised at this response.

'No, Batal. Your friend is currently imprisoned for breaking the rules. Did you not tell her she cannot go out alone? No matter, she is not worthy of you.'

'What?!' Saeed shouted. 'Where is she? She is meant to be my wife. Why may I not marry her? I will teach her everything she needs to know. She will not break the rules again, I promise.'

166

'Enough!' the reply came shooting back. 'It is not permitted. Now explain to me how this woman,' he looked at Maryam, 'can serve the caliphate without treachery?'

Saeed was getting better at not showing his emotions. He steadied himself and replied. 'She is a seamstress, sir. We will need many more uniforms for the fighters and for the women we will recruit. She can sew them.'

The Mudhir looked at the guard. 'Take her to the prison for now; let me think about this. Woman? What do you say? Will you save your life and defy your Christ? Will you sew for Allah?'

Maryam nodded and dropped her head. She spoke softly; her voice was still hoarse. 'It has been deemed I should sew; that is my talent and I will use it however it is decreed.'

'Take her away. I will talk to her again tomorrow.'

Saeed tried to catch Maryam's eye, but she looked away.

He looked pleadingly at the Mudhir. 'Can you not... '

'We have plans for you. If you help us in our work and if the girl behaves and learns, maybe we can give her back to you. It is in your hands, Batal. You must work hard for the caliphate. Someone will come to see you soon.'

'What plans? What do you want me to do?' Saeed asked but was waved away.

He went back to his house. It seemed so empty without Mari. When he was sure he was on his own and no one could hear him, he sat on the floor and wept for what he had become and for what he was now compelled to do in the future.

'Ahmed, why did I not listen to you? Maybe together we might have made it home. Mum, will I ever see you again?'

49

Mrs Lone Senior was at the station at exactly ten in the morning. Karen had borrowed Barry's office for the occasion and went to collect her from reception.

'Yes, Mrs Lone. You wanted to see me?'

The old lady was upset. 'I don't know where to start. It is all such a muddle,' she began.

'Is it about your granddaughter?' Karen asked.

'Yes. I want to know about my granddaughter. It was her picture in the papers the other day, wasn't it? She came to see us and... '

'Please continue, Mrs Lone.'

'I… no, we turned her away. My husband, you see… ' She paused to collect herself and began again. 'It is like this. We were so proud of our son when he enlisted. He was always so active and fit, a bit of a troublemaker really as a youngster. But his father and I both thought soldiering would make a man of him. So when he first told us, we were happy. We never thought then that he was in danger. The world wasn't so bad in those days. But he got on well. So well that he was selected for the S.A.S. And that we knew could be dangerous.'

'Ah, yes,' Karen said, remembering the emblem she'd seen on Mohamed's uniform.

'We both tried hard to persuade him to leave but he said he had signed up and there was nothing we could do. He began to change. I suppose it was the men he was with. He had to be like them. And he would come home to see us. He told us he had begun to eat bacon regularly and he drank in pubs and never went to the mosque anymore.'

'I can see that might be difficult for you,' Karen spoke to fill the pause.

'It was very hard. Too hard. Then he told us he was going to Iraq. My husband did not believe we should be fighting in Iraq at all. Now everybody says that, but not then. He argued with

168

Mohammed so much but he was adamant he would go.' Mrs Lone began to dab her eyes with her fingers. 'Then one time he came home to tell us he was getting married. At first, we rejoiced. Maybe he would settle down with a nice girl and leave the army, but he brought a Catholic girl home with him and my husband could never forgive him for that. We all wander from time to time, he said, but marriage is for life and you should not marry outside your own kind.'

'And so you lost contact with him?'

'Yes. Then we got a letter from the army telling us that he had been killed in action. Killed fighting Muslims. My husband could never understand that, even though war is complicated and not necessarily about faith. I know that. But from that moment on, he decided that he had never had such a son.'

'And what did you think?'

'He was my son. I still loved him dearly whatever he did.'

'But you never contacted his wife?'

The old woman shook her head and looked down. Karen felt her grief. 'I'm sorry.'

'His wife wrote to us after he was killed. I saw the Irish stamp on the letter so we knew it was her. My husband sent the letter back. We never read it. I had no idea Mohammed had a child until...'

'She turned up on your doorstep?'

'Yes. It was such a shock at first but I looked at her and I could see my son in her face, and it made me so sad. But my husband didn't want to know.'

'But now you do?'

'Yes. I saw her face again on the television and it made my heart ache for my son. Now I want to know all about her and I want to do anything I can to help to find her and bring her home.'

'All I can do is ask Sinéad – your daughter-in-law – if she would be willing to see you.'

'Yes, that is all I ask.'

'And your husband?'

'I haven't told him. He is a stubborn old man but I, too, saw his face when the girl's face came up. He was moved, I'm sure of it. I will bring him round one day.'

'I'll see what I can do.'

After Mrs Lone had gone, Karen mused about what she had said. She remembered how hard it had been for her growing up without a mother and empathised with what Mari might be going through. She'd had terrible rows with her father but there had always been somebody else to turn to.

Mari knew her paternal grandparents didn't want anything to do with her but then again, she loved her nana in Ireland. So why not go there? It could only be that she had a better offer. From someone whom she had feelings for. And what better, stronger urge than first love? Yes, she decided, it had to be Saeed.

Karen rang ahead and went straight over to see Sinéad. She opened the door and saw the weight of the world was etched on Sinéad's tired face.

'Have you got anything?'

'No. I'm just here to assure you we are doing everything we can.' Karen followed her inside. ' But there is one thing I need to tell you; ask you actually. Your mother-in-law came to see me. She wants to contact you. She seems genuine.'

'It's a bit fuckin' late now!' Sinéad screamed.

Niamh came running out of the kitchen. 'It's never too late. Be gracious and accept it. You need people around you, people on your side at a time like this.' She looked to Karen for support.

'It's entirely up to you. And there's no hurry. Give me a call when you've thought it through.'

'Yeah. I will.' Sinéad was now calmer.

Karen turned to go, then turned back. 'There's just one other thing I'd like to ask you. Your husband. Did you know any of his friends? Did you keep in touch with any of them?'

Sinéad looked puzzled. 'No. Not really. I mean, they all came to the funeral here. Well, not a proper funeral – they did something for him out there. But we laid a stone for him. And his mates brought a special wreath for 'Wolf.' But no, I haven't seen any of them since. Is it important?'

Karen hid her disappointment. 'No, not really. I'm just trying to build a picture, that's all. Thank you.'

With each step she took down from the flat, Karen's determination to find Mari increased. A plan was beginning to formulate and by the time she got in her car, it was halfway there. She sat there for a while until her thoughts were interrupted by a banging on the car window. It was Niamh. She wound the window down.

'I'm glad I caught you, officer. Sinéad says she'll see her mother-in-law. Give her Sinéad's number, will you? She promised she'll speak to her. She's in a terrible state. You are doing everything you can, aren't you?'

'We are.' Karen reassured her, and she meant it.

50

Mari was not coping well. After being in the cell for a short while, she'd shouted at the female guard. 'Tell Selina. She'll help me!'

'Selina?' The guard taunted her in perfect English. 'Why, she's the biggest bitch ever. She's why you're here.'

With her heart sinking, Mari looked around the cell. 'I need the toilet.'

'There's one there. Use it, bitch,' came the reply.

Mari squirmed for as long as she could before she could hold it no longer. She tried to squat over the bucket but only managed to knock it over.

Two guards came over to watch her and laugh.

'See how the pig loves its own shit! ' one yelled.

'Have you no decency?' Mari shouted back, but the only reply she got was more laughing.

She cried for the rest of the day until she was too tired to cry anymore. Then she lay on the grubby mattress and sobbed herself to sleep.

She woke feeling angry and began to think about how she might escape but her thoughts were interrupted by the sound of doors opening and people talking. She looked up to see a middle-aged woman in a white dress and blouse. She was thrown into the cell next door.

Mari sat still but saw that there was a window through which she could talk to the new inhabitant. When the noise of the guards talking subsided, Mari whispered to the woman.

'I am Mari. Who are you?'

'You're English? I have the same name as you. My name is Syrian for Mary.'

'I'm half Irish... ' Mari began

Maryam was curious. 'Why did you come here to such a place?'

'My boyfriend asked me.'

'That was foolish. And he betrayed you?'

'No. Saeed loves me. I made a mistake.'

'Then where is he? Why hasn't he come to save you?'

'I don't know. Why are you here?'

'Because I am Christian and they wanted my house. I could have stayed if I had forsaken Christ.'

'Then why didn't you? Does it matter more than your life?'

'Of course. It is for my soul.'

'What do you think they will do with us?'

'You are young and pretty. They will probably give you to service the men.'

'No!' Mari exclaimed. 'I thought they were religious. They surely won't do that to me.'

'Maybe not. Maybe if you become Muslim. I am too old for that. They may chop off my head or they may set me to work. I am a seamstress and they may want me to sew for them. But only if I convert.'

'But you said... '

'I believe that God has a different purpose for me now. I will go along with it until I find out what He wants of me.'

'You're very brave. I'm so scared now.'

'We can pray together, silently, when the guards cannot hear us. You will be strong. God will make you strong.'

***

Saeed sat at home, still fretting about Mari. When he heard a knock at the door, his heart leapt. Was it her? Had they released her?

No. A young man stood there smiling back at him. 'Batal? I am the director. Are you ready to be a film star?'

'What?' Saeed was distraught at his appearance and confused by his words. 'What are you talking about?'

'I make movies for the caliphate.'

'Are these the plans they have for me?'

'No idea. Call this an audition. We need to see how you look on screen. I need to see you. Come, my car is here. We are going out to find a good location.'

Saeed, now curious, followed him to the car, a red SUV. He saw that there were two other men already inside, one in the front passenger seat and another in the back. Should he go with them? Might they bring Mari back to him if he did what they wanted?

'Batal,' he announced through the car window.

'Welcome,' said the man sitting in the back. He had an English accent. The other did not speak.

Saeed got into the car and the director took to the wheel. He drove them out of the town and to an area of beautiful countryside with grassy knolls and trees but nothing which could identify their location.

The director got out and walked around looking at the position of the sun and any distinguishing features. 'Here,' he decided and pointed. 'Sit here. Under this tree.'

As the three men got into position the director went back to the car. 'I'm getting your lines. We will read them first then shoot for real when you have learnt them.'

He returned and handed out the scripts which were all in English and marked One, Two and Three. 'You speak in the order you sit. Now, remember, this is for your home audience. You all know how wonderful life is here so all you have to do is portray it to those out there. Smiles, enthusiasm, fervour, passion... '

Saeed was sitting in third place. He had never done anything like this before but he remembered Abu Munib's words; he had to try for Mari's sake.

The scripts were not long and so well written that the three men needed little prompting. The first run-through went without a hitch.

They were given a few minutes to learn their lines then the director said, 'Let's try to get it in one.'

Saeed gulped when he realised that this was now for real.

The man from the car, who did not speak to him, went first and seemed particularly adept. The second man went off-script several times and the director seemed very pleased with him.

'That's even better than what I have written. Well done.'

When it was his turn, Saeed remembered his words but he stumbled a little. He gave the director a worried glance.

'Do not worry, my friend. It is your face that everyone will be looking at.'

174

Saeed was bemused by the experience; he certainly wasn't experiencing the camaraderie they were portraying, but it was over and not especially painful. If that was to be his role here, he could cope with it and he began to hope that it would be. Anything was better than taking part in what he had just experienced.

Once again, there was no talking in the car except by the director when he was dropped back at his house. 'Well done. I'll let you know.'

51

It was Sunday, and both Karen and John were having a lazy day until there was a brief mention on the TV about the S.A.S.

Karen jumped to attention. 'What do you know about the S.A.S.?'

John smiled lazily at her. 'What do you want to know?'

Karen frowned. 'What do you mean? What does a forensics expert know about the army?'

'I know something about everything,' John teased. 'Ow. We'll run out of cushions at this rate.'

'Just tell me,' Karen snapped.

'You've met him.'

'John, you're being especially annoying. Who are you talking about?'

John sighed. 'I'm sure I told you. Uncle Gary used to be in the S.A.S. Why do you want to know?'

'Really?' Karen's eyes popped open. 'Uncle Gary? That sweet old man?'

'That's the one. And he's not so old.'

'Mari's father was in the S.A.S. I've just discovered that.'

'And how does that help you with your investigation? He's long dead, isn't he?'

'I don't know. But can we go and see Gary?'

'He retired years ago. You're not going to get the S.A.S in on this.'

'I just want to know a bit more about their procedures.'

John smiled. 'He seemed to like you, which, as you know, is unusual for my family. I'll ring Dad and get his number if you like.'

'Do it.' Karen listened carefully when John made the call.

'What's Uncle Gary's number? Karen's got a question for him.'

'Yes, I told her that too.'

'We can only ask.' John scribbled down a number and waved it at Karen. 'I'll call him now. OK?'

Luckily for Karen, Gary was enthusiastic. 'Of course.' He said to John. 'I'd be delighted to see you and your lovely young lady. Come on over.'

'This will be an interesting night,' John said. 'It's ages since I've heard him speak about the old days. You can drive, I'll keep him company on the whisky.'

When they arrived, after exchanging brief pleasantries, Karen got stuck in. Gary leaned forward, curious to hear what she wanted to know.

'Gary, if I were to tell you about a girl who'd been enticed somewhere out in the Middle East, possibly Syria, how would you go about getting her back?'

'Syria? You mean to help or to join up?'

'Possibly tricked into joining up.'

'I'd say nothing. It's almost impossible to breach those terror organisations; only the top guys could do it and it wouldn't be worth the effort for a girl. She'd probably be dead by now anyway.'

'You mean because she's a girl?'

'Yes. Cannon fodder, really. Unless they're as mad as the men. They're just used and spat out like used gum.'

'But if you *knew* she was alive?'

'Even then, tough one. We used to get involved in kidnap cases but only if the captive was of other importance. You can't risk your top guys for everyone. Hard but true. Now, who do you mean?'

'Supposing it was the daughter of one of yours?'

Gary sat up, interested.

'Well, there might be some willing to have a go. Not serving soldiers, though. They'd not get clearance. Am I getting it's someone you think I know?'

Karen nodded. 'Mari Lone.'

Gary interrupted her. 'The girl on the news the other day?' He thought for a minute. 'She's not Wolf's daughter, is she?'

Karen sat up. 'Yes. You did know him then.'

'I did. A brave man and an expert soldier. One of the best. So how did she go out there?'

'I don't know for sure she is out there but she's nowhere in England and was last seen getting off a bus at Birmingham airport in the company of a woman who might be a terrorist escort.'

'OK. But why? Is she a fanatic? Wolf wasn't religious at all, as far as I knew.'

'If she's there, I think she was enticed by a young lad. So what do you think?'

'Are you formally asking me to rescue her?'

Karen laughed. 'No, of course not,' she lied, and he knew it. 'I'm just exploring ways in which it could be done.'

Gary laughed in reply. 'Well, when you know what you want, let me know and I'll tell you if it's possible. Now, can I get you a drink?'

'Just the one, I'm driving,' Karen said.

Gary, Karen, and John chatted happily over a couple of drinks, but Gary seemed increasingly impatient for them to leave. Finally, he picked up the phone and looked at Karen. 'Now, I'm not promising anything, but I do know someone. He made a call. 'You know you were looking for a bit of action?' he waited for an answer. 'Good. Because I might have something right up your street, you mad bastard. You'll probably die, but that never stopped you before. I just need to see if I can wangle a little Intel out of a few mates in the morning.'

Gary downed his Scotch. 'It's about time I had a bit of excitement too,' he said.

52

Mari and Maryam were kept in the cell for three days until one of the council guards came to collect them. They were taken to a house where they were told to get washed and changed into clean undergarments and burqas which were laid out for them on a chair outside the bathroom.

Maryam let Mari go first. After four days in the cell, for Mari, this was like luxury, although the water was cold and there was no shampoo so she had to wash as best she could with the old bar of soap provided.

'Now I feel better,' Mari said, emerging from the bathroom wrapped in an old towel with wet hair. 'What do you think they are going to do with us?'

Maryam shook her head. 'We will have to wait and see.' She went into the bathroom leaving Mari to dry off and get dressed. When she, too, was ready they went downstairs to where the guard was waiting.

'Follow me,' he commanded. He walked them to the Mudhir's office where the guard let them in.

The Mudhir looked imposing in his full robes and regalia. He sat on a small platform from where he could look down on them.

'I have decided to grant you mercy,' he began. 'You,' he pointed at Maryam. 'You will go to our factory where you will make clothes.' Maryam nodded.

He turned to Mari. 'You will join the other women who look after our menfolk.'

Mari's heart sunk, guessing what this meant, but Maryam spoke out.

'If I may, Your Excellency, this girl will make a good seamstress. I can teach her well. She wants to become a good Muslim like me and hopes that she may soon be with the man she loves again.'

'Silence, woman!' the Mudhir barked, but his face looked contemplative. 'It may suit me if she does this. It will encourage Batal to work harder for us if he knows she is being looked after. He and his pretty face is becoming useful to us.' He looked at

Mari. 'You will join her but you will both receive religious training and you will both be tested. If you fail, then you,' he jabbed his finger at Mari, 'will be put with the other women. If you pass the test, we may find a husband for you.'

'But… ' Mari began.

'Enough!' the Mudhir waved his hand, and his guard pushed them out of the door.

Their guard took them outside and along a street. After walking for a few minutes, they arrived at a big white building. Neither of them could read the sign outside, but it was clearly not a prison.

'Is this the factory?' Mari asked as they were taken inside. The guard took them into a small room with bars on the window and waved at them to sit down. He left and shut the door behind him. They heard a key turn in the lock.

'No escape here,' Mari muttered.

'There will be no escape for a long time. Do as they say. Shush now, someone comes.'

They heard a key in the door. A man wearing a large turban and dressed in long black robes came in. He said something in Arabic. Maryam answered. 'I speak a fair amount and understand more.'

'And the girl?'

'No, she does not speak it.'

He spoke in English while looking at Mari. 'You will be taught Arabic and then both of you will receive instruction in the Quran and Sharia. After a short time, you will be tested on this. You must understand that your life is at stake if you do not pass this test. If you behave and you succeed, Allah may accept you into this sacred caliphate, and you may become citizens of this state. If you fail, you will not. Do you understand?'

Both women nodded.

'You come with me.'

Maryam was taken away leaving Mari on her own until the teacher returned with books, paper, and pens.

'Now you learn.' Mari listened to him as if her life depended on it because she knew that it did.

180

Maryam had been taken into a large sewing room on the ground floor. There were several women already working with the supervisor sitting at a desk in the front. She stood up and faced Maryam.

'You are very tall. I am Nazia. How well do you sew?'

'I am Maryam. Very well. Test me if you like.'

Nazia pointed at a roll of white cotton fabric on a table at the side.

'Make me a thobe and pants for a man six foot high and three foot wide.'

Maryam nodded. 'May I have...?'

'There are scissors, pins, and measuring sticks on the tables there. Use that machine in the corner.'

Maryam got to work straight away. In less than an hour, the suit was ready. Nazia picked up the thobe first and held it up against her. She checked the pants by pulling the sides and checking the elasticity of the waistband. She smiled.

'This is good work. My husband will wear them tomorrow. I will tell them that you have done well.'

Maryam nodded. 'Thank you.'

'Here is a list of things that we need to make. Start with the drapes. They are for the Mudhir's house. Can you read Arabic?'

'I know the numbers. What fabric shall I use?'

'There. The red and gold,' she hesitated. 'Ah, but first you should make night clothes for you and the girl.'

'The white cotton?'

Nazia nodded. 'Take what you need.'

At lunchtime, Mari was returned to the others in time for afternoon prayers.

'How are you getting on?' Maryam whispered. Mari gave a weak smile in return before she was summoned back to her studies. Maryam returned to her sewing.

When the day was done, Nazia took both of them to the canteen where they were given a modest meal of chicken and rice which they both ate hungrily. When they had finished, Nazia returned to speak to them both. She was carrying the nightclothes Maryam had made.

'You will be staying here from now on. Come with me.'

They were taken upstairs to a large room at the top of the factory laid out with camp beds. The windows were so high up and small that they didn't need bars.

'There is a washroom at the end of the room and a tap with clean water you can drink from. I have to lock you in now. I will see you in the morning.'

Both women were very tired after their long day.

'How were your studies?' Maryam asked in Arabic.

'Good evening. You're welcome.' Mari replied to Maryam's amusement.

'Well done. I'm sure you will do well,' she smiled.

The beds were small and basic but comfortable enough for tired eyes. Mari felt herself drifting off as she listened to Maryam's soft chanting of hymns. 'God bless you,' she whispered.

53

Maryam and Mari were already up when Nazia came to let them out. 'Follow me,' she instructed. 'I have to take the girl to her lessons then I have a new task for you.'

They followed her down the stairs to the room where Mari's teacher was waiting for her.

'Good luck.' Maryam said as she followed Nazia to the workroom. There, she saw several huge rolls of bright orange fabric on the back tables. She shuddered at the sight.

'We have to make clothes for prisoners,' Nazia said. 'If I give you an image, can you make them?'

'Of course,' Maryam said. 'It would be my pleasure to sew for you.'

The woman handed her the picture. Maryam recognised it as something she had seen on the news a long time ago; it was a prisoner from Guantanamo Bay.

'This is simple. What sizes do you want?'

The woman thought for a moment. 'I do not think they will be used for long. Make one size. Regular.' she paused. 'And make one or two bigger ones just in case.'

'I will start straight away,' Maryam replied. 'I will need large sheets of paper to make a pattern. And I will need orange cotton, too.'

Nazia shook her head. 'I only have black or white. Use black. The paper, I will have to get. Wait here.' She hesitated for a moment, looking at Maryam.

'I will not try to escape,' Maryam told her, already making her way to a sewing table.

Nazia nodded and left to get the paper. By the time she came back, Maryam had already cut some swatches of fabric and produced some sewing samples. 'I have set the machine up. All I need now is the pattern.'

'Good.' Nazia smiled. She watched intently as Maryam spread out the paper and using her hand, began to measure out the shapes she needed to make the outfits. Once the paper was cut, she rolled out the fabric, doubled it up and pinned the pattern to it. She paused to look at the woman.

'I need scissors. Not these,' she pushed the small pair she had been given aside. 'I need big scissors. Do you have some?'

Nazia did not even pause this time. She unlocked a drawer in her desk and handed her a pair with shiny blades.

'Thank you,' Maryam replied. She meant it. She had no intention of trying to attack Nazia or even escape. She had found a new purpose in life.

By the end of the day she had completed five garments and she explained to the woman 'I will be faster tomorrow now I have the pattern. How many do you need?'

'I have been asked for five hundred.'

'Then please can you make sure that these are correct. Can you get someone to try them on before I carry on?'

'You are very dedicated,' Nazia said. 'I was expecting you would not cooperate.'

'I am a seamstress before anything else,' Maryam replied. 'And I will work for whoever needs my services. Even Allah.'

The woman smiled broadly at her. 'Then my job will be so much easier. Thank you, Maryam. I will do as you say. The guard will come soon to take you back to the school, but if you carry on like this, I may be able to find a house for you to live in. Who knows? If you convert we may yet find you a husband too.'

Maryam laughed at that. 'I was married once. That was enough for me.'

Nazia laughed in sympathy. 'I know what you mean.'

'May I ask one favour?'

Nazia looked interested. 'Of course.'

'In my village, I used to make toys and dolls for the children from my scraps. May I use the scraps here?'

'Yes, of course you can. What a nice idea,' Nazia said. 'Maybe we can sell some; there are so few toys here.'

Maryam smiled. 'That's a good idea.'

That night she asked Mari in Arabic how she was getting on.

'Much better, I think. He says I have to start reading the Quran tomorrow.'

'That's good. Keep going. I have found that the woman who runs this place is reasonable. She treats me well. They have even said I may leave this place if I sew well.'

'That is good for you, you have your use but what am I good for?'

Maryam didn't answer at first. She had heard many terrible things about what happened to young girls but she didn't want to scare her. 'Maybe they will let you learn to sew? I can ask if you like.'

Mari brightened up. 'I can cook, too. Maybe they'll give me work if I try hard enough. There's just one problem.'

'What is that?'

Mari continued. 'I wasn't a good Catholic but I do believe in God. Saeed told me that Allah was the only true God, but the Allah here seems to be hard and cruel. How can I ever leave God for Allah?'

Maryam sighed. 'It is indeed hard but it is not the God who is at fault, it is the men. We have the same God but a different way of reaching him,' Maryam confided. 'He will understand what you do and will forgive you.'

'Thank you, Maryam. That helps a little.'

54

Karen, who believed in no God except the one who believed in justice, came home from another fruitless day. As usual, she checked her emails before settling down to eat dinner with John. He was just serving up when she yelled at him.

'Hang on, that guy from the CTC has just emailed me. It must be important.'

John sighed and put their dinner back in the oven.

'Look at this.' Karen beckoned him over. 'He says it's a propaganda video by the terrorists. They've just received it. He wants me to see if I recognise anyone.'

Karen played the footage on his laptop. Three young men were sitting on a grassy spot under a tree. All dressed in black and with rifles slung over their shoulders or in front of them The first one spoke very eloquently.

Karen spoke first. 'He's British! Bloody hell!'

'That's a quality film too. Professionally done,' John commented.

They watched, mesmerised, as the second man spoke. Then the camera closed in on the third.

Karen frowned and moved closer to the screen. 'Oh no!'

'What? It's not...'

'It's Saeed. Damn. I must ring him.'

'Saeed?'

'No, you twat. The CTC guy.'

John lightly touched his rumbling stomach while Karen rang the officer at the unit.

'Positive ID. The third one. That's Saeed Rahman. One of the missing.'

'Thanks. I thought it might be. We'll be right on it.'

'Where did the film come from?'

'We intercepted it on the web. We're trying to get it taken off.'

'Can I tell his parents?'

'Absolutely not.' He rang off.

John looked at Karen. 'Can we eat now?' He didn't wait for an answer. Minutes later he was munching his way through the pizza slices while Karen nibbled the edges, still deep in thought.

'Eat. You have to eat.'

'I know.'

After they had eaten, Karen sat at her laptop and began searching. 'They're too late,' she said.

'Too late for what?' John looked up from the papers he was reading.

'That video. It's on Twitter and every other social media platform. If his parents see it, they are going to be devastated. Especially that I didn't tell them first.'

'But aren't they, you know, too old for social media? I'm sure my parents wouldn't have a clue.'

'They have a teenage daughter with loads of friends. Saeed is a good-looking lad. I expect he's broken a few hearts already.'

'Ah,' John nodded. 'What are you going to do?'

'I'll ring them now. I need to keep them on side. I'll tell them I've just seen it online. That's not quite lying, is it?'

John shook his head. Karen took out her mobile, blocking the number before she called.

'Mrs Rahman? I wanted to let you know that I have seen some footage of Saeed...'

'I have just had a phone call from the imam. Razia has played it for me. Is it real?'

'I'm afraid it looks like it, Mrs Rahman. Saeed seems to have joined them.'

There was a silence at the other end, then very quietly she spoke. 'That is not my son. Someone must have persuaded him to do that. He is a good boy. Even the imam said so.'

'I expect he was brainwashed. Mrs Rahman, did Saeed know the imam's son Nadeem?'

'Yes. Such a nice boy. Why do you ask?'

'It's just part of our investigation.'

'Why? You don't think that he could be involved with all this, do you?'

'We're checking into everything, Mrs Rahman. I'll let you know what we find. And Mrs Rahman, please tell me if you hear anything at all from your friends and relatives about this. And tell them to watch out for young family members.'

'What? You don't think there are others, do you?'

Karen chose her words carefully. 'If Saeed has been talked into doing something like this, and we don't know for sure yet, but if he has, there may be other boys and girls preparing to do the same thing.'

'Oh no. That's too horrible to contemplate.'

'I know, Mrs Rahman, but it's very serious. Who knows what threat this terror group could bring to the UK? You must tell me if you hear anything from him too. Some of them, I'm told, use social media to try to persuade their friends to go and join them.' Karen hesitated. 'His cousin Selina has been on Twitter. Under an assumed name.'

There was a long pause followed by an almost whispered reply.

'I didn't know, but we feared it. I'll tell everyone I know to look out for their children.'

'Thank you, Mrs Rahman.' Karen put her phone down.

'Are you getting somewhere then?' John asked.

'Maybe. The guy at the unit told me Selina's been recruiting. And we've got a little dirt on the imam's son. It looks like we may be getting closer to knowing who's been persuading people to go out there.'

'Good. Now, will you just relax a bit? You look exhausted.'

'In a minute. I just need to look something up.'

'I know what your minutes are. They're hours. I'm going up to read in bed. Don't be long. I don't want to find you still here in the morning.'

'You know me so well,' Karen smiled.

John rolled his eyes.

55

In Pakistan, Jafar Rahman answered the phone to a frantic Maria. 'What is the matter now?' he said.

'Have you not seen that wretched film? The one with Saeed?'

Jafar sighed. 'One of the boys in the market showed it to me on his tablet. He remembered Saeed. But there is no sign of Ahmed. But I must assume they are together and well. Ahmed is a timid boy, always thinking. He wouldn't want to be on film. Not like your Saeed.'

'What are we going to do, Jafar?' Maria wailed. 'They cannot still be in the mountains, can they? So where are they? Now even Ibra is very worried.'

'Put him on.'

Ibrahim's voice sounded. 'Maria is right. It's been too long. We must get them back.'

Jafar paused. 'You're right, of course. I'll go again to the market and see if anyone knows anything. I will also talk to the police.'

Laila appeared. 'Who was that on the phone?'

'My sister-in-law, Maria. She is very worried about Saeed.'

'I am worried too. They've been away too long.'

Jafar tried to hide his worry. 'He's fine, I'm sure. But just to be sure, I will go out now and see what else I can find out.'

Jafar went straight out to the market where he asked everybody he knew if they had seen his son and nephew or knew about their travels. He was answered with shaking heads.

'Go to the airport,' one told him. 'Take a photo of him. If he was going far it would be by plane.'

Jafar had to agree. 'That is true. My nephew had already travelled from England. Maybe his plan was always to go further.'

He went home and found a photo his wife had taken of the two boys together when Saeed had first arrived.

'No news of them?' Laila asked.

189

He shook his head. 'I am going to the airport to see what I can find out.'

'The airport? Do you think… Please hurry. I am so worried myself. We should have done something before this.'

Jafar took a taxi to the airport and began asking at the information desk, where a man and a woman sat. The man was on the phone but the woman answered him.

'Do you know the airline or day they flew out? The airlines should have a list of names of all the passengers.'

'Thank you. I think I do.'

One by one, Mr Rahman approached each airline desk but they all said the same thing. 'We cannot give you that information. You must see a policeman.'

Frustrated, he went back to the enquiry desk. This time, the man spoke to him.

'Listen. I do not know your son and his cousin but I do know that sometimes people are flown to Iraq. They say they are going to a school but everybody knows it is really a training centre. See that airline there?' he pointed. 'Give that man a few rupees and tell him I sent you. He may help you.'

Jafar went over to the desk.

'I've already told you… ' he began, but Jafar nodded his head towards the information desk.

'He told me to give you this.' He opened his wallet discreetly.

'Follow me,' the man said, slipping the proffered notes into his pocket. 'But I am not promising anything.'

Jafar followed the man into the security area where he sat down at a workstation and called up a date. The footage showed all the passengers who had boarded flights on the days in question. He ran the film on fast but stopped it each time he saw two figures checking in.

'No,' said Jafar, 'that's not them.' Then *no* again and again until at last. 'That is them! That is them! What do I do now?'

'You go to the police and you tell them your son and his friend flew out on this flight on this day.' He wrote down the details. 'And they said their reason for travel was to attend a school. Then you hope that they will look into it for you.' He looked Jafar in the eyes. 'And if they don't, you will have to go yourself.'

190

'A school? The other man said it was a training camp. Do you think...'

'Almost certainly,' the man laughed. 'If it was a real school, it would be overflowing by now.'

Jafar began to despair. 'Surely my Ahmed would not have gone to a training camp?'

'If he went, then from what I've heard, he'll be dead by now. By fighting or by not fighting.'

'Don't say that!' Jafar snapped. 'Don't you dare say that.'

Jafar left the airport and made his way to the police station on foot. After waiting ages, he was finally called into a room where a policeman seemed to be disinterested.

'But my son is a national of this country. You have a duty to find him.'

'Yes indeed, Mr Rahman. But as we have already told you. He is eighteen and has reached the age of majority. He is quite entitled to go to Iraq if he wants to.'

Jafar reached for his wallet but was met with the raised palm of the officer's hand.

'We are not accepting bribes here, Mr Rahman. I will put it on the list and we will look for your son as soon as we can.'

With a heavy heart, Jafar went back to the airport and sought out the man at the enquiry desk.

'No luck?' Jafar shook his head. 'The police will not help,' he said. 'Is there anything you can do to help me?'

The man shook his head. 'But I am sure if you go to Iraq and ask the right people, they will tell you. Maybe even the police will be more helpful there.'

56

Jafar went home, now feeling despondent. He told his wife what he'd heard. 'Laila, we have no other choice.'

She agreed straight away. 'Just find him and bring him home,' she told him. 'Bring our son home.'

Jafar packed a small bag, took a taxi to the airport and bought a one-way ticket on the first available flight to Erbil. It was a long flight and inevitably, he got into conversation with the man next to him.

In his frustration and stress, the entire story came spilling out. '... and so I have to go to find him.'

The man he sat next to had been attentive. 'I may be able to help. My uncle is a taxi driver at the airport. He knows everything that is going on. I'll find him for you and see what he knows about this so-called school.'

With the small relief from the offer of help, Jafar endured the rest of his journey in hopeful anticipation. After the plane had landed, the man, as promised, looked out for his uncle. They had to wait nearly an hour before his taxi appeared.

'Uncle. Can you help this man please?'

The taxi driver listened to the story, shaking his head at every sentence. 'I am very sorry, sir. I have heard of this school. It is no school that I would want my children to go to. They teach how to kill but most of all, they teach how to hate. If their pupils cannot hate enough, they are killed. If they hate a great deal, they are sent on to more training where they learn to hate so much they *must* kill.'

Jafar listened, his hopes sinking. 'I must find out what happened to my son.'

'Did he have hate in his heart?'

Jafar shook his head. 'Only questions.'

'Then go to the police station. The bodies of those who don't make it are usually dumped on the road somewhere. But the police will know. May Allah help you if they have found him.'

'Thank you. Will you take me to the police station?'

'Of course. No need to pay me. I'll wait for you too.'

'You are very kind.'

It was a short drive to the station. Jafar rushed in to see an officer sitting at the desk in the lobby. 'I'm trying to find my son. I fear he went to a training camp.'

The officer looked up and spoke as if this happened every day. 'There are some unidentified bodies. We collect them. It's easier for the relatives to come to our city to identify them. There are never papers with them. I can show you if you like.'

Jafar breathed in deeply before he answered. 'Please.'

The officer called out to the back office. 'I need someone on the desk, please. I am going to the mortuary.' Someone appeared straight away.

The officer turned to Jafar. 'You have transport?'

Jafar nodded' Outside.' The two men left the station. Jafar spoke to the taxi driver who was still waiting outside. 'But you must take payment this time,' he added.

At the mortuary, the officer spoke to an attendant and asked him to bring out certain bodies. He went out through thick plastic curtains and came back with a trolley with a sheet-covered body on it.

Jafar was almost overcome with grief. It all seemed so matter of fact. Daily life, even. But here might be his only son, murdered by animals who said they believed in Allah.

The attendant pulled back the sheet. The body was yellow, and the eyes shrunken back into the head. Both arms and legs were missing. Jafar was horrified, but it was not Ahmed. He shook his head.

'Get the other one,' the officer said. The attendant wheeled the first one back to the refrigerated unit emerging a few minutes later with another. This time, the officer pulled back the sheet; it was Ahmed.

Jafar gently touched his face and scanned every inch of his body to see what had happened to his son. The body was covered with bullet holes, large lacerations, and bruises but it was intact.

'This is my son.' He began to weep. 'Who are these monsters?'

The officer pulled the sheet back over the body.

'Please come with me, Mr Rahman. We will need to make arrangements for you to take your son back to Pakistan. There are funeral directors who will do this for you, but you will need to sign the release papers here.'

Jafar nodded. At least there was something for him to do but then he remembered Laila. 'I must tell my wife. May I use your phone?' he asked.

'Let us go back to my office.'

In his grief, Jafar had almost forgotten about Saeed, but in the time it took them to get back to the station he remembered him. He wondered how the one boy could be so integrated into terror while his own was rejected. *Because Ahmed argued*, he guessed.

Ibrahim was devastated to hear the news. He made the usual platitudes but that wasn't enough. When he told Maria, she was heartbroken.

'We have to find our son, Maria. And we can't leave Jafar on his own. It's time I got involved too. I'm going to ring him and I will do whatever he wants me to do.'

He made the call while Maria paced around the room.

'Brother, I am going to come out to see you as soon as I can get away. I want to find the evil monsters who did this to Ahmed. It seems that Saeed is still alive and safe, for the time being. But I must find him and bring him back home.'

'Thank you, brother. I, too, want to find Saeed. What made them separate? What were Ahmed's last days? I need to know. Yes, we will be stronger together.'

Maria was both pleased and scared. 'But it is too dangerous,' she cried. 'I could not bear to lose you too.'

'It has to be done.' Jafar said. 'We know he is alive, and for the time being, he is also safe. I will make my preparations soon. This is my final word.'

57

After the filming, Saeed moped around his house for every minute that he was not needed for anything.

Selina came to see him to tell him that her husband had been killed in operations. She seemed unconcerned with this. 'He is in paradise now,' she said. 'He is so lucky to have died for the cause.'

'Have you no heart?' Saeed replied. 'Did you not care for him?'

'There is no point in love except that for Allah and the caliphate. Our reward is in the afterlife.'

'But I love Mari. How is she, do you know?'

'Mari is being well looked after. She will make a good wife one day for someone who will not break her heart when he too is killed.'

Selina sat closer to him. 'I am looking for a new husband, Batal,' she touched his knee.

Saeed shrank back. 'Mari is my love and my wife-to-be,' he told her. 'I will wait.'

'Then you will wait forever,' she spat, getting up. 'You are a fraud.' She stormed out without looking back.

Later there was another knock on the door. Saeed, half expecting Selina's return, ignored it at first, but when it continued, he gave in and opened the door.

'Oh, it's you,' he said to the director.

'Batal. I have good news for you. Amazing news. You are an internet sensation! You're going to be our new poster boy. the Mudhir told me he'd been thinking about how best to use your talents and now he says the way is clear. You will be the face of our films and the man to whom interested parties will ask questions.'

Saeed said nothing at first, but it seemed to him that this was a double-edged sword. He would be spared fighting – which he had heard was getting more dangerous every day – but back home, he would never be forgiven. Although he realised, there was not much chance of going home. Unless there was some way... and his mind began to whir. *Maybe this is Allah's wish after all.*

'That sounds very good,' he enthused. 'I would be delighted to take such an esteemed position.'

'Good. We start with a new photoshoot tomorrow. Come to my house now and we'll talk it through. You will become world famous, Batal. It will be such an honour for you.'

Saeed followed him to his house. There, he saw a very tall woman holding some bright orange clothing accompanied by a guard waiting outside.

'Ah, sorry. I forgot. Please come in and wait for a minute, Batal. I must talk with this woman for a moment.'

He nodded for the woman to follow him. She and Saeed went into the house, and while Saeed waited in the entrance hall with the woman's guard, she went into the main room with the director.

Saeed tried hard not to listen.

The door opened and the director told the woman to wait in the hall for a moment. When she emerged from the room, Saeed caught her gaze. He stared at the mesh covering her eyes, sure that he knew who she was. The guard was standing near the door.

Saeed dared not speak but she did. 'Tell me. Why did you save my life?'

He whispered three words to her. 'My mother. Maria.'

Maryam's eyes smiled at him. 'Maryam Maria Mari. We are all the same name. We are connected.'

'Mari?' Saeed said, but before she could reply, the director reappeared. The guard jumped to attention.

'Yes, it is fine,' the director said to Maryam. 'The Mudhir has told me to tell you that you can proceed. You may go.' He waited for her to leave with the guard and turned to Saeed. 'Batal, please come in.'

Saeed entered the main room and was amazed at all the technology and gadgets displayed around the room.

Forgetting for a moment, he spoke in English. 'Wow! This is amazing stuff!'

The director beamed at him and replied in kind. 'Yes, I thought you might approve. If you like, I'll show you the ropes one day.'

'Very much so. Are you British too? Your Arabic is so good.'

196

He nodded. 'Dual heritage. My father made me learn. Look, I hate the weird shit going on here. But I have no choice unless I want to lose my head too. They pay me, I never get my hands dirty, and I get to work with all this stuff.'

Saeed hesitated. *Is this a trick to out me?*

'You can be like me too, if you like,' the director continued. 'I know that one day we'll probably be blown to smithereens, but until then, we might as well make the most of it.'

'What is your name?' Saeed asked.

'They used to call me Harry. But here I'm Abdulla.'

'Saeed.'

'Saeed. Pleased to meet you.' The two young men shook hands.

58

Karen walked into work the next morning with a bit more of a spring in her step, but before she had got to her office, Barry stepped out of his.

'Can I have a word?'

'Formal or informal?' Karen asked as she followed him in.

'Informal.'

'Definitely!'

Barry waved his arm towards his desk and waited for her to sit opposite him. 'Karen, you have settled in reasonably well. I've had a few comments about your attitude to certain members of staff.'

'Such as?'

He smiled. 'I can't say. Let us leave it that you can be a little sharp with people. From where I sit, I can't condone it, but I can accept that it might have been, how can I say it, deserved. Our admin department seems to have tightened up some of their procedures since your arrival. How do you think you are getting on?'

'Well enough,' Karen said, never one to sing her own praises. 'I'm finding the work challenging, which is always good.'

'Yes, Karen. I try to maintain a light touch and I think you are handling the missing young people situation very well. How are the cases coming on?'

'Not good. I'm learning a great deal about terrorist practices, and I'm sure that both of them have been enticed out to Iraq or Syria.'

'And have you been in touch with the CTC?'

'Yes, although they put me in a bit of a spot the other day. The video, you know of the three boys?' Barry nodded.

'One of them is Saeed Rahman. The unit knew this already but wouldn't let me tell the family.'

'They have their reasons.'

'I fudged it, but I told his mother. We must gain the trust of these families or we will never get anywhere. If they think we are hiding stuff... '

'I agree. But you haven't had the training that they have. Next time, push your case but don't defy them. Make up with them. We don't want to lose intel because they don't like how you operate.' It was Karen's turn to nod.

'So update me.'

'Mari Lone was almost certainly trafficked or escorted to Turkey. I've contacted the police out there and they say they are investigating but I'm not sure they are. Saeed is already in the hands of the terrorists. I have no idea what we can do about him. And we've discovered that Selina Ali is Saeed's cousin. And strangely, her mother hasn't been in touch for ages about her disappearance.'

'What are you insinuating?'

'We're sure Selina is already out there. She's been tweeting about the cause from somewhere. The CTC have told me that much, and no, I haven't told her mother. We have a potential sighting at Birmingham Airport, but we can't confirm it. And maybe her mother likes what her daughter is doing.'

'Have you contacted the British Army?'

Karen was surprised at the question. 'No. Not yet I assumed they wouldn't get involved. Besides, the CTC would have passed the information on, wouldn't they?'

'Yes, but not necessarily to try to get him back. Although I share your reasoning that they won't try. It seems that too many of our young men are going out there. Still doesn't hurt to ask.'

'Right, sir. Will do.'

'And how are you getting on with Omar?'

'Very well. He's a good, solid man. And he speaks Urdu. That's very impressive.'

'Perfectly observed. Thank you, Karen, that will be all.'

Karen almost ran to her office to get on the phone but took care to smile sweetly at the admin assistant she had been rude to the day before. She knew she was meant to hear the *'Cow'* that her smile elicited. It made her smile even more. *I'd have done that too.*

Ringing the army was a frustrating business. At first, she was handed from one person to another and left on hold several times. Eventually, she spoke to a liaison officer and when she repeated her question for the umpteenth time, she was met with a strange response. 'The subject is known to us and normal procedures are being followed.'

'What does that mean? Did she go to Turkey?'

The phone was clunked down.

'Damn you!' Frustrated, she rang Gary to tap his brain. She relayed the words that the army spokesman had said.

'What does it mean, Gary?' Karen asked over the phone.

'I think you know what it means.'

'Bloody hell. Does everyone speak in code in the army?' she paused. 'OK. They know Mari is out there, they won't risk anyone's life to get her, but if the opportunity arises they'll act.'

'I said you'd know. But that's not the only way to do things.'

'Go on.'

'There may be people who are interested in helping.' Gary said. 'No promises. You heard my call the other day. They look after their own and many people remember Wolf. He was a good soldier, and if they can help, they will.'

'What would it involve in theory?' Karen asked.

'In theory, someone would have to access the Intel which tells them where she is. Then they'd get an idea of how difficult or not it would be to get her out.'

'So supposing she was in a prison or something?'

'Probably impossible without storming the place and that would be too visible. She would have to be somewhere where she could be nabbed quickly and quietly.'

'So when is someone going to ask the questions?'

There was silence at the other end.

'I won't lie, and I won't tell you anything either.'

'OK. Where does it start? Turkey? Should I go out there?'

'Under no circumstances.'

Karen grinned. Just what she wanted to hear. 'When do I get my ticket?'

'You don't. Not until I say and only if I'm sure John won't kill me.'

'John?' Karen laughed. 'OK, I'll go chase up the paperwork instead'

59

Remembering Barry's words, Karen rang the CTC and spoke to the officer she'd talked to before.

'Hands up,' she said. 'I did tell the family but they would have seen the video anyway and I did want to get their trust.'

She heard a sigh at the other end before the reply came. 'OK. What do you want to know?'

'Selina Ali. I'm pretty sure she's out there. Any confirmation of that?'

'Not yet. We haven't managed to shut her down, either, but it's likely.'

'What's her Twitter name?'

'And there was me thinking you're a detective.' The line went dead.

'Oh, John,' she mused out loud. 'What would I do without you.' She picked up her phone and rang him.

'Hello, my love. What is your command this time?'

Karen had no time for small talk. 'Twitter. You know how useless I am on there. Selina Ali. Apparently, she's been tweeting for the caliphate. Can you find her name, please?'

'On it, Sweetums.'

Karen went over to Omar's desk. As she approached she saw him flinch without even looking up.

'Have you got anything on Nadeem yet?'

He shook his head. 'Nothing yet that links him to Isis. I've searched online for everything I can think of. The CTC have nothing either.'

Karen heard her phone ring and went back to her desk. 'John.'

'Pen?'

'That was quick. How... '

'It was an anagram,' John guessed her question. 'Clever.'

'OK, shoot.' Karen wrote down the name on a piece of paper. She looked at it. 'Clever?' She ended the call and took the paper over to Omar.

'Here, this is Selina's Twitter account. She might have let something slip.'

'OK, Karen.'

Karen went back to her desk. She needed to think, and after running something through in her head several times, she rang the CTC and spoke to the officer she had been communicating with.

'I'm thinking of going to Turkey to see if I can find this woman and get her to take me to Mari. Can you get me the appropriate contacts? And I mean appropriate.'

'Not a chance in hell.' The call ended.

Karen looked up to see Omar looking very animated. He got up and came over. 'You're right. He's retweeted a couple of her posts. Old posts from a few months ago. Nothing about Isis, just general stuff. But there's definitely a connection between them.'

'Great stuff,' Karen beamed. 'It's time we interviewed him.'

'Barry?' Karen looked up as he approached.

'Sorry, Karen. Other developments. Unless you've got something spectacular for us, I'm going to have to move you to another case.'

'Oh shit,' Karen said. 'I thought that only happened at my old office.'

***

Not so far away, in a pub in a leafy suburb somewhere in Southeast England, four men sat talking loudly about football; or so a passing stranger might have guessed.

Gary sat at the helm of the round table. The others, all in their mid-forties, sat opposite in a fan shape. Tom, a tall white man, got up to collect their drinks on a tray and handed them out. They all raised their glasses.

'To Wolf. One of the best forwards ever.'

'Hear, hear!' The glasses were raised and quickly downed. Tom had ordered two rounds, and a barman was quick to resupply the team.

'So you all know why you are here?' Gary looked around the table.

'Teambuilding,' Tom said with a wink.

202

'That's right.' Gary nodded. 'As you all know, I'm too old to be much use on the field. But I'm the manager, and what I say goes.'

As one, they leaned forward to hear him.

'You know the objective. We have to win the trophy. No point in coming second, we'll be destroyed out there if we fail. It's do or die.' Gary sat back. 'Now, who's going to be our striker?'

They all looked at Ali, a thick-set man of Middle Eastern appearance.

He laughed. 'I'm more of a mid-fielder, an organiser.' He looked at Joe, a tall black man with a big smile. 'He'd be a good striker. He knows the lingo.'

Joe laughed. 'It's true I know a bit about it. And quite a few players come from Nigeria these days.'

'You'd have to get your dick chopped,' Tom chipped in.

'It already is,' Ali grinned.

'When did you see my dick?' Joe was surprised.

'Just curious in the changing room.'

Joe laughed. 'I was born a Muslim. It didn't last. But I suppose it would help.'

Joe went quiet. The others looked at him expectantly.

'He's having one of his turns again,' Ali laughed.

Joe grinned again. 'Gary, remember that story about black footballers wanting to switch sides because of racism?'

Gary looked puzzled and shook his head. Joe raised an eyebrow sarcastically. 'Write it for me, will you?'

Gary smiled. 'Aha! And there we have it. Genius. Consider it done. Now then, back to the game, lads. What else do we need to do to prepare?' He looked at Tom. 'How are we going to get some practice in? Do we have any friendly teams?'

Tom nodded. 'I've got a few contacts. Something on overseas turf would be good. Ali?'

'Oh, yes, I have relatives everywhere in the force. Some are even straight.'

The others laughed but Gary's face fell. 'That reminds me. There's a copper here who wants to get involved. Well, to be fair, it's her show.'

'No way,' the others said almost together.

'Who is it?' Tom was curious.

'My nephew's girlfriend. She's been wanting to get her hands on that trophy for a while. She's the reason we even know about it.'

'A woman? No chance,' Joe spluttered. 'I'm all for equality, even women's football, but I don't want one on my team.'

Ali was more circumspect. 'If we're going to play our first round in Turkey, it could be useful to have someone in there with the locals. Keep an eye on things. Make sure there are no crossed wires.'

'Aye. It's a thought.'

'I'll confirm nothing yet,' Gary said. 'We're a long way off even playing yet. First team meeting in here next week. Agreed?'

'Agreed,' came the chorus.

'Good,' Gary said. 'Now let's get some pints down us. Last drinks for a while; we have to get ourselves fit.'

60

14th March

The days had rolled on. Saeed and Harry were getting on like they'd known each other for years. Since no one else understood the complexities of what Harry was doing, they could take time out to muck around with things whenever they wanted. Harry had rigged up several video games which could be switched off in an instant in case anyone walked in. There was no one to challenge them, so they spent their time with as much fun and laughter as they could get away with.

'So how did you get into filming?' Saeed asked.

'A bit like you. I was a rubbish soldier but I told them I could help make films. So I found my niche. It's better than the alternative and at least I'm acquiring skills. Look at this one.' He showed an execution video to Saeed, who was both disgusted and fascinated.

'See,' Harry explained. 'They don't actually cut off his head here; it's all for show. That bit actually happens here.' He played a short clip which Saeed watched with revulsion. 'But even these guys won't show it exactly how it normally is. It's too bloody when done with a knife. Not that they care about sensitivities, of course, it's just that they want the movie to look good and it makes it seem clean and simple.'

Harry switched on some more footage. 'These are the films I like shooting.' It was a clip of fighters, all dressed up with their clothes blowing lightly in the wind. 'This is like Hollywood,' Harry said. 'If I ever got out of here I would have a career I'm sure. So would you as a leading man.'

Saeed laughed. 'Me?'

'Oh, yes. They want a new film. Just you. You have to be all sexy and appealing. They need more girls to come out here. They're running out of women.'

Saeed blushed. It reminded him how much he missed Mari.

'Have you got a woman?' Saeed asked.

Harry shook his head. 'Not really my bag. But I can't say that here. They might think I'm gay and you know what they do to gays, don't you?'

Saeed shook his head. 'I've never even thought about it.'

'You know that big, tall building? The hotel? They take them up there and throw them off.'

'Why?'

'Cleanses the soul of sin. Shit knows where they got that from. Not sure they had any tall buildings back then. Anyway, back to the babes. I've drafted a script.'

Saeed shook his head. 'Can't I write my own? Your last one was rubbish.'

Harry laughed. 'Of course you can. I have to check it, but I agree. Sexy talk was never my forte.'

'How much do I have to say?'

'You have to talk for just three minutes, so everything must count. Where will we shoot it? Where shall I put you?'

'In the bedroom?' Saeed suggested.

'Perfect. But my room here is very dull. Maybe I should get that woman to rustle something up?'

'Good idea,' Saeed said. 'Shall I come with you to speak to her?'

Harry paused for a moment. 'Look, I've been told to keep an eye on you. I don't know why, but it doesn't look good if I leave you on your own here with all this stuff unattended.'

Saeed frowned but understood his point. 'What should I do then?'

'You go on your own. I have no idea what *romantic* is. You must convey your message yourself and tell her how you want it to be.'

Saeed hesitated. *Would they allow him to talk to her? Was he trusted enough?* 'Is that proper?' he asked as generally as he could.

'To be seen with her? Under a black tent, who knows who is there? I won't tell. Besides, even I know she is old enough to be your mother. I trust you.'

Saeed laughed at the suggestion. Yes, why shouldn't he be trusted? He was the face of the caliphate, after all.

206

Even so, he was cautious when he went to the factory to talk to Maryam. Only her eyes conveyed her recognition of him as he walked in. The manager looked up with interest as he approached.

'I have a job for the seamstress,' he said. 'The director wants her to make some props for our new film.'

The manager beamed with pride. 'She is a good worker; it will be an honour for her to do this and for me. What do you need her to do?'

'She needs to decorate a room in my house so it looks most appealing.'

The manager clapped her hands. 'Go, Maryam. Go with the handsome soldier. You will be safe with him.'

Maryam got up. 'Thank you. It will indeed be an honour. I will need some paper and a pencil and a tape measure.'

The manager opened her drawer and handed her a small notepad and pencil. 'Take a measuring stick from over there,' she pointed.

Maryam took the stick and other items and followed Saeed out of the factory building and into the street, keeping well behind him as he walked to his house.

'Is it safe to talk in your house?' she asked.

It had not occurred to Saeed that it wouldn't be, but now he was put on alert. He turned his head slightly towards her as he spoke. 'I do not know.'

They walked the rest of the way in silence to his front door which he opened for her.

'The director wants to make a film to encourage more young women to come out here. He wants you to create a romantic bedroom.'

Maryam gasped, but when she spoke, it was calm and collected. 'Show me the room'.

Saeed took her to his bedroom. 'This will take a lot of work,' she said. 'The walls must be pink. We can have new drapes. Maybe hang some curtains around the bed. We will need a carpenter. Let me measure and I will draw what I want.'

When she was finished they walked back. Maryam spoke quietly to him.

'You are not one of them. Why do you do this?'

Saeed, desperate to speak to someone about his torment, trusted her with his innermost worries. 'What else can I do? Will they not kill me if I do not obey? They have already taken my girlfriend.'

'You must do your God's work and I know that your God is also mine. He would not want this evil to spread.'

'I know. But I am helpless.'

'You are about to make a film which will be shown all over the world. Think what your message should be.'

After he had walked Maryam back to the factory, he returned to see Harry with her measurements and drawing.

'She suggests a canopy over the bed where she can hang drapes. Oh, and the walls should be painted pink.'

'She is a diva then,' Harry exclaimed, taking the paper from him. 'But she is probably right. I'll sort what I can. I have a good budget to work with but not much time. They are keen to get this out soon.'

That night, Saeed tossed and turned; Maryam's words rang in his ears. He was about to send a message to the whole world. What should it say? At last, he fell asleep and dreamt about his old school. There was a large blackboard on the wall and he was writing endless equations on the board. Then the equations turned into chemical formulae. He woke suddenly.

'That's it!' he shouted. 'I will send a message to the world.'

61

Mari – with a great deal of help from Maryam at night – had finally mastered enough Arabic to get by. But now she had been moved on to the religious training and was finding it very hard. Maryam could offer little advice on this. Worse still, the food was not agreeing with her, and she felt nauseous a lot of the time. However hard she tried and however much she told them she wasn't feeling well, they still beat her if she got things wrong. She guessed what was going on with her body but didn't dare admit it to herself – never mind anyone else.

After a particularly hard day, she was pleased to see Maryam and hear all her news. Maryam herself had suspicions about Mari's condition.

'Mari, I have brought you a little present.' She reached into her robes and brought out a small but beautifully stitched rag doll in a bright yellow dress. Mari reached out to take it, then burst into tears.

'Thank you so much. It's beautiful. I will treasure it,' she said through her sobs.

'And it will make a lovely toy for the little one when it comes,' Maryam nodded.

'I don't know what you mean... how did you know?'

Maryam laughed. 'Two women living so closely together? It's not difficult to work out. Are you sure?'

'My period is late. But that could be all sorts of things. It's not fair. My first time... ' she began to cry.

'Poor girl,' Maryam hugged her. 'Maybe they will look more kindly on you if they know your condition?'

'Maybe.'

Mari slept that night with the doll tightly grasped to her chest. The next morning she kept it close to her by putting it in the pocket of the simple shift dress Maryam had made for her to wear under her burqa. She was feeling a little better and tried hard to concentrate on the lesson.

Suddenly the door flew open and the Mudhir walked in. 'Girl? I have good news for you. Selina has requested that I find you a husband. If you prove you have truly turned to Allah, then I will allow you to marry him. What do you say?'

Mari didn't know what to think. Could she trust Selina? Could the prison guards have been wrong about her? Maybe she knew how much Saeed loved her. It was possible.

She turned to face him. 'Yes, If it is Allah's will.'

The Mudhir turned round and beckoned to someone behind him. Mari was bursting with anticipation; it had been so long since she had last seen him. But it wasn't Saeed who came in. Instead, it was an old, obese man with a knotted beard. Mari couldn't hide her despair and disgust.

'But I thought... ' she began.

'This is Allah's will.' the Mudhir glared at her. 'You will show respect.'

'I can't marry him. I'm promised to Batal. I'm pregnant with his child!' she shouted.

Both men looked at her. The old man approached her and slapped her hard across the face.

'Then I will use you until you become too fat for me. After that, you will be thrown into prison with the other kaffirs.'

'So be it,' said the Mudhir, grabbing her arm. 'You will agree to marry him. Say it!' He shook her hard until she weakly gasped 'Yes.'

The man grabbed Mari by the arm and pulled her out of the classroom. He marched her out of the building, along the road to his house to the amusement of the people walking there.

'Have fun,' a man shouted.

Inside, he dragged her upstairs to the bedroom. Despite her fists, beating on his chest, he pulled off her burqa and tore off her dress and underwear until she was naked. She lay curled up on the bed, hiding the little doll amongst her clothes. He disrobed, revealing his aged body. Mari remembered Saeed's body. Young, firm, and beautiful. This man's was a travesty.

'You can't do this to me!' she screamed. 'It is rape!'

'Not at all,' the man said as he began to force himself on her. 'You are my wife. For now.'

'Saeed!' she cried in English as the man brutalised her. 'Save me, Saeed!'

210

When it was over, the man spat at her. 'Clean yourself up, whore. You must cook for me.'

Mari turned her head to the pillow, but she refused to cry.

62

Saeed had been formulating a plan. But first, he had to show Harry his script. If Harry rejected it, his plan would fail. He turned up at Harry's door as arranged and handed him the papers.

Harry snatched it and jumped on the sofa to read it. His expressions were of increasing delight. 'Wow! I had no idea you had so much passion in you, Saeed. You are already a babe magnet. Now they will be coming in their thousands just to see you and to listen to your sexy words.'

'It's not too strong, is it?' Saeed asked.

'Listen, buddy. I am not a girl, but even I'm interested. Let's shoot it and see how it looks. I can play around with it afterwards if necessary.' He looked at his watch. 'The carpenter has put something together for the set. How about a game or two while we're waiting?'

'Cool,' Saeed said, relieved at Harry's reaction.

The boys played a video game for a while until they heard a knock on the door. Saeed opened it to see the carpenter standing there with some long pieces of wood at his feet.

'Take him to your house, Batal; I will fetch the woman. The furnishings should be ready if she has done her job properly.'

Saeed took the carpenter back to his house and showed him the bedroom. The man nodded and put the wood down. After taking a few measurements, he began to construct a frame over the bed, making it look like a four-poster. He hadn't quite finished when Harry arrived with Maryam. She carried a large bag containing the drapes while Harry held his camera and tripod.

Maryam looked at the construction. 'The wall should be pink.'

'It wasn't possible to find pink paint here. You will have to make do,' Harry snapped.

Maryam turned to him but did not speak. Instead, she moved the small bedroom chair over to the bed and stood on it to arrange the wispy sheets of chiffon and silk around the frame.

'My word! It looks very Arabian Nights,' said Harry.

'Very nice,' Saeed added. 'Will it do?'

'Oh yes. Now you,' Harry pointed to the carpenter. 'Please escort this woman back to the factory.'

Maryam turned to him. 'What about the drapes?'

'Oh, I'm sure Batal can sort those out.' He looked over; Saeed nodded. He looked at Maryam, willing her to understand that he had taken heed of her words. She bowed her head and left with the carpenter.

While Saeed put up the new curtains, Harry quizzed him. 'Now, do you know your script?'

'I do.' And as he said it, Saeed felt his heart beating so fast he thought it would burst.

Harry nodded. 'Then we'll have a dry run.'

Saeed stared at the camera.

'Smile. You must smile.'

Saeed forced a smile and then began his speech. At just three minutes, there was a lot to get in. He talked of Mary, her exalted status in Islam and how girls could emulate her. He talked of marriage and happy families, and then he talked of how he had wasted his time at school learning unimportant things like maths and science. All that was really needed was a love of Allah, and for that, there was no place in the world like the caliphate.

'Nice,' Harry said. 'Now look sexy.'

'How do I do that?'

'I don't know. Raise your eyebrows a little. Tilt your head. Yes. Perfect.'

When they shot it for real, Saeed put in the passion. When he talked of his education, he held up sheets of paper bearing chemical formulae and he ripped them up very effectively in front of the camera before smouldering down the lens.

'Excellent,' Harry enthused 'That's a wrap. I'll come back to you if we need any more.'

'When is it being shown?' Saeed asked.

'Today. As soon as I say I am happy with it. There's no time to waste.'

When he had gone, all Saeed's tension was released and he fell back on his bed and wept.

63

Karen, who had never entirely dropped Mari and Saeed's case, finally had a lucky break. This time, it was a call from the CTC officer she had been liaising with.

'I've got something that might interest you,' he said.

'I'm coming over as soon as.' She checked in with Barry.

'If they're calling you, I'd say go. Any other progress?'

'Yes,' Karen said. 'Omar was beginning to pick up something on the imam's son. He's possibly the UK contact. And quite a big fish. I'm hoping the CTC have finally pinned him down,'

'Good luck,' Barry said, holding up crossed fingers. 'It would be a great morale boost to get these kids back.'

Karen didn't need telling twice. She was off like a shot, making her way to the CTC offices.

'OK. Whatcha got? ' she asked the officer.

'Quite a bit. Sit down, and I'll go through it.'

Karen sat, ears pricked. 'Go for it.'

'Firstly,' the man said, 'we're not getting as efficient help as we'd like from the Turkish police. It's a manpower and communications thing. They're perfectly cooperative but... '

'But you want me out there to liaise?' Karen's eyes were gleaming.

'Yeah. I'd support you going out. It may mean trudging through CCTV though.'

'I'm used to that,' Karen said. 'What about Nadeem Khan? Is he the recruiting sergeant?'

'We're getting closer. He's probably using aliases all over the place. Don't worry, we're watching him.'

'Good. Anything else?'

The man smiled at her. 'Oh, yes. Something really interesting. I think you'll like this.'

'What?' Karen leaned forward.

'It's a new film from your friends out there. We're still analysing it, but it shows Saeed Rahman very much alive and well and doing his bit for the caliphate. Bring your chair round this side of the desk and I'll play it.'

Karen moved the chair and watched, fascinated as the officer played the film.

'Shit. It's definitely him. What the fuck is this one about? It looks like he's about to seduce someone.'

They watched the video together, Karen's mouth falling open. 'Bloody hell. They must be desperate for women out there. Has this been shown anywhere yet?'

'Not widely. This is only hours old. It's from one of our sources but it won't be long.'

'I'll warn the family this time. I'll go there now.'

The officer remained silent. Karen took this as consent. 'Just one thing? Can you send me a copy? I'd like to have a better look myself. There's a lot going on in that and I know someone who might be able to see things in it that I can't.'

The officer raised an eyebrow.

'It's fine. He's one of us. Forensics.

'OK. But don't tell anyone I sent it to you.'

Karen looked around. 'Secrets here?' she laughed.

'And in return, promise you'll tell me anything you hear about it.' He picked up his mobile. 'The family might know more than you think. They might slip up. Any time, day or night.'

'And you'll do the same?'

'Maybe.'

'Maybe's not good enough. I outrank you,' Karen shot.

'Not here you don't. Listen. This is just one case to you, we have hundreds. You can't possibly know what repercussions there might be. '

'OK, OK,' Karen interrupted. 'Deal.'

'What's your number? I'll send it now.'

***

Karen made straight for the Rahman's house. Maria let her in and to her surprise, Sinéad was there too.

'I thought we should be together at a time like this,' Maria explained. 'Connection or not, we both have missing children.'

215

'Is your husband here?'

'No. He is away on business.' Maria looked a little shifty, Karen wasn't falling for it. Why would he go away at a time like this?

In her most commanding voice, she spoke. 'Where has he gone, Mrs Rahman?'

Maria was in no mood or shape to defy Karen. She spilled. 'He's gone to Pakistan. Saeed's cousin Ahmed went with Saeed to wherever they went. But Ahmed has been murdered. His father wants to find the killer and my husband has vowed to help him. They are going to go to Iraq together to find Saeed.'

Karen sighed. 'I understand, of course. But I can't say that it's the right thing to do. When did he go?'

'Two weeks ago.'

Karen shook her head sadly. 'And you couldn't persuade them not to go?'

'There was no point. Why did you come here? Do you have any news? If you can't help us, what do you expect us to do?'

Karen conceded that there was no answer to the last part of the question. 'Do you have recent photos of them? We can keep a look out.'

Maria looked around. Her eyes fell on a framed photo of the two families. 'It was a while ago, but Ibra and Jafar haven't changed that much. Except for their thinning hair and growing bellies.'

Karen snapped the photo on her phone. 'Mrs Rahman, the reason I came to see you today is that I wanted to warn you. Saeed has made another video. I thought you should know before others tell you about it.'

Maria shook her head. Sinéad looked angry. 'What about Mari? What are you doing about her?'

Karen couldn't answer her honestly. 'We're doing all we can,' she said.

'You keep saying that. But it's been weeks now and you're no closer than you were when she first went missing. You're useless, you lot.'

'What is this video?' Maria asked.

'It's just Saeed this time. He's encouraging girls to go out there.'

216

Maria shook her head. 'There is no hope for him, is there?'

'I can't say,' Karen said. 'The footage is only days old. So at least we know he's still alive.'

Maria answered for her. 'But for how long, Sergeant? Please, Sergeant Thorpe, please find him and bring him back.'

Karen didn't answer; there was nothing she could say except 'Goodnight, Mrs Rahman, Mrs Lone. I'll let you know as soon as we have any news.'

64

Karen went home that night frustrated and angry. Sinéad's words had hit home. She did feel useless. John was waiting for her as usual but she was not in the mood for chatting. John, used to her moods, cooked for the two of them while she sat at her desk going through her laptop.

Suddenly, she called him over. 'John? You're good at maths. Come and look at this.'

Pausing to place their plates in the oven to keep warm, John went over. 'What am I looking at?'

'Well, it's just a long shot, but could this be some sort of message?'

Karen had frozen the screen at the point Saeed was showing sheets of what he called his *homework*. John peered closer.

'Strange. That's not how you'd formulate that.'

'What?'

'Yes. I think it *is* something. Give me some paper.'

Karen grabbed her notebook and tore out a page, handing him a pen from her bag. 'What is it?' she pressed.

'It's the oddest chemical formulae I've ever seen. They're not represented by the first letter.'

'What are the chemicals?' Karen asked.

Magnesium, Argon, Radium, Iridium,' he said.

Karen frowned, thinking it through. 'M.A.R.I. Mari! She squealed. 'It *is* a message. What else? What about the sums?'

'Thirty-five point nine five,' John wrote down the number. 'And thirty-nine point zero-one-six seven. How odd. No, not odd. Coordinates?'

'What? Like on a map?'

'Maybe. But there's no direction. Let me look again.' He peered at the screen. 'Look, there's a tiny arrow there. North? I can't see the rest; it's too indistinct. Can I use your laptop?'

'Of course. Go ahead.' Karen got up while John took her place and started typing.

'Well. This looks likely. Not good though, from what I know.'

'Where?' Karen was almost bursting with excitement.

'He's in Raqqa.'

'Oh shit!' said Karen. 'Syria? That is going to be hard.'

'I'd better ring... ' she stopped herself.

John looked up. 'Who?'

'What?'

'Who? You said you had to ring someone.'

'Oh, yes. The guy at the CTC. I'll ring now and see if I can catch him. Thanks, John.' She kissed him on the cheek.

'No!' he ordered. 'There's a perfectly good lasagne there and it's getting cold. '

'You're so masterful,' Karen teased, but she was hungry, and she agreed a few minutes wouldn't make much difference.

She ate in rapid time, washing her food down with her usual wine. 'Fab,' she said, still swallowing as she picked up the phone and rang the CTC officer. 'He's sent a message.'

'We know. He and the girl are in Raqqa.'

Karen was furious both that they had worked it out and that they hadn't told her. 'You said you would tell me.'

'Hold your horses, I was just about to.'

'Oh. Thanks then.'

'What about the other message?'

'What message?' Karen's mind was whirring furiously.

'He outed the imam's son.'

'What? Where? Can you haul him in?'

'No. But it's enough to up surveillance on him. Oh, and about your trip.'

'Yes?'

'We're compiling a list of everyone we think went out there. Dates, faces etc. The Turkish police don't want to get involved with tracing Brits, but they're cooperating. They're allowing us to use their systems. When you get out there, we want you to run through the list.'

Karen clicked off the phone and went back to her laptop. She re-ran the footage twice and then realised she had heard the word imam. 'John, look at this?'

She wrote down the script, and sure enough, if you took every third word. See your imam, daughter, and son. You must hate the infidel. Preacher not teacher knows best.

'You get: Imam Son Hate Preacher. John? He's pointing the finger at the imam's son. So they are really on the ball. John?' she turned to look at him, but he had nodded off on the sofa. She rubbed her hands together and picked up the phone again.

'Gary? It's Karen,' she whispered. 'They're in Raqqa. There's a new video. He sent a message.'

'And it's recent?'

'They're certain it was done in the last 36 hours.'

'That's good news,' Gary replied.

'What? Is it? I thought that was the stronghold.'

'It's central. A real location. Much better than somewhere out in the bloody desert or a cave.'

'Oh,' Karen cheered up. 'That's good then.'

Karen remembered her news. 'But there may be another complication. I don't know if it's relevant. Saeed's father has flown out to join his brother. They're in Iraq to try to get him back. This afternoon, I thought Saeed was done for. But if he's really trying to finger them, well, maybe we should try. But we can't let these men get into trouble.'

'Send me full details of both of them. I'll try to head them off; they won't know where the kids are yet, it'll be guesswork on their part.'

'OK. I've got photos of them both, and I'll dig out the rest. And there's more good news. I'm officially working with the CTC. They're sorting out my trip to Turkey. I'll let you know.'

'We'll be in touch,' Gary said.

65

18th March

The whole office seemed to be gossiping about the latest race storm when Karen arrived the next morning. She walked past desk after desk covered with freebie newspapers opened at a page showing a photo of a black man under the heading **EX SAS SOLDIER LOSES FIGHT FOR EQUALITY.**

'I thought the army was getting better,' Karen said as she walked to her desk.

'May I?' she grabbed the paper from Omar as she walked past and sped-read the article out loud. '...his parents, who are devout Muslims, haven't heard from him for weeks and are worried that he may be seeking work as a mercenary.'

'That's terrible,' Omar said. 'And typical.'

'That'll keep the army busy then. But it's not our field. Can we get back to finding criminals and missing children, please?'

Karen sat at her desk, but something was chiming in the back of her brain somewhere. Shrugging it off, she called in to see Barry.

'Mari Lone. We're pretty sure she went to Turkey and then on to Raqqa. The police out there are meant to be on the case, but we're not getting very far and her family are getting anxious. Saeed Rahman's almost certainly in Raqqa too. We'd thought that he'd become one of the bad guys, but it seems like he's trying to help us from the other side. He's in the thick of it, but if we can get him out, we should.'

'And how do we do that?' Barry asked.

'The CTC want someone out there, in Turkey. There's a woman there operating across the Turkish border with Syria. They think she's the escort taking our kids from Britain to Turkey and then on to Syria. It's probably how Mari got there. They want someone to help track down this woman. It might not help Mari but it might stop others. I was wondering... '

'Let me guess. You want to go out to Turkey to be the liaison person.'

Karen's mouth fell open. 'How did you know?'

'DCI Winter did brief me about you, Karen. I'm only surprised that it took so long for you to ask.'

Karen grinned at him. 'I won't go until I'm sure I can achieve something, I promise.'

'So when is that?'

'Next week, I suspect.'

'I shall keep it under review. If I think we can help, I'll authorise it.'

'Thanks, Barry.' Karen got up to leave.

'Just one more thing,' Barry said.

'OK?' Karen was curious.

'What's all the chat about out there? Anything to do with your case?'

'No,' Karen replied. 'At least, I don't think so,' she hesitated. 'But it might be. It's a racial equality case. There's an ex-soldier, he took them to court for race discrimination.'

'And how could that have anything to do with our case?' Barry asked.

Karen shrugged. 'I don't know. It's just a feeling I've got.'

Barry looked perplexed as Karen left his office muttering, 'SAS.'

***

Ex-SAS Officer Joe Malik, who was sitting in a bar with Gary, was also looking at his picture in the paper. 'That's a pin-up face if ever I saw,' he said admiringly.

'I'd pin it up with arrows on a dartboard any day,' Gary shot back.

'I'm flying out to Baghdad tomorrow,' Joe replied. 'Do your bit, you bastard. I want a fucking welcoming committee.'

'I will,' Gary grinned. 'You won't be disappointed. Tom and I have been very busy. The story's getting out everywhere.'

'Tell me more,' Joe smiled back.

'I'll tell you that the Middle Eastern network is in overdrive. All over Iraq and Syria, we've got reports of an ex-SAS soldier looking for paid work and there are rumours that he's willing to bring others with him.'

'So I'm going to be in demand?' Joe grinned. 'I like the sound of that.'

'Yes, and with one man in particular. the Mudhir. He's the not-so-big cheese in the council in Raqqa. Thinks he's a big fish but he's small fry. He does hold the purse strings though, so the military will want him on board. Nasty piece of work by all accounts.'

'And how do I get to him?'

'You don't. You play it cool. Unless we've screwed up, you'll be contacted within twenty-four hours of getting off the plane. So you stroll around, smiling at everyone and let the bastards guess who you are and what you want.'

'Sounds good to me. What about here? I don't want to be pestered by the red-tops. Have you called the dogs off?'

'I have. They know nothing except that I'll cut off their bollocks if they try to get to you.'

'And the women?' Joe laughed. 'They've got bigger bollocks than the men these days.'

'They're the more sensible ones. They've asked for the real story when it's all over. Now, drink up. Haven't you got some packing to do?'

***

In Raqqa, the Mudhir's team had been thorough. They had not only heard the rumours about Joe Malik; they had thoroughly investigated them, and their sources all confirmed what the newspaper article didn't say but had hinted at. They had told him as much.

The Mudhir rang the military commander, who had also heard the rumours. 'What value would a man like that have to us?' he asked.

'Incalculable. If nothing else, we could torture him for his secrets. But as a fighting force, as you know, the S.A.S. is often considered the best in the world. With someone like that who could navigate security, we might even take out a big target. He'll know Americans and how they operate. Imagine what we could do if we took out one of their generals.'

The Mudhir stroked his bearded chin. 'What do we know about him? From the beginning, please.'

'He was a highly decorated soldier. But he was passed over when a promotion came up and it was given to a white man with lesser experience. He was taking them to court for millions. There was a very public spat with his unit. Actually, it was not that public originally. We had to search hard to find it. But more recently, a journalist from the British Press found out and published the story in all the media.'

'So he's the genuine article?'

'Oh, most definitely.'

'And do we know where he is?'

'No. Not yet. But we do know that he is seeking work in the region. We also know that we are not the only ones looking to acquire his services.'

'Then let it be known we will pay the best price.'

'I will.'

66

19th March

Joe arrived in Baghdad in the early afternoon. He'd planned well and was looking through his old contacts. There was one in particular: the leader of a small rebel group he had worked alongside years before. The man was no longer active but kept his ear to the ground. Joe had arranged to meet him in a coffee shop. He ordered food while he was waiting. Then the small, wrinkled man appeared and joined him at the table.

'So, my friend, you have cut off your wings, I hear.'

'Yeah. What's it to you?'

'And you are looking for gainful employment.'

'Your lot can't afford me.'

'My lot, as you say, are almost all retired. We are trying to live a comfortable life if we can. But there is so much trouble still around us.'

'Who will pay then, old man?' Joe smiled. 'Who's got the big bucks? I've got a hot troop of men and we're looking to make some serious moola.'

'Maybe you can get the most from Daesh, but they might also make you part company with your head.'

Joe laughed. 'They wouldn't. But I'm curious about how they operate. I have sympathy with what they're trying to achieve.'

'You are Muslim?' Joe nodded. 'How did I not know this?'

'Because we had a different enemy and a different cause last time. We were deposing a tyrant and look what we did. We destroyed a country. Maybe I owe it to them to help build a new one.'

'I see your point. And how do you propose to join them?'

'I'm expecting them to find me.'

The man laughed. 'Your arrogance knows no bounds. But you are probably right. If someone as lowly as I know you here, they certainly will and they have been struggling of late. They are building up for a new offensive. Military skill like yours is beyond price. Head for Qa'im. They will pick you up before you have time to scratch your arse.'

'Thank you, old man.'

'And you be careful. They are not like we were. They do not believe in mercy except that which comes with death.'

'I understand.'

Joe hired an old jeep and drove to Qa'im. It was a boring and uneventful four-hour drive but as he approached the town, he saw two fighters waiting in a truck by the side of the road. He was not wrong in supposing his former friend, who was well respected in the region, had tipped them off. He also knew that his friend would have gained assurances about his safety. He pulled up and waited for them to reach him.

'Small welcoming party,' Joe observed as the men got out and approached him. 'How did you recognise me?' He grinned broadly.

'Small army of one?' The man spat on the ground. 'We heard there were more.'

'Oh, I'm not going to display all my wares at once. Not until there's some understanding. But I'm not hanging around if there's nothing on offer.' He made a move to go back to his jeep.

'Stop,' the other man said. 'Come with us. You can talk business in Raqqa. Leave your car; you will need it to return and pick up your army tomorrow. Come with us now.'

They passed over the border to Syria without incident. After another four-hour drive, they reached Raqqa. It was gone eleven, local time.

'Big man, we will talk tomorrow. Tonight you rest. We have a nice hotel where you can stay. You want female company? Yes?'

'Is this your famous hospitality?' Joe asked with a knowing smile. 'A man can get lonely away from home and my team would sure like confirmation of what comforts there will be out here.'

'Of course. Follow me and we will see what we can do.'

Joe chose his words carefully. This just might be an opportunity to find the girl quickly, he thought. She's bound to be in some sort of captivity. 'I like them pale,' he elaborated as they walked.

'Our recruitment drive is not yet complete. But there is one who might find favour in your eyes.'

Joe was taken to a room in the prison building. It wasn't quite as bad as the cells but it was basic. Inside, several girls with empty eyes, most wearing grubby-looking clothes, were sitting on shabby sofas and chairs. Joe scanned the faces; all were uncovered. His eyes fell upon one with fairer skin than the others. She looked right at him with anger and he saw Wolf's eyes looking back at him. 'That one,' he said.

'I will bring her to you shortly. Now I will take you to your hotel.'

Joe was escorted to the hotel where there were good facilities. It seemed that the regime was trying to keep some semblance of civilisation. Along with generously sized twin beds, he noted a comfortable sofa laden with several cushions in his room and a large bathroom with a bath and walk-in shower. He made good use of the shower to wash off the dust of the day's travel.

He changed into light clothes and then went downstairs to the restaurant where he was given a passable meal. He noted that most of the other occupants, judging by their attire, were fighters. Some sat with women, their wives, he assumed. They looked suspiciously at him and after eating, he didn't hang around. Instead, he went to the reception area and told the man at the desk he was expecting company. 'I'll be in my room.'

When the knock came at the door, he opened it to reveal the girl dressed in a burqa. He couldn't see her face but he sensed it was Mari.

'Thank you,' he said to the concierge as he pulled Mari into the room.

Now he had a serious dilemma. If he revealed his mission, he might give the game away but he was so upset by her appearance that his heart wanted to give her hope. He decided he would give her that in another way.

He spoke to her in English. 'Don't worry, girl. I'm too tired now to take advantage. Have you eaten?'

'You must say that I satisfied you or they'll beat me,' she said angrily.

'I will say that. I have a daughter your age. '

'Why are you here? You don't look Arabic.'

'That's a long story. But I'm a soldier. Enough now. Are you hungry?'

Mari visibly relaxed. She nodded. 'Yes. Please, I am very hungry.'

'I'll get you something. Can I trust you to stay here?'

'Yes. The hotel is well-monitored. I can't escape.'

'So you've been here before?'

'Yes. They married me, but the man they gave me to wasn't happy. I couldn't read the Quran to him well enough. So now I am here to serve the men I am told to.'

Joe almost felt a tear coming, so he made for the door. 'I'll get you something.' He went downstairs to the restaurant, his mind racing.

Could he get her out here? No, the security was tight. Could he ask to take her with him? That would be too weird.

What about marrying her? Maybe. But not now. Drop hints? Set the scene. Yes, that might work.

He returned with a large plate of fried chicken which Mari ate hungrily.

'You take the bed,' he told her. 'I'll be fine on the sofa.'

Mari took off the burqa and pulled back the sheets.

'What's with the toy?' He had noticed the little doll dressed in yellow tucked into a pocket of her dress.

'My friend made it for me. She says it will keep me safe.'

Joe smiled at her. 'That's good. Sleep well, Mari.'

'How did you know my name?'

'I guessed.'

67

20th March

Mari and Joe were woken by a knock on the door. Joe jumped off the sofa and put on the courtesy dressing gown. He threw the cushions back into place as he talked. 'I'm sorry. I think they're here for you.'

'I know,' Mari nodded. 'But thank you for last night. I feel much better for it.'

The knocking began again. Joe opened the door for the guard to come in and collect Mari.

'Well?' he asked.

'Good,' Joe nodded as she was taken away.

After a good breakfast, he was approached by another guard in the reception of the hotel. 'You must come with me,' the man said.

Joe was taken straight to the council chambers where the Mudhir and the military commander were waiting for him. They sat at a round table.

'I hope your entertainment was satisfactory,' the Mudhir began. 'That one has not been popular.'

Joe grunted in response.

He was offered a drink then they got down to negotiations.

Joe pitched high. 'Two million for me and one each for my men.'

He was met with disbelief from the commander. 'A million dollars for each of your men and two for you? That is greedy.'

'It's chicken feed to you and think what you'll gain.'

'Do you have current intelligence of your unit?'

'Hell, yes. The formal routes have been severed of course, but some things don't change. Besides, it's more our skills you need. I was thinking more of training. Getting your boys into shape.'

The military commander nodded his head furiously. He looked at the Mudhir. 'We need that training,' he agreed. 'The fighters we buy are expendable. But properly trained soldiers are worth their weight in gold.'

'I think not that much,' the Mudhir interjected. Let us settle on something more reasonable.'

Joe fought a hard bargain but tactically agreed to a small reduction. 'Five mill in total for me to divide up.'

There was a long pause. Joe looked suitably adamant.

'We have a deal,' the Mudhir nodded.

'When will you return with your unit?' the commander asked.

Joe looked thoughtful. 'I'll come back with my second in command. Then we will start talking logistics. When we are all agreed, you will pay us the money and we will return for our troops.'

'We will pay you only when you are all here.'

'Then we will not come,' Joe bluffed.

It was the Mudhir's turn to think. He was under clear instructions to secure this deal. 'As long as either you or your second in command remain in Raqqa, that will be acceptable.'

Joe stood up, grinning broadly. 'Nice doing business with you. Where's my taxi home?' he joked.

'I will send for him.'

'Just one thing.'

'Yes?'

'The girl. I might want her again. Throw her in too.'

The Mudhir looked at him for longer than Joe was comfortable with before replying. 'We have other plans for her but I will think about it.'

'What plans?'

Joe had gone too far; the Mudhir was getting either suspicious or irritated. 'I suggest you concentrate on getting your men together.'

'Of course. Nothing else matters as much as that.'

***

After what seemed like days rather than hours, Joe arrived back in Baghdad and made straight for his hotel. Ali was waiting for him in reception. When they were sure they were alone, they talked.

'Great to see you. It's going really well. I've seen the girl; poor kid. Doesn't know what's hit her. But she's used on approval, and I've said I'd like her again, so there's our chance.'

'That is very good news,' Ali replied. 'So when do we head out?'

'Day after tomorrow, maybe the day after. We may need to accumulate a team here, just for show. They're watching us closely, especially my old mate. Is Turkey sorted?'

'Yes. My cousin is looking out for this policewoman. He will make sure she has a free hand with the records she wants to see. Remind me why we need her?'

'We don't. We just don't want her getting in the way. Gary says she thinks she might be useful, that's all.'

'Ah,' Ali nodded.

'Any sight of the boy's father and uncle?'

'No. No chance to look around. Do we have descriptions? We can look out for them when we go back.'

'I'll see what I can do.'

While Ali settled in their room, Joe rang Tom to update him about Mari and ask what they had on the two men.

'I want to come there to track them myself. I think they've probably followed the boy's route from Erbil,' Tom said.

'And the policewoman?' Joe asked.

'Coming out with me tomorrow,' Tom said. 'Gary wants a word,'

'You have no idea how much all this means to me, Joe,' Gary said. 'You know what those bastards could do to you if they get you. You do me proud. I only wish I could be with you.'

'We'll be fine, Gaz. You take it easy. You can write my obituary if you like. But make it spectacular!'

Joe waited for Gary's hearty laugh, then put the phone down and turned to Ali.

'You probably heard that. No sign of the boy, but we're not so bothered about him. It's the girl we've got to concentrate on.'

'Wolf saved my life once,' Ali replied. 'I owe it to him to do what I can.'

'He was an exceptional bloke.' Joe agreed. 'One of the best.'

68

Maria Rahman was very unhappy. Already frantic about Saeed's disappearance, her husband Ibrahim was now somewhere in Iraq with his brother Rafar, and neither of them had been in touch for days. She found some solace in the mosque by praying for their safe return.

When the imam was free of his duties, he sought her out. They walked outside and talked together. 'Tell me, Maria. What news do you have of Ibrahim and Saeed?'

'Still none,' Maria replied. 'It has been a few days since he last rang me. And I miss Saeed terribly. It is an awful thing to lose a son to these terrible creatures.'

The imam didn't respond. Maria looked at him. 'How is your son? Such a lovely boy.' She noticed the sadness in the man's eyes. 'Is something wrong?'

'I am very worried about him,' the imam replied.

Maria was shocked. 'How so?'

'Because I have been hearing rumours about him recently. I think he may have been mixing with the wrong sort.'

'Oh my goodness. What do you mean?'

'I could not believe it. But last night, I heard him.'

'What was he doing?'

'He was talking to someone on his laptop. He was talking about bringing killing to the streets of London. And he said that he was going out to join the caliphate.'

'What? What did you do?'

'I challenged him, of course. He laughed in my face. And this morning, when I woke, he had already gone. I don't know what to do.'

'You must tell the police,' Maria said. 'Suppose he was helping to plan an attack?' The imam hesitated. 'What's wrong? Has something happened?'

He sighed. 'The police have already been asking me questions about him. I have been trying to pretend it couldn't happen. But I could not live with myself if he has brought harm to anyone. You are right, Maria; I will ring them now.'

***

Karen took Gary's call with glee. John's ears pricked up at the unusual sound of happiness in her voice.

'OK, what's going on?'

'That was your uncle Gary.' Karen paused, needing time to think her answer through.

'And why is he ringing you?'

'You know I'm going to Turkey, right?'

John got closer and looked her in the eyes. 'Yes, but that's for a short liaison role with the authorities to help identify the escort. Mainly looking through CCTV, you said.'

'Yes. With the CTC.'

'And what's that got to do with my uncle?'

Karen chose her words carefully. She knew that Gary's pal had found the girl, but she didn't want to arouse John's suspicions. 'Well, he knows someone who's sort of going there too. And he might help look for the missing girl, Mari.'

'Not to Raqqa!' John's mouth remained open.

'I'm only going to Adana. No one will let me go further than that.'

'What do you mean no one?' John asked suspiciously.

'The force, silly. And the CTC. I'm working very closely with them now.'

'What about the imam's son? Have they got anything on him yet?'

'Not quite, but they're building up a picture.'

'When are you meant to be going then?'

Karen didn't answer.

'Karen...'

'Tomorrow. It's only for a few days. Less still if we make good progress.'

John went silent.

'John?'

'Karen, you have a way of getting in trouble wherever you go. Now you tell me you're walking into the arms of terrorists?'

Karen frowned. 'Of course not. I'll stay at the base. I don't know my way around. I'll be at the police station and the hotel. That's all.'

John turned away. He spoke quietly. 'I don't believe you.'

'What did you say? Now you're being stupid, John.'

John snapped. 'Do as you bloody well want. You always do anyway.'

He swore. Karen knew John was especially angry if he swore. She'd almost hoped he would offer to come with her; he had before. But last time he had taken a holiday. This was no beach resort.

They went to bed, not talking to each other.

69

21st March

Karen woke up to a space next to her. John had already gone to work. *He must be sulking,* she thought as she looked at her watch. *He never gets up that early. Still, he'll be pleased to see me when I'm back.*

Her mind swiftly returned to her travels. She was far too anxious about the flight, packing, and making sure she had everything she needed, to dwell on him.

She double-checked her schedule, tickets and, most importantly, directions. She was a nervous flyer, having only flown abroad once before, and that time, she had John to hang on to. She travelled light, with one small suitcase. She took a taxi to the train station and then got on the tube. But when she got off, she was horrified at how large the airport was compared to the one she'd been to before. She navigated her way to the check-in, went through security and even managed to find a seat in the café where she treated herself to an espresso.

When she'd had her first sip, she rang Gary for an update.

'Ali has confirmed his cousin knows you are going there. He's up to speed with our operation, your police, and the police in Turkey. He'll approach you if and when he can. Just make sure you don't say the wrong thing to the wrong people.'

'As if!' Karen laughed.

When the flight was called, the nerves took over and she had to run to the nearest Ladies. But once she was on the flight, and plugged into earphones, she began to relax a little. That's when she began to think about home. She was tough, she knew that, but she was hurt. She had become so used to John supporting her without question that when he turned his back on her, it stung her deeply. She was even feeling quite nauseous. He'd had plenty of time to think about what he'd done. He could have contacted her before she got on the plane. Was he not bothered about her at all? Or maybe he was just busy. Karen had to admit that she always was.

When the plane took off, she had something to distract her. She pulled down her messenger bag and began to read through her notes. This was more like it. Her role was clear: to find this woman who seemed to have escorted people out of the country. And hopefully, Gary and his friends would find Mari too. At the least, they might persuade the woman to reveal the route and that would help them stop others from going.

**

Nadeem had been spooked by Saeed's video. He had watched it over and over again and although he didn't quite catch on to what Saeed had done, he was sure that he had been dropped in it somehow.

He had also developed the feeling that he was being watched. There had been noise on his phone lines, even people disappearing out of view when he walked down the road.

Then his father had come home early and caught him talking to the Mudhir on Skype. He'd joked about it, laughed it off. But his father had begun to ask him some serious questions. It was the final straw.

He'd always expected to travel to Raqqa, but not quite so quickly. But when he raised the alarm with his contact, the arrangements were made that very night and a ticket was emailed to him. He'd acquired a false passport many months ago. He had no luggage to worry about. Everything he needed was packed in his rucksack, which he took on the plane. He was looking forward to a whole new life.

He didn't notice the young woman with dark, cropped hair and eyes closed tight. He walked to his seat at the back and sat down. Above everything else, he was excited; this was the greatest adventure of his life. He thought of his father. The man he had once loved and looked up to had now been revealed to him as pathetic. He'd begun to despise his father's wishy-washy ideas and his so-called community spirit.

He dreamed ahead of the time to come when his father would come to respect him when he realised what he, Nadeem, had been part of. He almost heard his father's words. *I'm sorry I doubted you, son. I can see now that you have taken part in something wonderful. The creation of a whole new world.*

Yes, it would start with the caliphate but soon it would be oh so much bigger than that...

***

As the plane began its descent, Karen gathered her things together. When it landed, she found herself trapped behind some slowcoaches seemingly determined to stop her from getting off the plane. The other lane seemed to be moving at a cracking pace.

When she was off the plane and in the queue for passport control, she was irritated. There seemed to be people everywhere, bustling around and so many people in front of her in the queue. Surely they knew she was coming, why did she have to wait?

She tried to go to the front to talk to someone but was rudely pushed back by others already queuing. Then she found she'd lost her place but she elbowed herself back in and waved her ID in the face of the man trying to edge her out. 'Police,' she said, just to make sure he understood.

The queue seemed to take ages and as it moved around the belt barriers, Karen looked longingly at the desks of the passport officers. As the queue shuffled round, Karen had different views of the other passengers ahead. One of them, a young man, was looking around furtively. She squinted; she knew that face. Who was it? *Nadeem!* She began climbing under the belts and pushing her way through. But as fast as she went, and she met a great deal of confused obstruction, he was faster. Someone was waving him through to the front of the queue for local travellers.

Aware of the commotion behind him, Nadeem began to run. Ahead of him, a woman whom Karen recognised from the CCTV images as Fatima was beckoning to him from the barriers.

That's her! Karen made it through the queue but security officers intervened. They held her back at the desk. She still had her ID in her hand but they didn't seem interested.

'Get that man!' she shouted, trying to wrestle herself from their grasp. 'Terrorist!' she yelled as if that would help.

Startled, they let go of her. Karen hurtled towards Nadeem and Fatima but Nadeem was too far ahead. He bolted through the gates and outside of the airport.

Karen lunged towards Fatima and managed to grab her. 'Take her!' she yelled at the security guards and as they seized the woman, Karen charged out of the exit, coming to an abrupt stop. There was no sign of Nadeem. He had disappeared.

Karen went back inside, where the security men were reluctantly still holding on to Fatima. 'Call the police!' She ordered. She followed their gaze to where a stout, well-dressed Turkish man was approaching.

'Good afternoon, Sergeant Thorpe,' he said. 'Pasha Kalmati,' he held out his hand. 'I was told you would make an entrance.'

Karen smiled at him and shook his hand. 'This woman, I believe, is responsible for escorting kids out of England. I caught her meeting Nadeem Khan, one of our suspects. He got away but she can tell you where he's gone.'

Fatima began struggling against her captors and was handcuffed in return.

Pasha addressed Karen again. 'We have booked you a room at the airport hotel. Take any taxi; I'll see you when I've dealt with this woman. Meet me at the police station.'

70

Karen checked into the hotel and unpacked. She fastened the clasp of her Swiss army knife to the belt on her jeans and covered it with a loose-fitting top. A quick face wash with a wet wipe later, she was ready. She looked at her phone, checked her WIFI settings, then looked at her messages. There was a note from Macy – reminding her about their get-together the following week – but nothing from John. 'Miserable git,' she muttered. *Or busy*, she decided. She picked up her messenger bag containing her precious laptop and made her way to the police station.

'Sergeant Thorpe. Metropolitan police,' she showed her ID to the first officer she saw.

The officer smiled back. 'Nice to meet you. We have great respect for our colleagues in London. I have arranged for you to look at our camera footage. But first, I believe you want to speak to Officer Kalmati regarding the incident at the airport.'

'Yes, please.'

He called to a man standing nearby. 'Take Sergeant Thorpe to the interrogation suite.'

Karen was led down the corridor and ushered into a viewing room where Pasha was waiting for her.

'Welcome to our humble station. May I get you something to drink?'

She noticed a jug of water and glasses on the table. 'A glass of water would be fine.'

Pasha poured her a glass. She hadn't realised how thirsty she was until she drank it.

'Have you found out anything?'

'We had an officer in a car trying to follow the boy but it was too late. He must have had backup plans. The woman is not cooperating. We are certain that the route goes up to the Syrian border, but it is long. We need to find where the rogue guards that take bribes to let them through are. Until then, there is little we can do.'

'So Nadeem's got away then?'

Pasha looked at his watch. 'By now, he will already be well on his way, if not already across the border with Syria. My guess is that he is heading to Raqqa. That is dangerous territory, even for armed policemen. We cannot cross the border; our only hope here is, as I say, to shut down the crossing. But even then, more guards will be bribed, and more openings will emerge. It is a long and thankless task.'

'At least we've disrupted their escort,' Karen said.

'Yes, we have caused them mild inconvenience. And she will be jailed whether she cooperates or not. But they will not care. There will be new ones ready to take her place.'

Karen thought for a moment. 'If there's nothing else I can do, I should get going on the list of possibly trafficked youngsters.'

'Indeed. Come.' Pasha took her out of the interview room and into another full of computers with screens. 'We will need evidence of the trafficking of people for her to be charged and tried. Visual evidence of her on-screen corroborated by a British police officer will be most helpful.'

'Good. I'll need to make a call and connect this.' She indicated her laptop.

'Of course. I can do that.'

Karen sighed. Now she was there; it was an office like any other. She had hoped for something more exotic. She knew it all had to be done, but she'd become used to Macy, and more recently Omar, doing the screen work.

Pasha connected her laptop and then showed her around the equipment. When the laptop fired up, she found a large file waiting for her in her inbox.

'Whoa! That's quite a list.'

Pasha looked over her shoulder. 'It certainly is.'

'I'd better start with the 'A's. 4 July 2013,' she read. 'Mo Ahmed. Let's see if we can find you then.' She began to search the footage.

When the day drew to a close, Pasha came in to see how Karen had been getting on.

'I've found a few. It's enough to convict the woman. And the girl I'm looking for, Mari, is one of them. But I have another problem now.'

'Tell me.'

'The boy who lured her out there. His father and uncle have gone to Iraq to find him. His mother is especially worried about her husband. I really should be doing something.'

Pasha nodded. 'I believe Tom is on their trail, but they did not go to Erbil apparently.'

Karen looked at him in astonishment 'Tom? I thought it was Gary?'

'No, definitely not. Gary is managing things from London. Only the younger ones with recent experience have left London. That's Tom, Joe, and my cousin Ali. ' Pasha stopped talking. Karen was grinning at him. 'You didn't know this, did you?'

'I had an inkling.' Karen nodded. 'I knew Ali had a cousin here. But not that he..., you, were a police officer. Tom and Joe, I know nothing about.'

'They make a good team,' Pasha said.

'So where am I going to be of most use now? Not Erbil, clearly.'

'Sergeant Thorpe. There is no place in the world less safe than Erbil for a Western woman. It is good that there is no reason for you to go.'

'Where does Tom think they are then?'

'Baghdad. Tom thinks that's where they flew to.'

'Surely I can help check the records just like I'm doing here? You must have contacts; can't you sort it for me?'

'I will see what I can do. Go to your hotel room. You must be hungry. I'll come over this evening to talk to you.'

***

When Karen had gone, Pasha rang Ali on a group call. 'Your policewoman is here. She's started work but she wants to be involved. She's talking about going to Baghdad.'

'I told her no,' Gary said.

'Baghdad's safe enough,' Tom said. 'If I had to go through all those records it would drive me nuts. Anyway, if we can get her there as a cop tracing Brits, that's official and the security out there is mainly British operated. She'd be safe enough.'

'What does Joe think?' Gary asked.

Tom handed the phone to Joe. 'I say bring her here. I've got enough pals around to look out for her. And if she puts a step outside the airport area, well, let's say it'll be covered.'

'Ali?' Joe looked at Ali; he nodded.'

'Ali's cool with it. It will help save shitloads of time if we know they came through Baghdad. We've got people here who'll know where they went from there.'

'Put Tom back on.'

'It looks like flights were cancelled from Islamabad to Erbil for a few days, so if we've got them definitely in, we can see if they flew out again. It cuts down the routes they could use.'

'OK. My nephew will probably kill me. Tom, get Joe to get her safe accommodation and call Pasha whatsit. Get her on the next plane over. If she's going to help, it's now or never.'

'On it,' said Tom. And before Karen even had a chance to put her head down for a nap, she found herself being put on a flight to Baghdad.

71

Saeed and Harry were playing a video game when they heard the front door being opened and slammed shut. the Mudhir himself came storming in. Harry was able to switch the screen before he entered the studio.

'Sir.' Harry nodded his head. 'How can we help?'

'We have a new film to be made,' the Mudhir answered. 'The Western brigade has made a significant capture of fifty prisoners and we want to tell the world about it.'

'That sounds like we need an epic production. Something much bigger than we've ever done before.'

'Do what you have to. Come to me when you have your ideas. This must be the best thing you have ever done. The whole world will have to take notice of this. We will make the other armies quake in their boots. You must make us invincible.'

'That will be an honour,' Harry replied. 'We'll start on it straight away. Are you going to behead any?'

'All of them. This will be a mass execution,' the Mudhir said as he turned away to leave.

'Shit,' said Harry when he had gone. 'That is going to take some organisation.'

Saeed shuddered. But despite his horror at the thought of it, he was interested in the filming. 'Tell me what's involved.'

'It's all about the visuals. You can't think of what's actually happening, or you'd go mad. We'll need trained executioners with razor-sharp swords and suitable outfits, including masks. Blindfolds and outfits for the prisoners,' he paused to take a breath, a really good location, at least two cameras, and I'll have to do storyboards and everything.'

He paused to look at Saeed.

'You any good behind a lens?'

'Me? No. And it's not my sort of thing. I'm better with the romance.'

'I don't think you've got a choice, mate,' Harry said. 'It's going to be all hands on deck.

'I suppose I can try,' Saeed answered, detecting the edge in Harry's voice.

'That's better. I need to look good too,' Harry said. 'In a different way, but still.'

'Of course. When do we begin?'

'Now!' Harry jumped up. 'Come on. Let's give you a go. And we can find a location too. We'd better start looking straight away. Let's go!'

Harry drove Saeed around for ages until he found the perfect spot. A piece of land devoid of any features and with nothing to throw awkward shadows. He looked around to see where the sun was coming from and spoke out loud. 'They're all going to be on one long line. Shit, how many? Fifty? I need to check that. It's a long line.'

He walked around waving his arms to illustrate his words. 'The sun goes down here, makes the light golden, very romantic. It gives them a sense of direction but no location. Each one will have his own executioner. I'm not sure how many we've got trained but I know they don't last long as soldiers. You're lucky in that respect.'

'But that's what I came here to do,' Saeed said. 'Although it's not turning out how I'd hoped.'

'You've got to forget about a love life,' Harry said. 'But if you know what to do, you can get a sex life.'

'Do you have a sex life?' Saeed asked.

'I'm sexless,' Harry said, going to the truck. He pulled out anything he could to represent bodies.

'Here.' He threw an old towel and some clothing over to Saeed. 'Start in a line over there. One long pace between each object.'

As Saeed began to disperse the objects, Harry went back to the truck and grabbed a cushion, a headdress, and a book. He counted out from Saeed's piles and placed his three at the end. Then he stood back and looked from one end to the other.

'OK. Now we need the cameras.'

They each took one from the truck. Saeed had never used anything so large before as he copied Harry and heaved it onto his shoulder.

244

'It's easy. You look here and press this when you're ready. It doesn't matter if you film too much, I'll edit it.'

'Got it,' Saeed nodded.

'You stand here,' Harry pointed to a spot. 'Now film from the towel to here.' He pulled up a blue garment and paced out to the halfway spot. 'And I'll film from there to the end.'

'I never realised how complicated it was,' Saeed remarked.

'Well, now you know,' Harry replied, still eyeing up the scene. After several tries from various distances, he was satisfied. 'OK. Let's go back. I have to speak to the Mudhir.'

***

Harry was in the Mudhir's office explaining his vision for the film. the Mudhir nodded his approval as he listened.

'Now for the finale,' Harry said. 'There will be fifty executioners all dressed in black with face masks. In front of each of them will be a blindfolded prisoner dressed in orange. The executions must happen sequentially, with a half second between them. We will film them all but show them in slow-mo. It will be like watching a ripple.'

The Mudhir was impressed. 'What do you need?'

'We have enough suits, but the black robes I want to design myself. And you, sir, need to provide fifty men capable of clean execution with the swiftest, sharpest blades to minimise the blood.

'We will need to do some training. How will you use Batal?'

'I will need him for the camera work. Besides, I don't think we should show him with the executions. Not with his new reputation with the ladies.'

The Mudhir grunted in agreement. 'Bring the seamstress to me. I want to speak to her myself. Tell her to bring her sewing tools.'

Harry went straight to find Maryam and talked to her as they went.

'Have you seen the girl Mari?' Maryam asked him.

'I haven't seen any girls in a long time,' he laughed. 'Why?'

245

'I just wanted to be sure she is safe. I think that the woman Selina doesn't like her and that she may be being treated badly.'

'Selina's a tough one, for sure. But it is none of my business. Come, woman, we are here and such talk will be frowned upon.'

***

When they arrived at the Mudhir's office, the guard looked at Maryam then spoke to Harry. 'You wait there; he wants to see the woman first.'

Maryam was ushered in. the Mudhir looked a little embarrassed.

'I need a new outfit,' he said. 'My wife is not so good at sewing anymore. Can you help?'

'Of course, sir. But first, I will need to measure you.'

Oblivious to Maryam's hatred of him, he submitted himself to her task. Carefully and efficiently, she took the measurements she needed and wrote them down in her notebook.

'I am done, sir. What sort of outfit do you require?'

The Mudhir frowned. 'Like this one, but more impressive. I need to look… magnificent.'

'Very well. In what colour or colours?'

'What do you think would suit me?'

Maryam frowned then studied him carefully. 'I have an idea. I will make something for you to see first, and if you do not like it, I will make another.'

He nodded. 'That makes sense. And if it fits properly, you can make me many more.'

'Thank you, sir.'

The Mudhir turned his head to talk to the guard. 'Call in Abdulla.'

Harry was summoned and ushered into the room.

'Tell the woman your requirements, please.'

'Of course. May we make use of your table?'

The Mudhir nodded. Harry and Maryam sat at the table, and Harry began to tell Maryam what was needed.

The Mudhir, looking bored, walked to the door. 'I have something to attend to, I will be back,' he said.

246

Maryam waited for him to leave before speaking. 'What is happening?' she asked.

'Another horrible mass execution,' Harry replied. 'I will try to make it as painless as possible. So, the first requirement is for thick blindfolds. They mustn't see what is happening to the others.'

'Good,' Maryam agreed. 'Poor souls. Who are they?'

Harry shrugged. 'I don't know. Mainly captured Syrian soldiers, I suspect. But there'll be civilians there too.'

'Any Christians?'

'Oh, yes. Probably. Do you know what I mean by jumpsuits? In orange?

Maryam nodded. 'When are they needed by?'

Harry shook his head. 'I don't have an exact date yet, but I guess it will be pretty soon.'

'It will take a while. Unless I had help...'

Harry winked at her. 'I'll see what I can do.'

Before they could say any more, the Mudhir reappeared. 'Is it settled?' he asked.

'The woman says she can do it quicker if she has help. There was a British girl brought out here. She has sewing skills.'

'I will see,' the Mudhir replied.

***

When Maryam and Harry had gone, the Mudhir walked around to the prison building where Selina sat in her office. She immediately stood and bowed her head. 'Your excellency.'

'I have had a request about the British girl who came here recently.'

'Mari?' Selina replied.

'Yes. She is good at sewing and the Syrian woman wants her assistance. What do you think of her?'

'She's useless,' Selina replied. I've been giving her cleaning duties but she doesn't know one end of a broom from the other.

'What else does she do?' the Mudhir narrowed his eyes.

Selina laughed. 'I lend her out to commanders from time to time, but they don't seem to like her much. She's not good at entertaining them either.

'Have you seen her sewing abilities?

Selina frowned. 'No. I don't think she's sewn anything. Besides, she is clumsy. The Syrian woman is good and efficient. But she would waste more time than she'd save training her up. And anyway, I doubt she would ever be any good.'

'As you say,' the Mudhir agreed.

72

22nd March

Karen arrived at Baghdad airport in the morning and was immediately intercepted by a police officer.

'Madam Thorpe. We understand the purpose of your visit and have arranged for you to complete your work here at the airport. You have a room reserved at the airport hotel and there are regular complimentary buses which will take you there and back.'

Karen took this in her stride. She knew that whilst women were allowed to join the police in Iraq, it was not something that was universally welcomed. And a Western woman might be even less acceptable.

She made straight for the hotel and checked in. But almost the second she sat on the bed to take off her shoes, she was overcome with fatigue and couldn't resist the urge to sleep.

It was two hours before she woke up, furious with herself for being so weak. She jumped in the shower then got dressed. She fixed her knife to the waistband of her trousers, then went downstairs to the reception area.

The receptionist greeted her immediately. 'Good afternoon, Miss Thorpe. Are you feeling all right?'

'I'm fine, thanks. I just needed time to catch up on my sleep.

The receptionist gave her a warm smile. 'Mr Saunders, of security, has been most concerned about you. He asked me to call you a taxi as soon as you come down. Please have a seat.'

'Thank you,' Karen muttered, running her hand through her hair as she sat down.

By the time she arrived back at the airport and got to the security centre, she was in full apology mode. She was astonished to be greeted by an English manager who escorted her around the security barriers.

'Good afternoon. I'm Nial Saunders, head of surveillance. How are you feeling now?'

'Much better. I'm not normally like this,' Karen explained. 'Tired, I mean.'

'Overnight flights are always tiresome,' Nial replied. 'You're not alone.'

Karen cheered up, and she was very impressed when Nial showed her to a large room which had a whole wall of screens showing live feeds from cameras around the airport.

He led her to a desk where a laptop was already waiting for her. 'You're already logged in as *guest*, Would you like me to get you started?'

Karen leaned on the desk and peered at the screen. She shook her head. 'It looks like the ones I've used before,' she said. 'So long as the commands are in English, I'll be fine. Which reminds me... '

'What are the Brits doing out here? He grinned. 'We won the contract in 2010.'

'Ah, I see!' Karen replied.

'Coffee?'

'Yes, please. Black, no sugar.'

Karen soon got stuck in. The system was easy enough; however, looking for two middle-aged men called Rahman travelling together was no easy task. It was a frequent name. Each time she found a pair of potential individuals, she checked the relevant CCTV footage but was disappointed.

After the ninth pair, she got lucky. There were two men, one in a western suit and one in loose trousers, tunic, and jacket wearing a fur cap.

'Got to be,' she muttered. She checked their faces; they matched. She studied the footage for a moment. The suited man was much taller than his brother who walked with a slight limp.

She looked back at the photo Maria had given her. Sure enough, Ibrahim was taller than Jafar.

'Sorted.'

The two men had arrived the day before, so she only had to check the footage after that to see where they went next.

Taking a sip of her coffee, Karen glanced up at the live screens. *What the hell...?* In the top right-hand corner, she saw two men walking away from the camera. Both in Pakistani attire and both wearing fur caps. She frowned. *They're about the same height as... Hell. He's got a limp. Has to be them.*

She charged out of the office, through security, and into the main departure lounge frantically looking around to work out where they were in the area. She heard a commotion behind her. Shouting. Somewhere, she heard the sound of an alarm beeping. *Was it them?* Looking this way and that, she made herself dizzy trying to find the right doors. *There!*

She just caught sight of two figures who matched the description on the screen. She ran after them as fast as she could and charged through the doors. But she wasn't alone. At the same time as two pairs of hands grabbed her, the outside air hit her like a wall of heat, and Karen did something she had never done in her life before; she fainted.

73

Nadeem arrived in Raqqa and was seriously unimpressed. He had expected to be greeted as a hero but the Mudhir hadn't even agreed to his request for a meeting. He'd been put through a rapid assessment process in the council building, like every other young man travelling there, and been told the bad news.

'My brother, we think that your services will be best used in our offices.'

'What? I came here to fight. To recruit others and to lead them.'

'You have already completed your service in that regard. You found us Batal.'

'Batal? Who's that? Where is Saeed?'

'Please come with me and I will take you to your accommodation.'

Nadeem slung his rucksack over his shoulder and followed the man outside to a dingy-looking apartment building a few hundred yards from the council building. He was given a key and told his room number.

'I will expect you back at our offices in half an hour.

Nadeem was even less impressed with his new lodgings. A small room, a single bed with a shower, and a tiny kitchen area.

'I will prove to you all how glorious a soldier I will be,' he said out loud. He threw down his rucksack, had a quick wash to freshen up then made his way back to the offices, checking his watch as he went. He was assigned to a desk in a big office and asked to put some papers in order ready for filing, which he completed with a scowl.

Later, he had some visitors. Two women, wearing the guards' headband, came up to his desk. One was more prominent than the other. He peered at the mesh over her eyes, wondering who she was.

'Hello, Nadeem,' a British voice said.

He realised who it was. 'Is that you, Selina?'

'Yes, Nadeem.' She sounded scornful.

'Greetings. You are making quite a name for yourself back in England.'

'You are not,' Selina scorned. 'And you are no fighter.'

Nadeem pouted. 'I will show everybody in time what I can do. This is only temporary until I acclimatise. There will be glorious work for me to do soon.'

'You wish,' Selina replied.

'Why are you here?'

'We have some small administration matters to deal with. *Small* administration,' she repeated to make her point.

Nadeem frowned. 'Do you know where Saeed is?'

'You mean Batal. Yes. He has wormed his way in with the media people. He was useless as a soldier, too, but at least he was pretty.'

'It sounds like you don't like him much.'

'He is nothing to me.'

Nadeem hesitated, thinking through what he wanted to say. 'I think he may have given me away, but I can't be sure.'

Selina narrowed her eyes. 'Explain.'

'It was just after the video came out, the one seeking girls. That's when I thought someone was following me.'

'And have you seen it, the video?'

'Not yet.'

Selina turned to her colleague. 'You sort out the expenses then come over to mine. There's something I want you to see.'

She turned back to Nadeem. 'You're not important enough. But if Batal has betrayed us, that needs checking urgently. Come with me.'

Nadeem looked around the office and caught the eye of his manager. 'She needs me for something,' he said.

The manager looked at Selina and bowed his head a little. He looked back at Nadeem. 'Go.'

***

Selina took Nadeem to her apartment near the prison. It was a modest affair in a small block, but still much better than the room Nadeem had been given. She gave him a glass of water. 'We will talk more when my colleague arrives,' she said, taking a banana from the well-filled fruit bowl on the coffee table. She didn't offer anything to Nadeem.

A buzzer sounded her friend's arrival. She stood up to open the door for her. 'Please meet Nadeem. He thinks he is quite the soldier. He is a mere son of an imam. He thinks that he alone can revive our fortunes here. I think he looks like a wimp.'

The woman laughed and replied with a northern British accent. 'He wouldn't have lasted five minutes at my school.'

'Two!' Selina corrected. 'Now you sit here on the sofa with me. He can sit on the floor. I want to show you both something. Watch carefully.'

She switched on the TV, found the video, and played it. The other two watched, fascinated.

'You are the son of an imam, are you not?' Selina asked him.

'Yes. You know that. But why do you ask me that?'

'Did you not listen to him? Listen to him. Hear the words which relate to you.'

She replayed the tape.

Nadeem shook his head. 'I don't understand.'

'Then you are even more stupid than you look.'

'Where can I find him?'

'You don't.' Selina glared at him. 'You will do as I say. You will go back to the offices and I will give you your instructions in time. Do you understand?' Nadeem nodded. 'You really don't want to mess with me,' she added.

When he had gone, both girls removed their burqas. Her friend looked at her. 'OK, so I'm stupid too. I didn't get it either.'

Selina laughed. 'You haven't spent enough time with cyphers yet. Watch this bit and count every third word.' She replayed the passage.

'Wow. And what does it mean if Batal wants to call him out? Batal is surely our top recruiter now, isn't he? I thought you had a thing for him once?'

Selina grimaced. 'He's no use to me. He still wants that girl.'

'So why can't she be with him?'

'Because she is a fraud and a tramp,' she laughed.

'And Batal?'

254

'He is a traitor. Even if Nadeem is completely useless, he is one of us. So for Batal to betray him, he is betraying all of us.'

74

Saeed and Harry were on location getting ready for the filming. the Mudhir arrived in his chauffeured car. He headed straight for Harry, swaggering as he showed off his new headdress and flowing robes, black-edged subtly with strands of gold.

Harry stopped what he was doing to talk to him. 'May I compliment you on your attire, sir? You look quite magnificent.'

The Mudhir, clearly pleased, gave him a broad smile. 'I wanted to ensure that it was appropriate for your film.'

'It is perfect. That will photograph nicely when the time comes,' Harry said. 'You look very dashing. Your seamstress has outdone herself. The outfits, too, were of exceptional quality.'

The Mudhir strutted around a little while Saeed put the cameras in position. 'This is a good choice of location and the sun is shining for us. This will be a perfect day for you, too.'

'When are the prisoners coming?' Harry asked. 'Are there still fifty?'

The Mudhir looked at his watch. 'In one hour. We had a little accident with one,' he laughed. 'But to make up the number we have found someone else who will be finding out very soon that he is on his way to paradise.'

'That's good,' Harry said, but Saeed saw the disgust on his face when he turned his head away.

'I will return when the prisoners have been loaded onto the trucks.' the Mudhir swept back to his car.

'How do you cope with this?' Saeed asked.

'I treat it as a job. Believe it or not, you get used to it. That's why they make kids watch beheadings. So they grow up with it as normal.'

'But they're humans.'

'I do what I can to help. I assure you,' Harry replied.

'Won't they struggle? What if they try to escape?'

Harry sighed. 'They've probably all been drugged a little. I hope so. I believe they're all told – in their own languages – that this is just a promotional film. That if they follow instructions, they'll be fine. They may have been told that they can go free once they've done this.'

'And they'll believe it?' Saeed asked, his eyes widening.

'What else do they have to believe in? Why wouldn't they? They know there is no way they can escape. Come. Let us check the positions one last time.'

The first truck was heard before it was visible, falling under the small hills of the area. As it got closer, they could see the whole convoy. First came the trucks carrying the prisoners. Behind them, in buses, were the executioners. the Mudhir's car was at the end.

Harry stood in position and waved his arms to guide the first truck to its designated parking spot, well out of camera. 'There!' He shouted and pointed. The truck came to a stop with the others lining up alongside.

Harry pointed for the buses to park even further away. He guided the car to a shadier spot nearer to the site.

Everybody got out of their vehicles – except the prisoners. With their hands tied behind their backs, they sat in silence, a gentle breeze rippling their orange outfits.

Harry first counted the doomed men, then spoke to the guards and pointed out the marked positions for the beginning and end of the row. 'OK, you can get them out now.'

The men were helped carefully out of the trucks.

Harry spoke to as many of them as he practically could. 'Please do not worry. This is just a film for our own purposes. I've been told that they want to exchange you for some of our captured fighters. This is just to show them we have you all and you are all still alive. Behind you will stand some of our people. They will appear in the film to prove that there are many of us and we are not violent. You will all be blindfolded shortly. This is so your family will not be distressed at seeing your faces. Kneel and stay still. You will be all right. You will be taken back to prison soon.'

The prisoners, some visibly shaking, knelt as they were told and Harry straightened them into line. The guards went swiftly along the line, tying black blindfolds over their eyes.

When Harry was satisfied, he walked over to the buses and beckoned the executioners forward. Each masked and dressed in long flowing black robes, they carried gleaming long-bladed hunting knives. No one seeing them would have doubted for a second what their role was. Harry checked them one by one, straightening and adjusting their black garments where necessary. When they were all assembled, Harry addressed them.

'Get in line. I want you to go to that tree; then, when I shout *WALK,* you line behind the row of prisoners until you are each behind one of them.' He paused to see that they'd all understood.

'When I raise my hand,' he continued, 'you hold your knife out like this.' He grabbed a knife from one of them and brandished it up high. 'When I lower my hand, you hold the knife like so.' He held his hand to his throat. Then you look to our leader. When he raises his arm, you,' he pointed at the man on the end, 'you sever the head. As quickly and cleanly as you can. Once the spinal cord is severed, the blood flow will cease. Have you all had practice?'

Nearly all of them nodded.

'Then you,' he pointed at the man next to him. 'You count *one* before doing the same. And so on. Do you understand?' He waited till all of them nodded. 'Good.'

Saeed took in the scene. He hoped no one could see him trembling. From their height and frame, he could see some were very young. He guessed that some would have been as nervous as the prisoners. He hoped they would do a decent job. That it would be as quick and painless as possible.

He gulped. The time had come.

75

Saeed watched as Harry walked over to where the Mudhir was waiting.

'They seem very young. Can they do this?' Harry asked.

'They have practised, but you may have to edit carefully.'

'I suggest we start immediately. We can do the speeches afterwards. I will superimpose them on the footage.' the Mudhir nodded.

'Thank you. One more thing.'' Harry said. 'The execution should be at your command, not mine.'

'Of course. What do you want me to do?'

'I will give the sign for them to hold the knives like so,' he gestured. 'You raise your arm for the actual execution. They will already have their eyes on you. When you drop your arm, it will commence.'

'Where should I stand?'

Harry guided the Mudhir to the right spot then got into his own place and studied the scene. Seemingly satisfied, he joined Saeed.

Saeed, still watching, felt his insides groan and twist. He guessed that some of the prisoners and maybe even an executioner or two had soiled themselves in fear. This film would be something far more revolting than anything he had ever heard of before.

'Batal?' Saeed turned to look at Harry. 'Start filming as we discussed. Point the camera in the middle and wait for the knife.'

Saeed glared at him. 'Why the knives? You said swords.'

'Be quiet,' Harry hissed. We have to work with what we've got,' Harry whispered. These are nearly as good and need less space.'

Saeed sighed. Poor, poor men.'

'Get back in position and start filming straight away. I can edit it later.' Harry grabbed Saeed's camera and tilted it a fraction. 'Keep it still at that angle.' He waited until he saw Saeed commence filming, then walked back to his own place.

'WALK!' he yelled, watching the executioners line up behind the prisoners. He paused and held his hand up high. Immediately, fifty knives were brandished.

Saeed's heart was thumping as he watched Harry hold his hand to his neck. The executioners followed. He looked over to the Mudhir, who stood with his hand raised and waited for what seemed like an eternity. His hand went down, and the executions commenced.

Harry's head dipped as he looked in his viewfinder.

Saeed held his camera steady but without looking at the scene. He wondered if it was easier for Harry to see through a viewfinder. A degree of separation, perhaps?

He couldn't hear anything. Was that because there was nothing to hear, or were his senses closing down? He counted slowly to ten before he could bear to look up. When he did, he felt calmer. It was over, and the prisoners, whatever their heavenly fate, could no longer feel pain or fear.

Harry strode over to the scene. 'Now we must straighten the bodies and arrange the heads,' he shouted at the executioners. 'Place each one neck down on the sand in front of the body.'

As the heads were being arranged, one of the youngest of the executioners seemed to be distracted by something. Harry gestured for him to hurry up. When he was satisfied that the heads were all in the right place and that he'd got every shot he needed, he approached the boy, who was now unmasked.

Saeed's heart sank at the sight. He must have been no more than eleven or twelve.

'What's the matter?' Harry asked.

'There is something strange here. Come and see,' the boy said.

The Mudhir approached them. 'Is there a problem?' he asked.

Harry shrugged. 'I'm about to find out.'

The boy had run back to the body of the prisoner he had just executed. He was pointing to the collar of the orange jumpsuit. 'See there. There is a cross in the collar of the suit.'

The Mudhir looked closely. His face changed from curious to furious. The boy was right. There, right behind what was left of the neck, was a cross picked out in black thread.

260

'By what infamy did this happen?' he bellowed.

'It's got to be a mistake,' Harry answered. 'An accident, maybe.'

The Mudhir wrenched his head to look at the next body. He saw another cross. 'There too. This is no mistake.'

He looked at Harry. 'This is your fault. You wanted to use the woman. Didn't you check these garments?'

Harry began to shake. 'I did,' he said. 'She must have put them in afterwards.'

'Pick them out. Pick out every single one with scissors. I will not take the chance. And make sure you edit your film so that none of these crosses is seen.'

'Of course, sir,' Harry held his breath.

The Mudhir rushed back to his car and shouted at his driver to get him back to his office as quickly as he could.

Saeed approached Harry. 'Are you all right?'

'Fine,' Harry gave him a big grin. 'I thought my time was up for a moment. But it seems not. Now, have you got any scissors with you? A blade will do.'

76

Maryam was working at her desk when Nazia hurried over, a guard looking behind her.

'Maryam, what have you done?'

'I have done nothing wrong,' she replied.

'Then why has this man come for you?' If you have brought my factory into disrepute there will be serious consequences for all of us.'

Maryam smiled. 'Please don't fret. I will take full responsibility for all of my actions. You will not be blamed for anything.'

'But what have you done?' the woman cried. 'What can have happened to upset our leader so much that he sends a guard for you?'

'That, I will have to find out,' Maryam replied as the guard seized her by her shoulders and marched her off the factory floor.

People in the streets stood and watched as she walked steadily in front of the guard. There was much muttering. She had become a well-known figure because of her height and stature.

'What can she have done?' they asked each other.

When she was pushed into the Mudhir's office, he ordered the guard to leave them alone.

'I command you to take off that burqa. I must see your face.'

Maryam complied and stood proudly before him in a simple white dress.

'I thought that you had some common sense, woman. I trusted you. How could you do this to me?'

Maryam was calm as she faced him. 'Sir, I do not know what has upset you. All I have ever done is to try and make the best garments for all my customers so that they should get some happiness from them.'

'Were you so stupid that you thought you could get away with it?'

'Get away with what? I don't know what you mean.'

'The crosses,' he snarled. 'The sign of the infidel. Sewn into our prisoner outfits.'

Maryam looked surprised. 'But that is my signature, sir. Every seamstress has one. At least the good ones do.'

'Your signature is a cross?' he asked.

Maryam nodded. 'I do the work of my God and He has decided I should sew. And therefore, I do. I sew in His name and for His glory. And especially, I sew to bring His peace and love to those who are about to die. I hope it will help their route to the afterlife.'

'Afterlife? Only Allah can decide that.'

He began to pace. 'I trusted you, Maryam. I even thought that we had something in common. I thought that if you had truly repented and turned to Allah, that things… ' he tailed off, 'that things might have been good between us.'

'I think that very unlikely,' Maryam replied.

'But this outfit that you made me, it is exquisite. It could only have been made by somebody with love in their heart.'

'My heart has always been filled with the love of my God and my Lord Jesus Christ.'

The Mudhir shook his head in sadness, his anger momentarily gone. Then he began to look puzzled; something preying on his mind.

He began to take off his outer robes, then searched with his fingers and worked his way to the neck. There, in golden thread, was not just a simple cross, it was the cross of Saint Thomas, complete with floral leaf edges.

'How dare you infect me with your despicable idolatry,' he screamed. 'I trusted you. You will be punished for this.' He raised his hand and struck her on the side of her head, making her crash to the floor. 'I must think what I should do.'

Maryam remained still as he paced around her, muttering as he went.

'… and you have proved you are no more than an infidel. Aha!' he wheeled around to look her in the face. 'Since you admit your guilt, there is only one fate that I can bestow upon you. You will be executed as soon as possible. And,' he leaned down to grab her by the shoulders, 'since you are so fond of your cross and your Jesus Christ, I think that I shall nail you to one.'

'It will be an honour indeed to die like my Lord,' Maryam said, head held high.

The Mudhir frowned, 'Then I will not give you that satisfaction.' He went to the door. 'Guard? Take her to prison while I decide what to do with her.'

When she had been taken, the Mudhir's cry of pure rage was heard through the whole building.

77

Karen began to stir. She opened her eyes to see white walls and a figure dressed in green standing over her, a woman in hospital scrubs.

'Our patient is coming round,' Karen heard a female voice say. She began to sit up.

'What the hell... '

'Please, Madam Thorpe. Please take it slowly. Let me help you sit up.'

Karen slowly wrenched her torso up from the bed. The nurse immediately stuffed a pillow behind her for support.

'Here. Have some water.'

Karen sat up and took the glass. She sipped the water while she collected her thoughts. 'What happened?'

'Oh, it was nothing serious, the nurse replied. 'It was just a simple case of exhaustion and heat. The security guards brought you straight here. You were very dehydrated. It's common after a long flight.'

Karen looked at her wrist where a cannula had been inserted. 'Ah, that's good. I'm never ill. Can I go back to the airport now?'

'You're free to go as soon as you like,' the nurse replied. 'But there's someone here who wants to speak to you. Do you feel able to? He says he knows you.'

'What's his name?'

Before the nurse could answer, a tall white man poked his head around the door. 'Sergeant Thorpe, I believe?'

Karen's eyes widened. 'Yes. And you are?'

'Let's just say I'm a friend of Uncle Gary's. You can call me Tom.'

Karen sat bolt upright. She looked at the nurse. 'It's all right. I do know this man.'

The nurse nodded. 'I will leave you alone then. Push the bell if you need anything.'

'The Rahmans. I had them; I could have... '

'No, you couldn't, as it happens. I was watching them just as you did your charge. Any idea how stupid it is to run through airport security carrying a knife?'

Karen blinked. Yes, it did sound stupid. 'I didn't think. What an idiot. I didn't go in that way so I didn't think of the sensors.'

'We've all done it,' Tom said. 'I explained who you were to your captors and left you to it.'

'Where is it now?'

'Don't worry about it. I'll get it back to you soon. It's a nice piece.'

'It was a present from Gary,' Karen smiled. 'What about the Rahmans then? Did you get them?'

'Well, you did give us the lead on them. I hot footed it after them. I caught them in a taxi queue outside; it wasn't difficult.'

'And?'

Tom shook his head. 'I couldn't stop them. They're two grown men and they're stupid enough to think that they can buy the kids back. I had to let them go.'

'Buy them? How much did they think they'd have to pay? I promised their mothers I'd find them.'

'You did your best. More than most people would have done.'

'But where were they going? Did they have a lead?'

'They mentioned Raqqa. I don't know how they knew that, but I guessed there was no point trying to persuade them otherwise.'

'I should have done more,' Karen said.

'There was nothing you could have done, I promise you. Now you have to promise to sit tight while we see if we can't do the job we came out here for.'

'You mean Mari?' Karen smiled at last.

'Yes, I do,' Tom replied. 'Joe and Ali are already on their way.'

'I suppose there's not much I can do now.'

'No way,' Tom said. 'Even I'm not going into Syria. You and I would both stick out here. But I'll catch up with you later so you can keep in touch.'

'Where's my phone?' Karen panicked.

'Look in the drawer,' Tom said.

Karen gasped with relief when she saw it there, then pouted as she turned it on.

'Expecting a message from someone?' Tom asked.

'Nothing important,' Karen replied. 'But before you set off, let me have your number.'

78

The Mudhir's fury had subsided. He had changed his clothes and ordered them to be burned. Now, he was sitting at his desk in a more reflective mood, thinking about how he would deal with Maryam. There was a knock on his door.

'Enter.'

His guard appeared. 'I have visitors here. They say they have important information.'

'Who is it?' He asked.

'It is Nadeem and Selina,' the guard replied. 'They say they have discovered a traitor.'

'Another one or the same?' the Mudhir wondered out loud. 'Bring them in.'

'Well? What have you to tell me,' he snarled as they stood before him.

Nadeem, holding his tablet in his hand, was trembling but Selina stood proud.

'We have found a traitor,' she announced. 'The film that Batal made. The one that everyone was so pleased with. It contains a hidden message.'

The Mudhir was astonished. 'Explain.'

'May I show you, sir? It is easier if you watch the film for yourself.'

The Mudhir grunted and waved his arm towards his meeting table. 'Sit,' he commanded.

Selina took Nadeem's tablet from him and propped it up on the table so that the Mudhir could see it. She leaned across him to set off the footage and increased the volume so that he could hear it properly.

'There is nothing wrong with that,' he looked at her.

'Listen again.' She reran the footage but this time, repeated the relevant words with Saeed on screen.

'But... ' the Mudhir was puzzled.

Selina rewound it and ran it again. 'See? Every third word. Imam. Son. Hate. Preacher. It is surely telling the world that Nadeem, who is the son of an imam, is a hate preacher. That is what they are called in England. Those are the people they try to arrest there.'

The Mudhir thought for a moment. 'Leave me. I will deal with this.' He gestured for them to leave and then called the guard in. 'Bring me the director. Bring Abdulla to me now!'

***

Harry had been expecting to be summoned, so he wasn't overly worried when he was called to see the Mudhir. When he arrived, he said the words he'd practised on the way there.

'Good afternoon, sir. I have been working hard on the film, of course. Oh!' he stalled. 'You've changed your outfit. But sir, we will need some more footage of you.'

'Not possible,' the Mudhir interrupted. 'In time you will have to sort that out. But this is something more important.'

'What is it, sir?'

'The film you did with Batal. The one to tempt the girls to come here.'

Harry's eyebrows shot up. 'Yes, what of it?'

'Are you not responsible for the words?'

'Of course.' Harry said. 'Hang on, no. I didn't write that one. Batal wrote his own. I have to admit it was much better than mine.'

'And you saw nothing wrong with it?' the Mudhir peered at him.

'No. Why? What has happened?' Harry gulped. He didn't feel quite so confident now.

'It was coded. It had a message in it.'

'What?' Harry's mouth fell open. 'It can't have.'

'The woman. You checked the garments, did you not?'

Harry began to tremble. 'Only the prototype. That was fine. I had nothing to do with the woman. But Batal... '

The Mudhir seemed to have grown in size and stature. His face was red with anger. Harry clutched at his stomach. 'Batal did what?'

Harry's words were garbled but intelligible. 'Batal spoke often to her.'

The Mudhir visibly relaxed. 'Good. That is all I need to know. Go now. I will deal with him.'

79

The Mudhir sat in his office, head in hands. How could he have been fooled by a boy and a woman? Yet still, he could not quite believe that Batal would trick him. He had been a huge draw and there were now many girls around the world embarking on their journey. No, he couldn't quite bring himself to believe the deceit and had his suspicions about the director. What young man wouldn't have his pick of girls? How do you test faith? And the thought came straight into his head. The best test of all. He could test Batal and Abdulla in a good and spectacular way.

He called the guard. 'Bring Batal to me.'

Saeed was collected and taken into the Mudhir's office. He stood there trembling.

'I am told you are a traitor! ' the Mudhir roared at him. 'Explain yourself.'

Saeed shook his head. 'What? No, of course I'm not a traitor. What do you mean?'

'The film, you wretch.'

Saaed looked perplexed. 'I thought it served its purpose well. Abdulla told me it was a success.'

'What about the words! The hidden message!'

Saeed shook his head. 'It's a simple text. The message is clear, isn't it?'

The Mudhir quoted the text, emphasising each third word. 'Imam's Son Hate Preacher.

Saeed looked bemused. 'I don't understand.'

The Mudhir was almost at boiling point. 'Batal. Did you mean to unveil the imam's son?'

Saeed looked surprised. 'What? Which one? There are hundreds of imams with sons who hate preachers.'

'Nadeem, you idiot,' the Mudhir was now on the point of exploding, but he managed to calm himself.

'Nadeem?' Saeed said. 'He is my friend. He is the reason I am here and helping you. I am happy here. I wanted to be a soldier, but Allah decided I wasn't good enough. So I do what I can. And now I'm just a simple actor but I am helping the caliphate in my own way.'

The Mudhir smiled at him. Saeed smiled back.

'Guard!' the Mudhir shouted. The man scurried in. the Mudhir watched Saeed carefully as he spoke to him. 'Prepare the central square for the execution of the infidel woman they call the seamstress.'

'Yes, sir.'

'Tell all the people to come; they will enjoy the spectacle of an infidel woman being executed.'

Saeed gulped. 'Is it necessary, sir?' he asked. 'She only made a few stitches. She's probably always done it and didn't think about it.'

The Mudhir peered at him. 'You saved her once before, Batal. Now you must admit that you were wrong. You shall prove your allegiance to the caliphate once and for all, or you will share her fate.'

***

The Mudhir led the way to the square. There were guards posted at all the entrances. Saeed followed, seeing the security already in place. As they arrived in the square, a small crowd was already gathering. The executioner was already in place, his knife gleaming in the thin sunlight.

There was much talking going on. 'Who is this woman?' they asked as Maryam, still in her dress with her hair piled in the topknot, was brought out by a guard.

'Why, it is the seamstress,' they began to realise. 'No one else is that tall. What can she have done?'

Some of them spotted Saeed and began to chant 'Batal! Batal!' as he walked past them.

A brave woman approached the Mudhir and asked him, 'What has she done?'

'She has forsaken Allah,' he replied. 'She lied. She is a Christian.'

More muttering rippled through the now-increasing crowd. Some secretly admired her defiance, Muslims, and secret

Christians alike. Others were full of venom. They spat and threw small stones and dirt at her.

Saeed stood nervously alongside the Mudhir. 'What is it, sir? Are we going to film this?'

'No Batal. This time we have a great honour to bestow upon you. You are to have the honour of executing this infidel.'

Saeed disguised his emotions well. 'This is indeed an honour, but why me? It is true she deceived us all but surely there are others who would love to do this to such a traitor?'

'Are you saying you will not do it?'

'Of course not. But I am not worthy of such an honour.'

Maryam looked up when she saw Saeed and smiled at him. the Mudhir grabbed Saeed's arm. 'See, she smiles. She is a friend to you.'

'No,' Saeed shook his head furiously. 'She only helped to make items for the films.'

The Mudhir approached the executioner and held out his hand for the knife. He handed it to Saeed. Saeed began to sweat.

'I've never done this before,' he said. 'Surely there is someone better?'

'You have seen it done a hundred times. Do it now,' the Mudhir ordered.

Saeed walked slowly up to Maryam.

'Do it!' she whispered in English. 'Do it now, or they will doubt you. I am ready to go to my Lord Jesus. I forgive you.'

Saeed stood behind her, his eyes filling with tears. The crowd began to chant. 'Batal! Batal! Batal!

He held the knife to her throat, but he could not bring himself to draw it across her neck. Instead, he cried out and dropped the knife.

The Mudhir picked up the knife and ran behind Maryam. She stood motionless. He grabbed at her hair, still tied, and held the knife across her neck. 'It could have been so different,' he whispered. In an instant, he drew the knife across her neck and severed her head. He turned it towards him and looked into her still-open eyes. 'I forgive you,' she mouthed. Startled, he threw her head towards the executioner and looked away.

'Seize him!' he shouted. The guard grabbed Saeed and marched him away. The crowd cheered, confused at first that Saeed had dropped the knife.

'Maybe he is just the poster boy,' some said. 'He is not a fighter after all.'

80

23 March

Joe and Ali were making good progress. They had taken it in turns to drive most of the night but stopped for sleep near the border town of Qa'im.

'Full English for me,' Joe said. 'Same for you without the bacon and sausages, bruv?' He nudged Ali, who was trying hard to ignore him.

'It'll be dry biscuits for the both of us, again,' Ali muttered. 'We'll eat like kings when this is all over.'

'It's a good gig though,' Joe said. 'I haven't felt so alive in ages.'

'And it's a very good cause,' Ali agreed. 'Wolf was like a brother to me. It will be a pleasure helping his family, even if he isn't around to hear about it.'

'It's probably the reason she got so screwed up,' Joe said. 'Poor kid.'

'How was she when you left?'

'Scared, all right. But at least she was clean and well-fed. And had a good night's sleep. I asked for her again in the hope they might take better care of her. Couldn't push it, they were getting wary.'

'Sick bastards,' Ali said. 'I ain't no saint, but I reckon I'd get into Jannah before them lot.'

'I'm sure you would,' Joe agreed as he opened the biscuits. 'Do you have a cousin at the border too?'

'How big do you think my family is?' Ali replied.

'Ten times the size of mine. Well?'

Ali grinned as he took a biscuit. 'Bloody millions of 'em. I'll ring him in a mo. Make sure he's on duty. We'll have to give him some dosh though, the others at the border will want a cut too.'

'Covered,' Joe grinned back. 'Better make that call. I'd better refuel.'

Joe took the wheel to free Ali in case of issues at the border, which turned out to be easy. The next part of the journey was harder going. 'I'll drive but pad your backside,' Joe said. 'It's a bumpy ride. Mine's only just recovered. I know some of the rough spots now. Hang on, who's that? Your cuz?' he looked at Ali, whose phone was ringing.

'Tom.' Ali replied, looking at the phone. 'Let's hope there's nothing up. Boss? What can I do for you?'

'The Rahman brothers.' Tom said. 'That's Saeed Rahman's dad and uncle. We're pretty sure they're on their way to Raqqa. Head them off if you find them, they'll only get in the way.'

'OK. What are we looking for?'

'One about Joe's height but without the muscle. The other is six inches shorter. Both left Baghdad in fur hats but what's the weather like there?'

'Hottish,' Ali replied.

'Damn. OK, well, the smaller guy has a limp. That'll help.'

'Oh, sure, bloody wonderful,' Ali replied. 'We'll do what we can.'

As they got closer to Raqqa, Joe began to get twitchy.

'What's the problem, bro?' Ali asked.

'We should have had a welcoming committee by now. They're meant to be expecting us.'

'Maybe they've got other plans. What's the lowdown?'

'We head to the checkpoint. The guards should either know me or about me. I do stand out a bit in town. No reason anyone should suspect us. We'd have heard by now if they did. In fact, we'd be dead by now,' Joe laughed.

When they approached the checkpoint, the guards did recognise Joe and waved the jeep through. Arriving in the centre of town, they were treated with great respect by the guards and soldiers they saw. Word of their coming to join up had got around.

Joe parked up as close as he could to the centre and they headed straight to the council building. They were immediately ushered into the Mudhir's office.

'Welcome, gentlemen. You have come at a very auspicious time. You must be Ali, the second in command.' Ali gave a little bow. 'I am honoured you know my name.'

Joe was more concerned about what he had heard. 'We have? What's the occasion?'

'We are about to punish a traitor. It will be quite a spectacle, I assure you. And the film will be, what do you say, Box Office. Everybody has been commanded to watch. They must know what it is like to defy Allah in his caliphate.'

'When? I was hoping for a little rest and relaxation with the girl.'

'There will be time for that afterwards. Come. The entertainment will start soon.'

Joe and Ali followed the council member out of the office towards the town square, exchanging worried glances.

When he was sure they were out of earshot Joe whispered. 'I'll seek out the girl; you try to spot the men.'

Both men's jaws dropped when they entered the square. A huge crate made out of railings had been erected in the middle of the square. It was surrounded by petrol cans and filled with straw. The crowds were gathering around open-mouthed.

'Enjoy!' said the Mudhir. 'I have official duties to perform.' He left them and went to address the audience.

81

The Mudhir had settled himself and was ready. He stepped up onto the small podium erected for his use and began to speak. 'Many of you will know Batal. Our wonderful, handsome young man who has served us well with his charming films.'

The crowd shouted his name. 'Batal! Batal! We want to see Batal!' They were expecting him to front the film as usual.

The Mudhir continued. 'But it is with great sorrow that I have to announce that he has betrayed the caliphate.'

There were strange glances exchanged amongst the crowds and muttering began.

'Yes, my people. He is a traitor!' the Mudhir shouted the last word so that they could see there was no doubt. 'Not only did he fail to execute the infidel, but he has also betrayed our brethren.'

The muttering continued until Saeed, dressed in a white thobe was brought out into the square. His hands and feet were manacled making it difficult for him to walk. The guard behind him kept shoving him forward, making him fall at times. He was dragged up again by his hair. The muttering turned to exclamations of shock as gradually people took in the miserable spectacle.

Saeed's journey towards the cage was slow and painful. His legs were beginning to bleed from the rough steel chafing at his flesh. But he remained silent. Every step seemed to cause him more pain, but still, he trudged on until he reached the cage. His final destination.

The guard manhandled him inside the structure and linked chains to his feet and wrists until he was fully secured with little room for movement.

The crowd held their collective breath while sheets of twisted fabric were wound around his feet and spread out to the edges of the cage. Another man walked into the cage to throw liquid over his thobe The crowd instantly recognised the smell of petrol. There were gasps and looks of horror as they realised what was about to happen.

The Mudhir was still talking. He had to raise his voice so that the people could hear him.

From the crowd, a man shouted out 'Saeed!' Saeed heard it and turned to look, but there were too many people to see where it was coming from. He bowed his head and waited.

***

From their position at the back, Ali, too, had heard the cry. He looked at Joe. 'The father?'

Joe nodded. 'Go see. I'll look for the girl.'

Ali left Joe to weave through the crowd towards the source of the cry. It was easy to recognise the two brothers but more difficult to get to them through the crowd. He pushed his way through with brute strength until he reached the brothers.

'Be silent,' he hissed to them. 'Or you will lose your lives too.'

They looked at him in confusion. 'That is my son,' Ibrahim said. 'How can I watch him die.'

'Then don't look.' Ali hissed. 'There is nothing you can do to save him now. You are too late. Stay with me and I will try to save you.'

'Who are you?' Jafar asked.

'Shush. Later. We must start getting out of here. Follow me.'

Jafar looked at Ibrahim, tears in his eyes. 'We can't take on all these people. Let's not make our wives widows.'

Ibrahim took one last look at his son and murmured a prayer. When he was done, he nodded. 'Let's go.'

***

Mari was in a poor way. Badly beaten by the last man she had been forced to go with, she hadn't slept for the pain. Selina had appeared unexpectedly to drag her from her cell. All she had for comfort was the little doll which she held in her hand.

'Where are you taking me,' she asked. 'I'm tired. I need to sleep.'

Selina turned to her. 'Look at you,' she scorned. 'You're a woman now and you still play with little dollies.'

'Maryam made it for me. Where is she? Is she OK?'

'Oh, you'll see her soon,' Selina said. 'Or at least her head. Stuck on a railing somewhere.'

'What?' Mari stopped still. 'What did she do?'

'I don't know, but she proved she was still an infidel,' Selina shoved her. 'Move. There is another spectacle about to happen, one which you really don't want to miss.'

Mari was marched through the now empty streets into the square which was heaving with people. The crowds parted as Selina approached. Her headband was known and feared by everyone.

Taking the best view, as close to the cage as she could get, Selina stood next to Mari, her vice-like grip holding Mari's wrist. 'See? This is the man you thought loved you. Now you will see what happens to traitors.'

'What? What are you saying?' Mari couldn't see past the people in front of her. 'What's happening?'

'Listen and learn,' Selina commanded. 'Hear what our leader has to say.'

Mari held the doll even more tightly. She said a prayer in her head. 'Why are they calling for Batal?'

'Because he is about to be executed,' Selina said with glee in her voice. 'He is a traitor.'

'No, not my Saeed?' Mari cried, understanding at last what was happening.

***

Joe wove through the crowd, trying to look at eyes as he went. Ahead of him, he noticed a ripple of people moving to let one of the female guards through. Being tall, he had a better view than most. He took a punt and pushed his way through the crowd to get to the front. Looking around in despair, his eyes caught the motion of something light against the sea of black. A small yellow doll grasped tightly in a pale hand. *It's her.* He made straight for Mari.

When he got close, he had to think quickly. He winked at the woman holding Mari's other hand.

'This one's for my afters.'

Selina was startled for a moment, but she, too, recognised Joe. She released her grip on Mari's arm and in a second, Joe whisked her away.

Joe's size made it relatively easy for him to push through the people, dragging Mari behind him. He headed for where he knew Ali had seen the Rahman brothers.

From the tone of his voice and the growing anger of the crowd's response, Joe could tell the Mudhir's speech was coming to an end. As the whole crowd began to bay for Batal's blood, Joe slipped round to the back and saw Ali ahead of him with the Rahman brothers.

Ali, with superhuman force, pulled the men away. Their places were soon filled with other members of the crowd.

'We must get out now!' Joe yelled to make himself heard above the crowd. 'While they are all occupied.'

Silence fell. They heard a voice. It was Saeed. He shouted out. 'Mari! If you are here, know that I'm sorry. I truly loved you.'

Ibrahim and Jafar began to struggle with Ali. 'We must go to him!' Ibrahim shouted.

Mari, too, tried to pull her arm from Joe's grasp. But he had the strength to hold her and help Ali. 'Just get them all out of here,' he yelled.

Between them, Joe and Ali managed to get all three back to Joe's jeep. Joe started the engine while Ali bundled them in the back and pulled a tarpaulin over them. 'Keep down,' he hissed.

When they reached the town checkout, Joe pulled up and grinned at them. 'Hey, you're missing a good spectacle back there.'

A senior guard stepped up to the truck. 'Where are you going? I thought we were having talks later.'

'Sure thing. Just getting some more of our team. I've had word that they've reached Qa'im earlier than expected.'

'Good news.'

'Cheers!'

Joe sped off again and out of the city into the vast countryside.

82

The time had come to light the fire and Saeed stood there alone, about to meet his fate. He had known he would die the moment he dropped the knife meant for Maryam, but he had hoped for a swift death. Now he knew his punishment was to be much worse than that. Yes, he was scared of being hurt, but more than that, he was ashamed of what he'd done. He began to shout over the noise of the crowds. First, he shouted to Mari, hoping that she would hear him and know of his love for her. Then he thought about Maryam.

'The seamstress was a good woman. She did not deserve to die. All she did was serve her God. But she didn't kill or maim or rape or whip anyone. All she did was sew. I go to my death ashamed. I am ashamed I came here to this fallacy of a caliphate. It is nothing but an evil empire.'

The Mudhir was furious. 'Light it. Drown out his words with fire.' But Saeed had one more thing to say.

'Allah is the God of love, not hate. Save yourselves, there is time.'

The smell of petrol was already filling his nostrils before the fire was started, but now he saw the guard approaching with a torch.

'This is what happens when you betray your brothers,' the guard shouted to the crowd. 'Let this be a warning to you all!'

Saeed remembered reading that in fires, the smoke suffocates before the flames burn, and he prayed to whichever god he thought might hear him that he would be spared too much pain. But when the flames were lit, they raced towards his petrol-soaked feet. Within seconds he was surrounded by a wall of fire. The pain was unbearable but he didn't have to bear it for long.

The crowd watched; some in silence, some cheering as his body twisted and turned in the flames until, at last, it fell forward and could no longer be seen in the fire.

***

The Mudhir stayed to watch until the flames began to die down. Nobody else dared move away until he did. 'It is finished,' he announced and turned away to go back to his office. He was still angry with Batal, but now he was also a little sad.

'He could have been someone really important,' he told one of the guards as he went back to his office. 'If he had not been so sentimental about that woman.'

He waited in his office for a while then called the guard.

'Where are the English fighters? Are they still watching the spectacle?'

'I don't know,' the guard replied.

'Don't just stand there! Get them. We have important things to discuss.'

The guard disappeared, only to return on his own fifteen minutes later.

'There is no sign of them,' he said.

'What? 'The Mudhir roared. 'What nonsense is this? Have you checked with the hotel?'

'Yes. They have not seen them.'

'Check with the town guards.'

'Yes, sir.' The guard took out his phone and rang the checkpoint. 'Ah,' he said, then he relayed what he had heard. 'They have gone to pick up some more of the team from Qa'im, sir.'

The Mudhir thought about this for a moment.

'That might be right. Call the guards on the road. Ask them to check in when the Englishmen depart. I will speak to them myself.'

'I will, sir.'

83

Joe was careering along at a breakneck pace; the guards stationed ahead were coming quickly into view.

'I reckon we take them out,' said Joe to Ali.

'Let's give them the chance to talk first. We might buy more time,' Ali replied.

Joe slowed down and pulled up at the checkpoint. 'Good afternoon, my man,' he smiled.

This guard bent his head to reply. He looked stern. 'You must be the English soldiers.'

'That's us. English to the core,' Ali grinned at the man.

'The Mudhir wants to talk to you.'

'Hey. That's cool,' Joe said, reaching for the phone. But before he took it, another guard walked around the truck and began to lift the edge of the tarpaulin. 'What have you got here?' he asked.

The first guard stiffened. His face showed his concern.

'Presents?' Joe looked at Ali, he nodded. 'Well, they wanted some training; let's show them how it's done.'

Both men reached for the pistols tucked under their seats. Joe took out the first guard whose phone dropped into the sand. Ali leapt out and hit the one at the back. There were two others at the checkpoint but they were slow to move. They began to shoot hurried, careless shots, no match for a steady hand and a true eye.

'Left,' Joe yelled and shot. 'Right,' Ali grinned. First one, then the other fell to the ground.

'Well, that was the easy bit.' Joe said. He picked up the first guard's phone to see if the Mudhir was still on the line.

He was. 'What is happening?' He yelled.

'We've done a bit of training,' Joe said. 'The lads here wanted to see how good our shots were.'

'You must come back now. We should talk.'

'Oops.' Joe dropped the phone and shot it to pieces.

'How long before the whole pack descends on us?' Ali asked. 'We'd better get going.'

The Rahman brothers and Mari lay stunned in the back of the truck, still covered by the canopy. 'Please can you tell us what is happening,' Jafar asked from underneath.

'Stay down out of sight,' Ali shouted. 'Just a little problem. All sorted now.'

Joe revved up and pulled out. 'The bigwig will still be wondering what's gone on. He'll get his guard to ring the checkpoint. Then someone will come out to check, find the stiffs... I'd say we've got a lead of twenty minutes. We don't know how good their comms are. We've transmitted fuck all so far, so even if we start now it'll take them time to tune in.'

'Sounds good so far. Where's the but?' Ali said.

'This is the only route in. So the first, whatever, to pass us on the way, will find our leaving present. They'll call it straight in. But they won't understand what's at stake straight away. They won't miss the girl, hopefully, and they won't know about the old guys, but they will want our blood for killing their watchdogs. And, of course, they'll know we ain't playing ball. If we get to the border, we have almost no hope of getting through.'

'But they won't know which crossing?'

'Doesn't matter. They'll have them all covered and we can't go too far off-road with this old crate. Get on to Tom. See if he can pull a few rabbits out of the hat.'

'Tom was always my favourite,' Ali smiled. 'At least, I'll tell him that as I ask him to save our arses!'

***

Tom and Karen were together in a borrowed office trying to work out where their colleagues were. Tom had put up a large map of Iraq and the borders and had marked up various areas with colours.

Tom's phone rang. He answered the call. 'Ali?'

Karen's head turned around.

'Where the fuck are you?' Tom ranted. 'The airwaves are quiet. Too quiet.'

'We're heading out of Raqqa, but we haven't got a chance.'

'And the girl?'

'Safe and well. And the Rahman brothers. But we're toast unless you can do something.' Ali explained what had happened.

'Hold on, I'll get back to you ASAP.'

'They've got Mari?' Karen's eyes were shining.

'Sounds like. And the old boys. But they've given us quite a task.' He pointed at the map. 'These green areas are relatively safe,' he told her. 'The red speaks for itself. This is the route they're expecting to follow: to the border here, by Qa'im. But that might not be an option now.' He looked at his watch. 'Shit. We're going to have to get some air power out there. I'm going to have to call in a few favours.'

'Airpower? You mean for speed?'

Tom nodded. 'I did a bit of ringing around before we came out. Just in case. There's an American squadron stationed just twenty miles north of the city. I'd better get going.'

'I?', Karen queried.'

'This time, yes. I can't risk any more fainting fits. I have to concentrate on the mission.'

'But I'm fine now,' Karen shouted after him as he ran out of the door.

'You're more important staying here,' he shouted back at her. 'If it all goes tits up, at least you'll know what the hell happened to us.'

84

Tom careered out of the office and jumped in his hired car. He put his foot down and drove straight to the airbase. He was greeted by guards at the entrance to the camp.

'I thought you guys left in two thousand and eleven?' he joked.

'Just what we need,' the guard quipped back.' A funny limey.'

'Hey, is Johnson around?'

'Johnson who? And get out of the car, buddy.'

Tom got out. 'You mean there's more than one Johnson? I'll have to think.' He stood still while he was patted down.

'Ex S.A.S.? the guard said.

'How did you guess?' Tom laughed.

'Same rotten sense of humour.' The guard slapped him on the back. 'I'll take you to him. Follow me.'

Johnson was a tall, broad man with a grin as wide as his chest and he used it when he saw Tom. 'Well, I'll be fucked. What the hell are you doing out here?'

'I may need to ask a favour.'

'You gotta be kidding.'

'We've got a situation, much as I'd love to catch up.'

'Fire.'

'Truck carrying three non-combatants, a rescued girl and two civilians. Heading east out of Raqqa, but no hope of reaching the border. They had to despatch a few enemies on the way... '

Johnson sighed. 'You Brits. Why the hell didn't... '

'Hands up. We had a good plan. It kind of went wrong.'

Johnson looked at the map pinned up behind him. 'Best we can do is send a 'copter out. Too much shit in the air to do much, but if we can pop up, over and down, it might just work.'

'Good enough for me,' Tom said. 'OK. Where do they head for?'

'Tell them to go south. Head to At Tanf; 33o 29' 0' North, 38o 41' 0' East. If they're still alive in two hours, we'll go on out there.'

'Any chance of some backup on the road?'

Johnson laughed. 'Don't push it, Tom.'

'But I heard you guys were on the verge of waging a new campaign in Syria? And it's being led by your old boss...'

'You're way ahead of yourself. Don't push it. Look, Tom, I won't make promises I can't keep. I'll do what I can. And sure, I'll give it a go. I'll ring the general.'

Johnson picked up his phone. 'These idiot Englishmen. They're in Syria to rescue a kid who got caught up in it all. They're finished unless someone can bail them out.'

'What's in it for us?'

'Target practice. You're using drones, right?'

'Yes.'

'The limeys are stuck in Syria heading southeast towards Qa'im. I've told them to go south now but they'll still be on the main route. My guess is there'll be lots of nice little targets heading out either after them or to meet them. Could work out well.'

'I'll think about it.' The general put the phone down.

***

Joe was pushing the old jeep as hard as he could, but it was not going fast. He'd seen the enemy's vehicles, all recently stolen from the Iraqi army; top-notch American gear. There was no way he could outrun anyone, and they were sure to be coming out towards them too. He was stuck for ideas but couldn't admit it. He looked at the dashboard clock. 'They'll definitely be on our trail now,' he said. 'They'll have found the guards' bodies. They're on their way.'

'OK, let's assess. Tom?' Ali said. 'I can find out if there are any safe places on the way. Maybe we can hide for a while, off-road somewhere.'

'Good idea,' Joe replied.

'Shit. I can hear something,' Ali was getting concerned.

Joe looked in his rear-view mirror while Ali turned round. Far away in the distance, they could make out a black dot.

'They're onto us.'

In the back of the truck, Ibrahim pulled back the cover so they could see what was going on. Mari and the two men were still

288

shell-shocked but were now beginning to understand their situation. Ibrahim leaned towards the front seat.

'So it seems that they are after us.'

'Yes, sir.' Ali replied. 'And it's not you they want. I doubt they even know about you or care about the girl. I'm afraid it's us this time.'

'Then what is your plan?'

'We could maybe drop you off somewhere and you can take your chances.'

'I have lost my son. I would rather die than give myself up to those monsters.'

'Me too.' Jafar said. 'Do you have arms? We can fight too.'

Joe laughed. 'You see that black shape behind us?'

The two men looked around.

'As soon as that dot gets to the size of a blob, that's when they can set their sights on us. Then they don't even have to catch us. They can just fire.'

'I see,' said Ibrahim.

'So we're going to die anyway?' Mari asked. 'Why did you come? Why risk yourselves?'

'Because we used to know a really good guy,' Joe began.

Ali carried on. 'Such a good guy. He was brave and probably saved all our arses at one time or another.'

Mari was confused. 'But who was he?'

Joe took over the conversation. 'His name was Mohammed Lone. And he was the bravest, nicest, smartest man I ever met.'

'And me,' Ali added.

Mari let it sink in. 'You're doing this for me? For him?'

'We sure are,' Joe said.

'He was that important to you?'

'Oh yes. That much.'

Ibrahim put his arm around Mari and hugged her. 'What a very special daughter you are. Now you must try to be as brave as your father was.'

'I wish I was as brave as Maryam. She tried to save me too.'

'She did save you,' Joe said. 'That little doll. I might never have found you without her.'

'I still have it,' Mari held it up. 'And Saeed saved her life. She told me.'

'He was very brave for such a young man.' Ali nodded. 'It's the size of a blob now,' he observed. 'Shit. What the fuck is that?'

85

What are you talking about?' Joe looked around.

'Listen,' Ali said. The occupants of the jeep fell silent. They heard a strange and unfamiliar noise in the distance.

'What the fuck is that?' Joe said. 'Where's it coming from? Don't tell me they've got 'copters. We've got no fucking chance.'

'That ain't any 'copter I ever heard.' Ali hauled himself halfway out of the window to take a good look. 'Well fuck me sideways. You're not going to believe this,' he said. 'It's only the bloody cavalry!'

'What? In the sky?' Joe was incredulous. 'Who could it be? The Yanks aren't in Syria.'

'They are now,' Ali corrected. 'And that's a drone, if I'm not mistaken.' They all watched out of the windows as the tiny object flew over their heads and shot a missile at the blob. They saw the earth shoot up around it, followed by a loud explosion and flames.

'If I ever say a bad word about the Yanks again, hit me.'

Ali's phone rang; it was Tom. 'My pal Johnson wants to know if you got his present.'

'Tell him we did, but next time to wrap it himself.'

'By my reckoning, you're two hours away from the pick-up. I'm booking you a taxi now. You've got the coordinates; the last bit will be on foot.'

'Good work, Tom!'

'Do you know what? It was fifty-fifty. Luckily, I had a few good pals from back in the day. Now make sure nothing else happens. I've got to tell that neurotic copper that we've got you all. I don't want to lie to her.'

'You go ahead and tell her,' Ali said. 'We've got a lucky charm with us. There's nothing coming after us, I reckon we've done it.'

Revived and newly encouraged, Joe put his foot down and they carried on along the road past Palmyra. Along the road, they passed a few vehicles wrecked and still smoking from drone attacks.

'Check the coordinates, Ali. We'll be getting close soon.'

'We're nearly there,' Ali said. 'It's about two miles on foot that way. Dump the jeep here. We'll just have to pray the taxi is on its way.'

The four men and Mari began their walk in the dust of the sandy terrain. They saw no one as they trudged along, each one of them thinking the same thing. Supposing no one came? They were alone, with a paltry few weapons completely exposed to anyone or anything that might come their way. They didn't even have the shelter of the jeep anymore.

'Hey! I hear something!' Joe shouted.

Ali swung around. 'Me too. Look!' He pointed, and they all heard, before they saw, the comforting sound of a helicopter in the distance. There were collective sighs of relief as it approached.

'It's definitely the Yanks,' Ali said.

Mari tore off her burqa and threw it to the ground but held tightly onto the little doll.

As the helicopter came closer, they instinctively waved as it descended.

'Is it all over?' Mari asked as she was helped on board by the pilot.

'Very nearly, Miss,' said the American. 'Very nearly.'

As they flew back to the camp in Baghdad, the pilot chatted to them as if it was the most normal thing in the world, but his words proved how extraordinarily lucky they had been.

'Hey, we've never ever got anybody out of there before. Kudos to you guys. I didn't think it was possible.'

'We had a plan,' Joe confided. 'But it got shot out of the water.'

'Tell me.'

'We were going to smuggle Mari here back to Baghdad. Then just not return. But then it got complicated with these gentlemen here.'

'In our defence, we didn't know anything about Mari,' Jafar said.

'True enough,' Joe said. 'Anyhow, we made it.'

The pilot turned to look at him. 'Buddy, do I know you?'

Joe laughed. 'I have had my picture in the papers.'

'Hey, don't say you're the disgruntled S.A.S man? No way!'

'The very same. You didn't recognise my picture?'

'Hell, no. And if I had, you might have got the drone first. We were convinced you'd turned. You were on our hit list, buddy!'

'Shit,' said Joe. 'I never thought... '

'Kidding! Tom told me all about it. Right from the beginning. I just didn't know I'd be the taxi service. By the way, I'm Johnson. Pleased to meet you.'

86

The journey back to the American base was the same in miles as they'd covered from Raqqa, but it was insignificant compared to what they had just come through. Landing there was almost as good as landing back in England. Johnson's hospitality couldn't stretch to flying them back to the airport, but Tom was already on his way to pick them up. Karen was left to organise rooms for the night and arrange flights back home. She rang Gary to confirm their safe arrival at the base. 'I can't tell you how grateful I am to you all,' she said. 'I promised Mari's mother I'd find her; I just wish I'd have been able to do more.'

'Karen, just think it was all down to you. If you hadn't brought us on board, God knows what would have happened to the poor child.'

'I won't take any credit,' she said. 'But maybe I helped stop that route at least. Poor Saeed. His mother will be devastated.'

'True. But maybe his story will stop other lads from going.'

'By the way. Have you heard anything from John?' she asked.

'Sorry. I've been a bit tied up. Do you want me to contact him?'

'No. It doesn't matter.' Karen ended the call. She waited at the hotel reception for them all to arrive. She'd decided against ringing Sinéad until she'd seen Mari with her own eyes.

When they turned up, Karen saw that Mari looked in a bad way. She was shivering and dressed only in a thin dress.

'Mari? I'm Sergeant Thorpe from England. I've been looking for you. How are you?'

'Better now, just a bit cold.'

'I'll sort something out for you. Are you up to speaking to your mother?'

Mari nodded.

'I just need to have a quick word with Saeed's father. Sit there a minute.'

Karen went over to Ibrahim and Jafar. 'I'm so sorry for your loss,' she said.

'He was a foolish boy but he didn't deserve to die like that. I must ring his mother and tell her. Thank you for trying.'

'I've booked flights for all of us going back to England tomorrow. We need to meet here at about ten in the morning.' She turned to Jafar. 'I'm sorry, I couldn't book yours.'

'That is fine. I will make my own arrangements. Thank you. It was already too late to save my son but I know you did your best for Saeed.'

Karen went to the reception desk and nodded her head back to Mari. 'She's in a bad way. She only has the clothes she's wearing. Could someone sort something out for her?'

'Of course,' said the receptionist. 'I will get someone from customer services.' She leant forward. 'What happened to her?'

'She was in Raqqa,' Karen replied.

That was enough. The woman was satisfied with the explanation. 'Poor girl. It will be our absolute pleasure to do this.'

Minutes later, a young and very kind-looking woman came to the desk and was pointed in Mari's direction. 'She's about my size,' the woman said. 'I'll find her something comfortable and bring it to your room.'

Karen went over to Mari. 'We're sharing a room, is that OK?' Mari nodded. 'Come on, let's get you upstairs and you can ring your mother.'

In their room, Karen picked up the phone. 'Do you want to tell her or shall I?'

'I'll tell her,' Mari said firmly. 'There is a lot to say.'

Karen rang the number and passed the receiver over to Mari. 'Mum?'

'Mari? Is it really you? Where are you? How are you?'

Karen discreetly moved away while the mother and daughter spoke. Then Mari called her over.

'Mum wants to speak to you.'

Karen took the phone. 'Thank you so much, Sergeant Thorpe. I'm so sorry I was rude.'

'No problem at all. Mari told you that Saeed didn't make it. He's dead, I'm afraid. Please don't mention anything to Mrs Rahman; her husband will ring her shortly.'

'Oh, poor woman. Poor boy. No, I won't say anything.'

'We'll be flying home tomorrow. We should get there at around six in the evening.'

'Thank you again.'

Karen put the phone down and looked at Mari. 'How about a nice hot bath?'

'That would be wonderful,' Mari said, beginning to cry. 'Is it really all over? Am I safe now?'

Karen held her hands. 'Yes, you're safe. Go on, get in that bath. And when you come back, there should be a surprise for you. Oh, and how about I order some food? I'm starving.'

'Yes, please,' Mari said, getting up. Anything plain would be good.'

When Mari had gone, Karen checked her phone again. 'What's wrong with you, John? When did you get to be so heartless?'

87

After Karen and Mari had gone, the men were left awkwardly together in reception.

Ibrahim was the first to speak. 'Who are you? What sort of men come out here to take on terrorists on their own territory?'

Joe answered first. 'That requires a drink and a sit-down. Care to join us?' He looked over to the seating area.

With pleasure,' Jafar replied for both of them.

Almost as soon as the four men sat at a lounge table, a waiter appeared to take their order.

'Two beers for us,' Joe looked at Ali. He nodded.

'A soda for me, and... ' Jafar looked at Ibrahim.

'I'll have a whisky. I don't do it often, but I think I need one.'

'Of course, gentlemen,' The waiter disappeared through a side door.

'So,' Joe began. 'What would you like to know?'

'Tell me from the beginning,' Ibrahim said. 'We have a few hours to fill.'

'We're all ex-S.A.S.' Joe said. 'Recently retired and all looking for action. There's another man in the group, Gary. He was our Major once upon a time. We all served together.'

'I had no idea we were in such exalted company,' Jafar said. 'But why this child?'

'Ah,' Joe said. 'Do neither of you know anything about her?'

Jafar shook his head, but Ibrahim answered. 'My son, Saeed, he helped her with her maths homework. My wife and I had absolutely no idea that they had feelings for each other. And it wasn't where he went at first. He was meant to be staying in Pakistan, with my brother here and his wife.'

'Well, we knew her father,' Ali said. 'Mo Lone. We called him Wolf.'

'Wolf Lone?' Ibrahim queried. 'I get it. Lone Wolf.'

'That's right,' Joe laughed. 'And he did often work alone. That's when he pulled off some spectacular hits.'

'We could talk about him all night. And we probably will,' Ali said. 'But that's why we're here. To rescue his daughter.'

'I see. And it was my son who tempted her away from safety. If it hadn't been for him...'

Joe interrupted. 'If she's anything at all like Mo, she'll have made her own decisions. I saw the fire in her eyes, even if she was being badly treated. Don't you worry about that. She's tough.'

'Tell me about your sons,' Ali said. 'I'm interested in why they would want to go to join them.'

Jafar spoke first. 'My son was a thinker. He would go to the ends of the earth for a debate about anything, but especially Islam. My belief is he found something of interest in what these devils were saying and it attracted him enough to make him want to go there and find out for himself.'

'And my son was bored,' Ibrahim said. 'He wanted a purpose. He was tired of going to prayers; he wanted to change the world.'

Joe, listening carefully, nodded. 'I can see how the two would encourage each other,' he said.

'They were as thick as thieves. Is that the saying?' Joe nodded. 'They were inseparable. I heard them chattering together late into the night, but I did not hear the words clearly.'

'And I thought they were chalk and cheese,' Ibrahim said. 'I remember on an earlier visit they quarrelled, did they not?'

Jafar nodded. 'And maybe they quarrelled again.'

'What happened to your son?' Ali asked.

'His body was dumped on the roadside and picked up by the Erbil police. If these wretched boys do not, as you say, pass muster, they are disposed of.'

'And if he was challenging their ideology...?' Joe said.

'Oh, definitely,' Jafar said. 'He would never give up on an argument. He could be very trying,' Jafar gave a little laugh.

'Whereas Saeed was all action. But I can't believe he had the desire to do so much harm to people. He was adventurous, but he had a gentle soul.'

'They were good boys,' Jafar said. 'And neither deserved to die like that.'

'That's right,' Joe said. 'It's all down to those bastards out there. And maybe one day, your true religion will win the battle and peace will return.'

'Until some other fucker gets a different idea,' Ali said. 'Sorry for the language.'

'Do not be sorry, my friend,' Ibrahim said. 'If it hadn't been for you and Joe here, we might not have made it back either. Then our wives would be widows as well as losing their only sons.'

'Now then,' Joe stood up. 'I'm starving. Anyone for supper?'

88

28th March

Karen woke to the sounds of Mari retching in the bathroom. She knocked on the door. 'Are you OK?'

'I'm fine,' Mari muttered. 'Must be something I ate.'

'Really?' Karen was surprised. 'It was very bland. Never mind. You can try on your new outfit if you like. You'll have to wear something to go down for breakfast.'

'I'm not sure I want anything to eat,' Mari said. She emerged from the bathroom looking unsteady on her feet.

'Here,' Karen patted the bed. 'Sit down and take it easy. We can order something in the room again if you like? They have room service. How about a couple of bread rolls or something?'

Mari waivered, then nodded. 'That's cool.'

Karen made the call, ordering a full-cooked breakfast for herself. They ate at a little table.

'I'm pregnant,' Mari said. 'How am I going to tell my mother?'

'After what you've been through, I'm sure she'll be right there for you. Do you know who the father was?'

Mari nodded. 'Oh yes. It's definitely Saeed's. It's strange but also quite comforting that there's something of him growing inside me. We didn't have long together but I knew he loved me.'

'That's an interesting way to think about it,' Karen smiled. 'I assume you haven't mentioned it to his father.'

Mari shook her head. 'I've not thought about telling anyone yet. It was just one day at a time when I was out there. I don't know what Mum will say, but I have to tell her first. She can help me tell his parents.

'I suspect they'll be pleased when they get over the shock. His mother and yours have become quite close while you've been missing. Now, we'd better get downstairs. The others will be wondering what we're doing.'

***

Karen and Mari went into the reception area to see all the men standing there.

'Well, don't you look a picture, young lady,' Joe said to Mari. 'How are you feeling?'

'Better,' she nodded.

Jafar approached her and gave her a little hug. 'You are a very brave girl,' he said. 'I must go to catch my plane now, but I truly hope we will meet again one day.'

He turned to Karen and shook her hand. 'And thank you, sergeant. Without you, my brother and I might not have been here today,'

'Pleasure,' Karen said. 'And spread the word. The fewer kids that get caught up in this evil, the better

'Very true,' he replied. He turned to the others. 'Goodbye, all. Safe journey.'

'Are we all set?' Joe looked around. 'Let's get to the airport.'

When they arrived there, Mari and Ibrahim were waved through, but Tom, Joe and Ali were stopped at security by a man with a British accent.

'What's going on?' Karen asked.

'It's these guys, ' the man replied. He looked at them. 'Do you think you can come into our country, run rampant and just fly out without question?' he grinned. 'Look I have the info on you guys from the CTC, but we've got to go through procedures. I'll make it as painless as possible.'

'But I'm OK?' Karen asked.

'Sure, you go ahead.'

'See you on the other side,' Karen waved.

Tom laughed. 'Come on guys, we knew this would happen, didn't we? It's all part of the fun.'

'Being strip-searched and interrogated isn't my idea of fun,' Joe said.

89

Karen sat next to Mari on the plane home. While Mari dozed, Karen spent much of the flight writing up notes and thinking about things. She still hadn't heard anything from John at all. While she knew he was cross with her, she was very cross with him.

When the plane landed and they disembarked, Karen saw that there was a welcome party waiting for Mari. Sinéad, Niamh, Maria, and Razia were there and a man she didn't recognise. She watched as Mari charged ahead and fell into the arms of Sinéad and Niamh. All of them were crying. 'This is your uncle Jimmy,' she heard Sinéad say while Ibrahim hugged his wife and daughter.

Karen turned to Tom, Joe, and Ali. 'I can never thank you enough for what you've done. We must meet up again to celebrate soon.

'It was our pleasure,' Tom said. Joe and Ali nodded.

'We did it for Wolf, too,' Joe added. 'But it's cool you were there to orchestrate it all.'

Karen shook hands with them and nodded towards the family. 'I'd better say my goodbyes.'

'Cheers, Karen. See you soon,' Ali said as they made their way out.

Karen joined the others. She looked around for John, but he wasn't there.

Sinéad came up to her. 'Thanks again, Sergeant Thorpe. 'Our family seems to be stronger than ever now. Mari's other grandparents have promised to come and visit. We're all going to try to get along now.'

'That's great,' Karen said. 'Mari will need everyone around her for a long while to come.' She wondered how they would take the news about the baby, but decided it was definitely not for her to say anything. She went up to Mari and hugged her. 'You take care now and keep in touch.'

'I will', Mari said. 'And thanks so much. I'm going to tell Mum when I get home.'

'Good luck.'

***

Karen made her way out of the airport. She heard someone calling her name. 'Karen?! Karen!'

She looked around to see Macy hurtling towards her.

'Hi!' Macy gave her one of her biggest hugs ever. 'I've come to kidnap you.'

'What the fuck?' Karen said. 'What's going on?'

'Hurry, it's costing me a fortune in parking,' Macy said.

Ten minutes later, Karen was sitting in Macy's car as she sped off towards Hertfordshire.

'What's going on, Mace?

'I'm not saying a thing until we get to the pub.'

'The pub? Well, I am hungry I suppose.'

Forty minutes later they arrived at The Crown. Karen walked in to find her old colleagues waiting for her. Bradley, Emma, and Phil were all there. Even Gary. There was no sign of Harris but then she saw someone else.

'Guv?' She said in surprise. She looked around for John, then felt a presence behind her. He put his chin on her shoulder. 'Don't be cross, it's not what you think. I've been busy here. Arranging all this.'

Karen turned around. 'What is it then?'

DCI Winter stood up. 'I have a little announcement to make,' he said. 'It's about the Cooper case.'

'The Cooper case?' Karen said. 'But that was years ago.'

'Indeed it was. But your colleagues here have uncovered a small injustice.'

Karen began to blush.

'Yes, it appears that after your suspension, when you were meant to be off work, you worked your butt off on a case on the quiet. And somebody else took the credit for it.'

'Harris,' Karen whispered.

'And he got a commendation. And although you were totally in the wrong,' DCI Winter emphasised, 'I think that it goes against the spirit of the force.'

'How on earth did you find out?' Karen gaped.

'It was a combination of all of your team,' DCI Winter nodded at them. 'Emma located the cases, John accessed the files and Macy tricked him into a confession.'

'Oh. So what happened to him?'

'He resigned. So when you finish your placement, there's a DI job back here with your name on it. Now, how about a little celebration?'

From nowhere, John produced a bottle of champagne in an ice bucket.

'Let me pour you a glass, my sweet,' he said.

Karen stared at him as if he was completely mad. 'No.' she said.

John frowned. 'I worked flat out for you to do this. Aren't you happy?'

Karen looked at him. 'I'm not sure. I blame the curry. I'm pregnant.'

THE END

Dear Reader,

The purpose of this story was to challenge myself and Karen Thorpe with this most difficult scenario; a young girl going missing and getting embroiled in a nightmare scenario.
Originally drafted in 2015; after hearing many news events around terrorism, it took a very long time to reach fruition for various reasons. I hope I have achieved my aims and produced an exciting, although sometimes brutal, adventure story.

As always, I couldn't have done this without the help of many people. My special thanks go to the talented and super helpful Awais Khan who agreed to be my sensitivity reader to help me ensure that where I had to touch on religions and cultural issues, I was broadly on the right course.

I would like to thank Andrea Neal and Sue Scott for their initial editing and Shelagh Corker for the final edits.

I would also like to thank Mark Pearce, Diane Warburton, Eleanor O' Farrell and Sara Drew for their eagle-eyed error-spotting, and all my beta readers for their helpful comments and corrections.

I'm sure that there will be another Karen Thorpe story to come in the not-too-distant future!

OTHER BOOKS IN THE KAREN THORPE SERIES

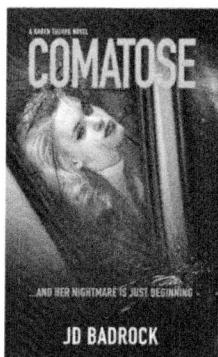

A PACEY WHODUNNIT!
A woman is left in a coma, and Karen's convinced it's no crime - despite the lack of evidence. When an indisputable crime is committed, Karen's hands are tied and even her boss isn't on her side.

SPOOKY COLD CASE INVESTIGATIONS!
Karen picks up her father's trail to investigate the disappearance of three little girls fifty years earlier. She doesn't believe in the supernatural, but what she discovers tests her to the core.

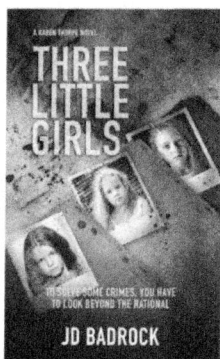

A MYSTERY TIED UP IN A CRIMINAL RING
An autistic artist with amazing powers of recognition and memory goes missing. But who's got her? The good guys or the baddies?

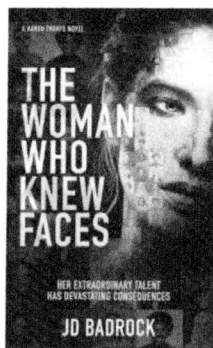

Books by Jane Badrock

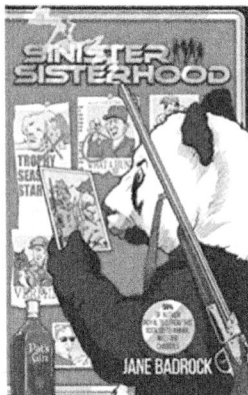

SINISTER SISTERHOOD

Elle's love life is a disaster. Encouraged by her Auntie. Pat, she takes on a new challenge and puts together a team of madcap women to take on trophy hunters and fight animal exploitation.

THE ICE MAIDEN

Maths student Maddie's life is being threatened - but why?
She has to solve her most critical problem ever...
Who is she really?
If she doesn't find out, she'll die!

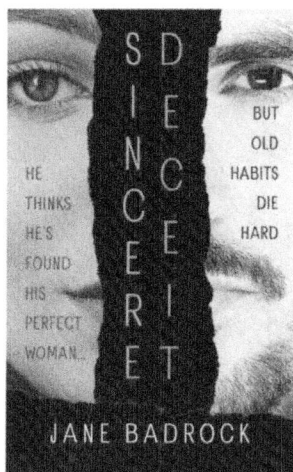

SINCERE DECEIT

**Successful financier
Michael is cheating on
new wife Frances...
until his terrifying
past comes back to
haunt him.
As his world falls apart
he realises that the
only one who can help
him, is Frances.**

HE
THINKS
HE'S
FOUND
HIS
PERFECT
WOMAN

BUT
OLD
HABITS
DIE
HARD

JANE BADROCK

THE SHOCKALOT BOX

**Pick from forty
twisted, tasty, tales
to create a
FIVE COURSE DINNER
OF DELIGHT!**

THE
SHOCKALOT
BOX

By
JANE BADROCK

Printed in Great Britain
by Amazon